BROKEN SHIELD

J.D. Rhoades

Dedication

This book is dedicated to my great and good friend, David Terrenoire. A kick-ass writer his ownself as well as a crackerjack blues harp player, David was the first one to suggest that BREAKING COVER was as much Tim Buckthorn's story as Tony Wolf's. Stay strong, David.

Contents

Part One

Chapter One

The girl was young, skinny, and as nervous as a deer under the harsh white lights of the truck stop parking lot. She kept looking back over her shoulder as she strolled between the lines of trucks. She was new enough that the high heels she wore were still awkward for her and she tottered a bit atop slim, bony legs. She wore a mini-skirt made of some fake leather material that barely covered her buttocks and a spaghetti-strap T-Shirt that did the same mediocre job of concealing her small, high breasts.

A man watched from the shadows between two trucks as the girl stopped at the driver's side of a large white Freightliner across the way. It was decorated with orange LED lights that outlined the doors and the tall sleeper cab that rose up behind the driver's compartment. They gave the big truck an almost festive appearance. The truck was running, the engine rumbling like a giant sleeping beast. The windows were covered by quilted panels stuck up by the driver while he grabbed a little nap in the sleeper. The girl knocked on the driver's door tentatively, then harder. He couldn't see the conversation that followed, but it didn't end well for the girl. She flinched back and nearly fell off the heels as a cascade of some liquid was ejected out the window, drenching her flimsy t-shirt. He could see the black lace bra beneath the material. "ASSHOLE!" she shouted as she stomped away. She tried to hold her head up with as much dignity as she could, but that effort was crushed by a peal of cruel laughter from somewhere else in the darkness, followed by a shouted comment in a rough female voice that he couldn't make out. Apparently it was clear enough to the girl; she hung her head and he could hear the sound of sobbing as she stumbled away. He considered for a moment, then followed, stepping out into the light and following her.

He was slim and wiry, dressed in blue jeans and a windbreaker that was too warm for the humid South Carolina summer night. He appeared to be in his early forties, but it was hard to tell exactly because of the NC State baseball cap pulled down to obscure his eyes. He had to shorten his stride to avoid catching up with the girl before she got where she was going.

The parking lot stretched out for acres around the garishly lit oasis of the compound that made up the "Interstate Travel Center" off a nameless exit on Interstate 95 in the marshlands of South Carolina, near the Georgia Border. The place was like a small town compacted into a few cinderblock buildings; along with the expected rows of fuel pumps, there was a diner, a convenience store, a bank, a Laundromat, a post office, even a tiny video store. A weary trucker could find nearly anything legal he needed in the complex, and most illegal things he could want in the shadows outside.

The girl stopped by a small white pickup truck with a white bubble light on top of the cab and the words "Dixie Security" in black letters on the side. A beefy man with a shaved head and a bored expression stared straight ahead as she voiced her complaint, waving her arms for emphasis and pointing back to where the trucker who'd thrown his drink on her was parked. Finally, the bald man had had enough. As the man in the ball cap approached, he told her harshly to shut up and get her skinny ass back to work. The girl slammed her hand onto the top of the cab in frustration. "You're s'posed to take *care* of us!" she shouted in a thick Southern accent made harsh and ugly by her fury. The bald man opened the truck door and shoved, nearly knocking the girl down again. He got out of the truck. He was dressed in a pair of khaki pants and a white t-shirt with "SECURITY" written on it in the same lettering as on the truck. He grabbed the girl by the throat, shoving her back against the truck. "Listen here, you little white trash cunt," he began, but he was interrupted by the man in the ball cap, who loudly cleared his throat, then said "Excuse me."

The bald man released the girl and turned around. "The fuck do you want?"

"I want you to deliver a message for me. To your boss." He began to unzip the windbreaker.

"A message?" the bald man said. Another man was getting out of the passenger side of the truck. This one was squat and even uglier than the first. The muscles bulging against his T-shirt shirt looked more like they came from a needle than the gym, the word SECURITY on his shirt stretched and distorted. "The fuck I look like?" the bald man said. "Western Union?" The two men laughed at this witticism, until the man in the ball cap drew an X26 Taser from the pocket of the windbreaker and shot the bald man with it. Two darts propelled by compressed nitrogen covered the distance in less than a second and embedded themselves in the flesh of his arm. He went rigid, then bellowed in agony as the electricity hit him. He collapsed to the asphalt just as the man in the ball cap dropped the Taser and drew a .40 caliber Smith and Wesson pistol from the shoulder holster under his windbreaker and pointed it at the other security man, who was charging around the front of the truck, a police baton in one hand. "Drop it," the man in the ball cap said. The security man drew up short, then dropped the baton to the pavement.

"You were holding it wrong, anyway," the man in the ball cap said.

"Wh—what?"

The man in the ball cap ignored the question. "Get over there and sit on the ground. Next to your buddy." The second security man hesitated, then lowered himself slowly to the ground where the first man was sitting up, groaning in pain.

The man in the ball cap turned to the girl. "Where do they keep the money?"

She was trembling, the fear making her shake as if she was the one who'd just ridden the lightning. "I...I don't know."

He looked at her for a moment, then turned to the second man. "Okay. You can tell the boss she's not the one who told me. But you know where it is."

The man's expression of puzzled innocence was so clearly false it was almost comical. "Where what is?"

"Listen to me, son," the man in the ball cap said. "No one here has to die tonight. Fact is, I'd rather not kill you. You're just grunts. But I am already way the hell over every line I ever recognized, and it would not trouble me one bit to but a bullet in as many knees and ankles and other non-lethal body parts as it would take to get you to cough up the money you've been collecting from this girl and the half-dozen others I've seen working this lot tonight. Now what's it gonna be?"

The bald man spoke up, his voice still tight with pain. "You got any idea who you're fucking with? Whose money that is?"

The man in the ball cap grinned. It was a savage smile, leached dry of all humor. "I know exactly whose money it is. That's why I'm taking it." He motioned with the gun to the second man. "Get it."

The man slowly got to his feet and turned his back to lean over and reach inside the truck. "You turn around with a weapon in your hand," the man in the ball cap said, "and you'll die. I guarantee it. Don't get yourself killed for another man's money or for your dumb-ass pride. None of that's worth dying for."

"Well, what are you dying for?" the bald man on the ground said. "Because you, my friend, are fucking dead."

"Maybe," the man in the ball cap said. "But not tonight." The second man came out with a white canvas bag. "Toss it over here." The bag landed with a heavy thump. The man in the ball cap squatted down, keeping the gun on the two security men. He picked up the bag and stood up. "Come with me," he told the girl. "When we get far enough away, I'll give you this money. You can use it to get out of the life." She stared at him uncomprehendingly, then shook her head. "No," she said. "They'll find me. And they'll hurt me."

"Just like they're going to find you," the bald man said. "They'll find out who you are. When they do..."

The man in the ball cap aimed the pistol to one side and fired. The girl screamed. Both men screamed as well, covering their faces with their arms. The bullet struck the left rear tire, which exploded with a report almost as loud as the flat bang of the gun. He shot the other tire. The truck leaned to one side, the loud hiss of the escaping air filling the night and nearly drowning out the girl's terrified sobbing.

"I know your boss is going to find out who I am," the man said, "because I'm telling you now." He started backing away. "My name," he said, "is Tim Buckthorn. Be sure you tell him. He already knows it, but he needs to know I'm coming for him."

He turned and vanished into the night.

Chapter Two

Two Weeks Earlier

The storm had passed, leaving behind a few ragged clouds, sailing by against a sky so bright and blue it looked freshly scrubbed. The yard surrounding Maddie Underhill's house was less pristine, littered as it was with small sticks and pinecones scattered among the larger branches. The high winds of the fast-moving system had taken their toll as it galloped through Gibson County; some of the branches were as big around as her arm. Maddie was sweeping the front walk, uncomplaining despite the pain in her joints.

"I'll get that, Mama," Maddie's son Rayvon called from the yard. He and his fifteen-year-old son Trey were pulling one of the larger branches to the curb. "Go on back inside." Maddie's only response was to wave off the offer with a wrinkled and age-knotted hand. There might come a day when she'd sit on her behind while someone else worked, she thought, but not yet. She went back to sweeping the walk, the wet pine straw stubbornly adhering to the concrete. She set her jaw, brushed harder, and said a quick prayer under her breath. "Thank you, Jesus," she said. "Thank you that all I have to worry about is this pine straw and some limbs." She thought of the pictures she'd seen on her TV the night before, scenes of devastation where the huge storm system had roared through the Southeast, spawning tornadoes and hellish winds, leaving behind a swath of devastation forty miles wide.

"And please be good," she added, "to all those people who weren't as lucky as us, and please take those poor souls who died to be with You in Your Heavenly Kingdom. Amen." She had no doubt in her mind that the prayer had been heard; Jesus was an unseen but constant presence in Maddie Underhill's life, as real to her and as close as the man and boy dragging that giant limb to the edge of the road where it could be picked up by the county. She glanced over at them and saw that they'd stopped dragging the limb and were looking at the sky. She followed their gaze, craning her neck to see.

The air was full of small fluttering things, falling slowly and erratically through the humid atmosphere. It took her a moment to recognize them as scraps of paper. The first one alighted delicately on the ground a few feet from where she stood, like a moth coming to rest. She stood dumbfounded as others followed, settling gently to the earth all around her. She bent over to pick one up at her feet, grimacing as her back reminded her why she didn't do that much anymore. She looked at the object in her hand as she carefully straightened up. It was a piece of notebook paper. The blue ink was smeared, running down the page in streaks, but she could make out the shape of a heart, with the symbols "T.L. &" inside it. She couldn't make out the other two initials. She almost laughed out loud with the shock of sudden recognition. She'd certainly seen plenty of similar foolishness in her thirty years as a teacher in the Gibson County Schools. Some young girl (or boy) mooning over some young boy (or girl) in the next row instead of paying attention to their lessons. She almost let the paper drop, but it seemed too much like littering, so she stuck it in the pocket of her housedress. Other bits of paper, and some scraps that looked like wet cardboard, were falling around her like snow.

"Where'd all this come from, Grandmama?" Trey had come up to stand next to her, holding out a soggy handful of paper.

"I saw a story about this," she said. "On the news. Sometimes when one of these big storms come through and destroys somebody's house, some of the papers inside get picked up and carried. I heard for miles."

Rayvon looked at the yard glumly. "Ain't gonna make this easier to clean up." He bent over to pick up a square piece of paper. "Look," he said. "Someone's picture."

She took it from him. It was a couple of young white boys, tongues stuck out, each one trying to put his fingers up as bunny ears behind the other one's head. Maddie made her decision instantly.

"We need to get all these up," she said. "The pictures especially. And save them. Be careful with them, now. These belong to someone."

"Mama," Rayvon said, "How are we gonna find out..."

"That's what I read about," she said. "Last time this happened. Someone put those pictures up on the computer. On that Facebook." She waved the photograph at them. "This is a memory to someone. Maybe even a precious one. We need to try and get these back to the people who they belong to."

"Mama," Rayvon said. She stopped him with the look that had frozen two generations of Gibson County schoolchildren into silence. "We have work to do, son," she said.

He sighed. "Okay."

The work went slowly. There must have been a couple of hundred bits of airborne flotsam scattered in the yard and the dirt road in front of Maddie's house, and even more on the roof. Maddie went inside and got a card table she'd used for extra seating at Thanksgiving. She set it up in the yard and put a blue plastic wastebasket next to it. As Rayvon and Trey brought her the scraps of paper, she sat in her folding metal chair and sorted them. The majority were too damaged to identify, and those went into the wastebasket. She started to put the photographs in a pile, and then decided to spread them out on the table to dry. Miscellaneous papers went in their own pile, except for one that Rayvon brought her. It was a death certificate, or at least two-thirds of one. She put that aside, as it seemed disrespectful to just shove it in the pile. Besides, it might provide some clue as to the source of the other papers, even though the name of the issuing county was torn off.

She looked up from her sorting to see Trey standing before her. He was holding a photograph in his hand. He had a strange look on his face. "Well, boy?" she said. "What have you got there? Don't just stand there like a moon-calf. Hand it here!"

Wordlessly, he did so. She looked at it. Her hand went to her mouth. She stared at the photo for a moment before raising her head, a grim expression on her face.

"RAYVON!" she called out. "Call the Sheriff. Right now. Get them out here." A thought occurred to her. "Ask for Tim Buckthorn."

Chapter Three

*B*uried alive.

　　She had sobbed herself into unconsciousness in the dark, and now she awoke in terror and that same impenetrable and hopeless blackness, the phrase whispering in her mind, settling down on top of any hope she might have felt like some mocking carrion bird, just waiting for the moment when she surrendered, waiting to strip the flesh from her still living bones.

Buried alive.

　　The power had gone out first, a few hours after the man had left. "I'll be back," he said, but now she doubted it. The sounds she'd heard above her in the house had sounded like the end of the world: the whistling wind building to a shriek, then mounting incredibly, unimaginably, insanely higher, becoming the roar she'd heard described by stunned-looking survivors on the news. "Like a freight train," they'd said, eyes wide and haunted with the memory. But to her it had sounded more like God's own buzz saw, a high-pitched, brutally overpowering drone that took over every corner of consciousness, blotting out everything but the raw fear. Then the other sounds, the cracking, rumbling, thudding sound of the house above her collapsing, falling in on itself, crashing against the door to the cellar, blotting out the last bits of dim illumination from the one tiny, filthy window she could see from where she'd been imprisoned. She thought she might go insane then, as that final scrap of grayish half-light that was her only connection with the world outside the cellar had suddenly vanished, leaving her in the pitch blackness with what sounded like the legions of Hell ransacking the world above her.

Leaving her *buried alive.*

She shook her head. If she kept thinking like this, she *would* go crazy. Something in her yearned for that, wanting so much to slip into the oblivion of madness, unfeeling, unknowing, until death took her. But something stronger inside her refused to just die. Her mom needed her. Even her dad, for all that he'd been responsible for where she was, didn't deserve what that would do to him.

She thought about her dad. The man who took her said he'd done it because her dad owed him money. So maybe Dad would come up with it. Maybe he'd come get her. The second after she thought it, she knew it was just a fantasy. She loved her dad, always would, but he wasn't strong. And certainly no kind of hero. The thought made her feel even more alone and helpless and small. And God, she was so thirsty.

Come on, girl, she thought. *Get your shit together. You're fifteen, not a baby any more.* A disaster like this would draw people from surrounding towns, even other states, to claw through the wreckage, searching for survivors. And the man who'd taken her wouldn't be likely to come back with all that going on. *Okay. So how do I get found?* She thought about a special she'd seen on TV, about people who'd flown to Turkey or someplace like that to rescue people from an earthquake. They'd used special dogs. *Cadaver dogs*, a voice whispered in the back of her mind. She shoved it back brutally.

Okay, dogs. They used their sense of smell. Well, she was thoroughly ripe after three days in a cellar, with a bucket for a toilet, so she was pretty well fixed there. Then she remembered the teams using sensitive microphones to listen for the sounds of people in the rubble. Well, that was fine, too. If she could get this damn duct tape off her mouth, she'd make enough noise to wake a graveyard. She tried to move. The rubble hemming her in on either side stopped her before the chain on her ankle did. The chain was fastened to an eyebolt driven into the cinderblock wall of the cellar. She moved towards where she thought she remembered the wall was, her hands held out in front of her. They were still chained together as well. After a moment, she collided softly with the rough block wall. She moved more slowly then, until her body was against the wall, her duct-tape covered cheek pressed against it. She began rubbing her face against the wall, wondering how long it took to wear through this many layers of duct tape. It was better than just waiting to die.

Chapter Four

She was standing on the porch as Buckthorn pulled the cruiser into the yard, her back as ramrod straight as always. Instinctively, Tim glanced at the dashboard clock with a little shiver of dread, then caught himself and laughed. He wasn't going to get a dressing down for being late for class. But Mrs. Underhill had that effect on people. He'd been to school functions with his sister and nephews and seen grown men and women instinctively check their clothing to make sure shirt tails were tucked in and skirts properly arranged when the old lady passed by. She was a legend to anyone who'd passed through the sixth and seventh grades at Pine Lake Middle School— feared by her students, the fear turning to reverence after a few years when they realized how well she'd prepared them, both for further study and for life.

He got out of the car, pulling his "Smokey Bear" hat on as he shut the door. She watched him approach up the walk, that familiar expression of skeptical appraisal on her face. He touched his finger to his hat brim as he stopped before her. "Mrs. Underhill," he said.

She nodded. "Timothy." Then the cool demeanor cracked and her face split in a wide smile. "Come up here and hug my neck right now, young man."

He grinned back as they embraced. He noted the slight stiffening and the quick, pained intake of breath and released the hug quickly. "You been all right, ma'am?" he asked.

She shrugged. "A touch of the arthritis, and my sugar gets bad sometimes, but I can't complain. Every day above ground's a gift from the Lord."

"Yes, ma'am," Buckthorn said. "You said you'd found something after the storm."

"Yes," she said. "Come on in. I made some ice tea."

The inside of the house was cramped but immaculate. They'd moved the card table inside, where it stood awkwardly between the easy chair and the old TV. Buckthorn saw that there were papers and photographs spread across the surface of the table. "So these fell from the sky?" he said.

"Yes," Maddie said, handing him his glass of tea. "See anything unusual?" She watched him closely as he shuffled through the pictures with his free hand, sipping at the sweet, cold tea with the other. Suddenly he stopped, the glass halfway to his lips. He picked up one of the pictures. "Holy..." he started, then caught himself.

"It's what I think it is, isn't it?" she said.

"Maybe it's some kind of joke," Buckthorn said.

Mrs. Underhill's snort told him what she thought of that idea. "That girl look like she's joking around?"

"Have you got a plastic bag of some..." he stopped. She was already holding out a small Ziploc bag. "I watch that CSI show," she said. "The original one, not the one with that silly red-headed man with the sunglasses. Bag it and tag it. That's what they say, right?"

"Yes ma'am," Buckthorn said, sliding the soggy photograph into the bag and putting down his tea to seal it. "Mrs. Underhill," he said, "I need you to come down and get your fingerprints taken. Not right now, but in the next day or so."

She nodded. "I figured. So if there's any prints on it, you can tell if they're mine, right? I'll bring my grandson Trey. He's the one who picked it up."

"Thank you. I'll need to talk to the Sheriff about this."

"Hmmph," she said. "Don't let him push this off on someone else, or some other department, Timothy. I know that man, and if there's a way to pass the buck, he'll find it." She put a hand on his arm and looked him squarely in the eye. "That picture landed in my yard for a reason, Timothy. It was meant to come to you. If anyone's going to help that girl, the Lord means for it to be you. I feel it."

"Yes, ma'am," Buckthorn said.

She nodded again, as if satisfied. "I'll let you get back to work, then. It was nice seeing you. Tell your sister I asked after her."

"You too, Mrs. Underhill. And I will."

As he walked to the car, he spotted Trey in the yard, working with the rake. A second glance told him the area where he was working was clear of debris. It didn't need raking. Buckthorn waited by the open car door until Trey leaned the rake against a tree and walked over.

"Trey," Buckthorn said, "looks like you grew a couple of inches since I saw you last."

"Thanks," the young man said. He stuck his hands in his pockets and looked down. Buckthorn waited patiently. Trey looked up, towards his grandmother's door. "Ummmm..." he said.

"Something on your mind, son?" Buckthorn said.

"I, uh, I just wanted to say thanks. For speaking up for me a couple months ago."

"No problem," Buckthorn said. "You did a dumb thing, sure. But I didn't see any reason to hang a felony on you."

The previous October, a number of mailboxes and fences in Gibson County had been destroyed by 'works bombs'—homemade explosives made by filling a two-liter soda bottle halfway with a mixture of water and drain cleaner, then shoving in a piece of aluminum foil, quickly screwing the cap back on and shaking. The chemical reaction inside the bottle generated a large amount of hydrogen gas very quickly, causing the plastic bottle to swell and explode with a loud noise and enough force to do damage to anyone or anything nearby. Repeated irate phone calls from residents who'd had their mailboxes destroyed or who'd been awakened in the middle of the night by loud booms beneath their bedroom windows had led Buckthorn to assign two members of the county's already understaffed Detective Division to the case.

Fortunately for them, one of the young men involved, a wannabe thug named Gerrome Tyree, had been bragging about what he and two others had done. Buckthorn wasn't surprised to hear that Tyree was involved, nor was he surprised to learn that one of his compatriots was another delinquent named Walter Bean. Those two had already made a few appearances on juvenile court dockets, and Buckthorn expected to have a professional relationship with them into the foreseeable future. But the involvement of Trey Underhill startled him. He'd known the family as solid citizens for years. The District Attorney had wanted to slam the young men hard with felony charges. Buckthorn had gone to bat for Trey and managed to persuade the D.A. to allow him to plead to a misdemeanor and receive a deferred prosecution. If he performed community service, paid for the property damage, and avoided further charges for a year, the case against him would be dismissed and his record wiped clean.

"So how's it been working out?" Buckthorn asked. "The DPA, I mean."

"Good. Got the community service done. Washing fire trucks down at the station in Fox Springs."

"Not a lot of fun."

Trey shrugged. "It was all right. The cool part was getting to hang around and talk to the firemen."

"Think you might want to do that some day?"

Trey nodded and smiled. "That'd be sweet."

"Come see me when you get to be seventeen," Buckthorn said. "I'll put in a word."

The smile widened. "Really?"

"Sure. But you have to stay out of trouble. And away from guys like Tyree and Bean."

The smile slipped a bit. "Not a problem."

Buckthorn saw something in his eyes. "They hassling you?"

Trey looked away. "Nothing I can't handle."

Buckthorn made a mental note to check on that. "Okay. You need any help, Trey, let me know."

The young man nodded, then looked back at Tim. "I will. And thanks."

"Not a problem," Buckthorn said as he got back in the car. Before starting the car, he looked at the picture in the plastic bag again. The girl bound to the chair, her eyes wide and pleading, couldn't be much older than Trey. There was something familiar about her that he couldn't place. Something in the eyes that called to him. He shook his head. She needed help. And he swore he'd get that help to her.

***

As it was in most things, Maddie Underhill's assessment of Sheriff Henderson Stark's character was spot on. He looked at the photograph lying on his desk, still sealed in the Ziploc bag, as if it was a squalling bastard child dropped down in front of him, one he had no intention of claiming.

"What the hell are we supposed to do with this, Tim?" he said.

Buckthorn repressed a sigh. Stark was good at two things: getting elected and saving the county money. He was usually smart enough to leave the actual law enforcement work to his Chief Deputy. Usually. Buckthorn was getting the sinking feeling that this wasn't one of those times. He briefly wondered whether he'd done the right thing by bringing the photo to Stark's attention, but there really wasn't any way he could think of not to.

"I think it's a proof of life," Buckthorn said. "Something a kidnapper sends to show the target that the victim's still alive." He pointed at the newspaper held by an out-of-frame hand directly beneath the chin of the bound, terrified girl in the picture. "See? Atlanta *Journal -Constitution*. From two days ago. Right before the storms hit. So she was alive then."

"Well, if she was in the path of that storm, and it hit wherever she was hard enough to take this photograph and a bunch of other papers up in the sky and deposit them here, she may not be alive now."

"Maybe not," Buckthorn said. "But we can't assume that. Not if there's a chance."

"We're not assuming anything at all, Tim," Stark said. He gestured at the photograph. "The paper's from Atlanta. So it's a Georgia case."

"Or South Carolina," Buckthorn said.

"Or Alabama, or Mississippi, or wherever. You said these systems can carry things for hundreds of miles."

Buckthorn nodded. "That's what I read."

"Point is, it's interstate, and it's kidnapping. Or worse. It's above our pay grade."

Buckthorn thought of Maddie Underhill's words: *It was meant to come to you.* But Stark went on. "As soon as I heard the word kidnapping," he said, "I called the FBI office in Charlotte. They're sending someone down."

Buckthorn wanted to shout at the man. But he realized that, for all his laziness and buck-passing expertise, the Sheriff was right. This was an FBI case. It didn't mean he had to like it. It may have been absurd, but he felt oddly responsible for this girl he'd never met.

"Okay," he said. "But there's a couple of things I'd like to try while we wait for the Feds to show."

Stark dismissed him with a lackadaisical wave of his hand. "Whatever. As long as it doesn't cost anything and you turn it over to the FBI guys as soon as they get here. Then we're out of it. Got that?"

"Yes, sir," Buckthorn said.

Chapter Five

"I swear to God, boy," Lamp Monroe said, "you could find a way to fuck up a wet dream."

"Hey," Lofton shot back, "I didn't plan for a goddamn tornado to come and level the house."

"I tole you to get me my money," Monroe said, the last word ending in a choked wheeze. There was a pause. Lofton could almost see the old man trying to get his breath, struggling to draw air enough to speak again through the slim tubes that ran into his nose from the ever-present oxygen tank that rode in a silver cart by the side of his wheelchair. After a strangled cough, muffled no doubt by his gnarled claw held over the phone's mouthpiece, Monroe went on. "I din't tell you to kidnap nobody. Nor lose 'em, neither."

"You said get it back," Lofton said. "You said you didn't care how."

"I meant show Preston some consequences. I meant break a finger. A leg, even. Kidnappin's a federal crime, boy. An' now, it might be murder."

"We ought not to be talking about this on the phone, Granddaddy," Lofton said.

"Just fix this shit, goddamn it," Monroe said, then broke the connection.

Lofton stared at the phone, fighting the urge to toss it across the room. Monroe had been running the family as long as anyone could remember. The legend of his ferocity still kept most of his children, grandchildren, nephews, and assorted hangers-on in line. The fact that they all made money—good money—off the businesses he'd founded back in the glory days of the Dixie Mafia helped as well. But,

Lofton mused, maybe it was time for a change. Maybe it was time for Granddaddy Lamp to step down. Or get stepped down.

***

"He wants to be like you," Patience said. She stood behind the old man and put her hands on his shoulders. She began massaging them, gently, but firmly, her motions practiced. She'd done many jobs in her life, including massage—both therapeutic and the other kind. Monroe closed his eyes and made a creaking sound of pleasure deep in his throat. "That's good, gal," he whispered. Then he opened his eyes. "That's the trouble," he said. "These young idjits think it's all about how bad you can be. No damn sense at all. No *judgment*."

"Mmm-hmmm," she said. "Maybe you've brought Lofton along too fast," she said. "Maybe he's gotten in over his head."

He patted her hand fondly. "You let me worry about that, gal. I'll see how he gets hisself out of this. Then I'll decide what to do about him." He squeezed the hand harder. "Right now, I'm cold."

"Well let me warm you up, then, hon," she said with the slow, lazy smile that was the only thing left that he could always count on to stir the blood in his old veins. He smiled back at her, his eyes taking in her lush curves. He'd told Patience more than once that she looked like a woman ought to look, not like these skinny girls the TV told him he should be wanting. Still smiling, Patience helped him up out of the wheelchair and guided him to the huge four poster bed. It was an antique, like everything in the old antebellum-style house. *Like Lamp Monroe himself*, she thought wryly.

She pulled back the covers and gently laid him down, still fully clothed. Sliding in next to him, she pulled the thick handmade quilts over them both and wrapped her arms around his skinny frame. He gave another happy little sound, like a baby's coo, and buried his face between her ample breasts. She kissed the top of his bald head and gently traced the lobes of his ears with her fingertips. In moments, he was asleep.

When she was sure he was completely out, she slipped silently out of the bed. He made a grunt of protest, for all the world like a restless infant, then rolled over on his side and curled up. She looked down at him for a moment. She was fond of the old bastard, she had to admit, and of all the powerful men she'd been next to, his age made him the least demanding. And, if she did this right, he'd be the one who ensured she never had to be any man's plaything again. She walked out of the bedroom and down a long hallway to where she couldn't be heard if the old man woke up. Some of the rooms of the old house had been emptied of furniture. The antiques in other rooms were covered by white sheets to keep the dust off. Lampton Monroe's world had shrunk to a few rooms in the great, rambling old house. His empire had shrunk as well, but there was still enough of it worth having.

When she was far enough away, she ducked into one of the deserted bedrooms and took her cell phone out of her purse. She dialed a number she knew by heart.

"It's me," she said, when the party on the other end picked up. "Lofton's gone off the reservation. He's made a mess." She listened for a moment, then spoke again. "Yeah. He took Preston's kid. Stashed her in of his houses up in Barrett. Then the house got leveled by the storms." Another pause. "I don't know if she's alive, but if she is, it's a problem. If you can get on top of it, he can't help but appreciate it." After a moment, her voice softened. "You too, baby. Miss you." She hung up and went back to the bedroom. Monroe was snoring loudly. She smiled at him, trailed her fingers gently over him beneath the covers. If the time came, and she hoped it never would, she was going to regret killing him. She hoped she could avoid that.

She sat down in the rocker next to the bed and picked up the murder mystery she'd left on the bedside table. Nothing to do now but wait and be patient. She smiled at that. She'd picked this name for a reason.

Chapter Six

Buckthorn left the Sheriff's office and went downstairs to where his own tiny workspace was located, in the middle of the cramped warren that housed the actual law enforcement operations of Gibson County. He sat down behind his desk and ran his hand through his thinning hair. Janine, the departmental secretary, appeared in the doorway. She read the news immediately in his face. "He punted it, didn't he?" she said.

Buckthorn spread his hands in a helpless gesture. "When he's right, he's right. It's a federal matter."

"But you don't like it," she said. "I can tell by the way you're grinding your teeth."

He sighed. Every time he went to his dentist, she'd shake her head and warn him that his habit of grinding his teeth when under stress was causing cracks in the enamel. "You're looking at thousands of dollars' worth of implants if you keep taking your anger out on your teeth," she said. "Or dentures."

"I'm not angry," he insisted.

"Your enamel tells me a different story."

Buckthorn had promised to try and relax. Then he'd gone back to work.

Janine went on. "By the time those federal guys get off their backsides, that girl could be dead. Or worse."

"So we make sure we've done everything we can by the time they get here."

She nodded. "I got the scanner set up, and we're loading everything that'll come out clearly into the computers. Except the picture of the girl. Soon as we get it all digitized, I'll put them up on a Facebook page I set up. Then we wait to see if anyone recognizes their pictures. If they do and get in touch with me, then we have an idea where the stuff came from."

He looked at her strangely. "You have a Facebook page?"

"Unlike some people, Tim, I live in the twenty-first century."

"I thought it was just for teenagers. Not for..." he trailed off.

Janine put one hand on her hip and looked at him over the tops of her glasses. "You want to pick your next words real carefully, Tim Buckthorn," she said.

"I didn't mean you were..."

She didn't give him time to finish. "Lots of people are on Facebook. I mostly use it to keep up with Judith and Jonathan." Buckthorn remembered that Janine's married daughter had moved to California with her husband, a captain in the Marines, and her son Jonathan was a student at Appalachian State. "Okay," he said. "Let me know when it's ready to go up. I want to take a look at it."

"Okay. We could use some press coverage on this. You think that girl reporter from WRHO'd be interested? The one who came down last time?"

Buckthorn felt a jolt of dread run through him at the mention of the last time he'd seen Gabriella Torrijos. An outlaw motorcycle gang had invaded Pine Lake, wreaking terrible havoc while trying to free one of their captured members. He'd lost several good men. He himself had been taken prisoner and beaten savagely by one of them. In the end, he'd had to kill the group's leader, along with another man. He shook his head to clear the images. It hadn't been Torrijos' fault. If anything, it had been the fault of...

Janine's voice cut through his reverie. "I said, you want me to call her?"

"Yeah," he said. "Or someone. Good idea."

"You okay, Tim?" she said.

His smile felt unconvincing, even to him. "I'm fine. I just don't like bringing the press into these things."

She nodded. "I hear you. But this isn't exactly your ordinary case."

"True," Buckthorn said. "So call her."

"On it," she said, and left.

Buckthorn leaned back in his chair and rubbed his hands over his face. In reality, he'd never really gotten over that terrible day. It was the first life he'd taken in the line of duty. Afterwards, he'd had trouble sleeping. He'd found himself having more and more trouble holding ordinary conversations. A woman he'd been seeing off and on had finally told him that if she wanted silence, she could get that alone at home. He hadn't dated since. Janine had gently suggested that maybe he should see somebody professional. He'd turned down the idea of a psychologist. If word had gotten around the tight-knit department that he was seeing a shrink, he told her, he'd never hear the end of it. She retorted that he didn't give his people enough credit. If he didn't want a doctor, she suggested, he could talk to her pastor. Buckthorn had changed the subject, not wanting to admit to her that he had begun to have his doubts about the existence of God .He'd buried himself in work, and slowly, the bad memories had weakened to the point where he could lock them away.

Work, he thought. *That's the solution.* He turned to the stack of paperwork on his desk that never seemed to get any smaller, no matter how much he hacked away at it. He was several pages into last week's incident reports when he saw a shadow move across his doorway. He looked up. Janine was standing there, an odd look on her face.

"What?" he said.

"We've got the pictures ready to go."

"Okay, I'll be there in a minute."

"And, ah, the FBI people are here."

"Well, I guess I better meet them first. They may have their own..." He saw the way her jaw was set, the slight tightening of the skin around her eyes. "Okay, seriously, what's wrong?"

"Actually, Tim, you've already met one of them."

"What do you mean I've...oh. Oh, no."

"Well," a voice from behind Janine said, "I've had warmer welcomes." Janine stepped aside, and a man entered.

He was short and stocky. His hair was shorter than the first time he and Buckthorn had met, and he'd shaven the beard and moustache. Without them, he was a thoroughly unremarkable-looking man, which is why he'd been so successful in his former job working undercover. From the looks of the suit he wore, he wasn't doing that any more. He'd moved up in the FBI.

"Agent Wolf," Buckthorn said.

"Deputy Buckthorn," Tony Wolf replied, and stuck out his hand. "Good to be back in Pine Lake."

Chapter Seven

Lofton Monroe stood in the sweltering heat and stared at the pile of lumber, piping and drywall that had once been a house. *There's no way the girl could be alive under all of that,* he thought. But at some point, someone would have to come and clean up the wreckage. At some point, they'd find the body. In a house that had his name on the deed.

He took out a bandanna and wiped the sweat from his brow, cursing himself for not using a safe house or even a motel to stash the girl. But he hadn't expected anything like this to happen. The storms had boiled up suddenly, driven by a savage three-week heat wave with temperatures soaring into the hundreds every day across the South. And Preston was supposed to have the money within a couple of days. That's what he'd said. Of course, that's what deadbeats always said. He'd been a mile or so away from the house, getting groceries, when the sky had turned black and the winds began to howl. He'd jumped into the truck and headed back as quickly as he could, vicious gusts of wind nearly buffeting the big vehicle off the road and the rain coming down so fiercely that at times he had to slow the truck to a crawl because he could barely see. When he got back to the house on its cul-de-sac, there was nothing left but rubble. There was no way he could have expected that. It wasn't fair of Granddaddy to blame him. But Lampton Monroe was never known for fairness. *A hard man*, people said, and they didn't know the half of it.

"Hell of a mess," a voice said behind Lofton. He jumped, startled, then turned around. Donovan was standing behind him, a toothpick dangling out of one corner of his mouth.

"The fuck are you doing here?" Lofton demanded.

Donovan ignored the tone. "Mr. Monroe sent me up here from Biloxi to see if ya needed a hand," he said. His voice retained just a hint of the Irish accent he'd grown up with.

"I'm fine. I've got this."

"Yeah," Donovan said. "I can see that." He took the toothpick out of his mouth and gestured towards the rubble. "She down there?"

"No way she could be anywhere else."

"Unless she got away."

"There's no way," Lofton said.

"We got to get the body out, then," Donovan said. "Can't have dead girls turnin' up on family-owned property."

It was exactly what Lofton had been thinking, but he didn't like hearing it. Especially not from Donovan. Hell, he wasn't even family. "And just how do you think we're goin' to go about that?" he said. "Use our hands?"

Donovan shook his head. "Front-end loader."

"Uh-huh. You happen to bring one of them with you?"

"No. But we can find ourselves one." He cocked his head slightly. "Ya hear something?"

***

Callie could feel the wetness on her face. She couldn't tell if it was blood or tears. The effort of rubbing the duct tape off had resulted in some painful scrapes. If she got out, would she be scarred for life? Boys had begun paying attention to her, but she'd always been shy about her looks. Even the beginnings of a zit were enough to make her painfully embarrassed and self-conscious. *If I've messed up my face...* she put that thought away for the moment. She needed to let people know she was alive down here.

"HEY!" she yelled as loud as she could, then waited. "HEY!" she yelled again. "DOWN HERE!" She listened for some response. All she could hear was a trickling sound, like running water. It sounded very near. She realized then how thirsty she was. She moved towards the sound, to the end of the chain that tethered her to the wall. She was startled when she ran up against what seemed to be a wall where one hadn't been before. *Maybe I've gotten turned around in the dark*, she thought. But no, the wall she was chained to was behind her. Then she comprehended what had happened. Most of the cellar was gone. The house had collapsed into it. She was in a tiny chamber that was left. The word came back to her from the T.V. program she'd seen. A void. That's what she was in. A void.

Buried alive, the voice in her head was nearly shrieking now. She took a deep breath and got hold of herself. She listened again for the water, then leaned forward. She suddenly felt a steady stream of liquid, flowing like a tiny waterfall from the rubble above her. She stuck out her tongue. It was warm and tasted of metal. She didn't have any idea what kind of nasty stuff was in it. But if she didn't drink, she risked dying of thirst. She opened her mouth and took a swallow, then another. Then another, until she'd taken the edge off her thirst. She leaned back. The panic was still there, but she thought of it as being in a little room, locked away like she was. The trick was not to let it out. If she did, she'd lose her shit. She'd forget what she needed to do. And then she'd die. She took a deep breath. "HEY!" she yelled. "HEY! HELP!"

She was lucky, she told herself. If she wasn't, she'd have died in the collapse. She wouldn't have found the water near enough to drink. If that luck held, someone would come to get her.

***

Lofton turned back to the pile. He wiped his brow again, straining his ears. He heard nothing but the sound of the slight breeze stirring the leaves of the few trees still standing. Then he heard it. It was unmistakably a voice, coming from beneath the ruins of his house. "Hey!" the voice said, faint but distinct. "Hey! Help!"

"Holy shit," Lofton said.

"We better get moving," Donovan said. "We need to get her out before anyone else does."

Lofton gestured at the empty lots around him. He'd bought the house shortly before the real estate crash had driven the developer into bankruptcy. He liked not having neighbors. "There's no one out here."

"Not now. But that won't last. Let's go steal a loader."

"And what are we going to do, even if we can dig her out?"

"We'll deal with that when the time comes. But we have to keep her quiet." He looked at the ruined house. "We'll be back, little girl," he said.

Chapter Eight

“Good to see you too, Agent Wolf,” Buckthorn said as he got up and extended his hand.

Wolf shook the hand, cocking an eyebrow at Buckthorn. “Really? I seem to remember last time we met, you said if I ever came back here, you'd throw me in jail.”

Buckthorn let go of the handshake, let his hand drop awkwardly to his side. “Yeah. Well. I was a little upset.”

Wolf nodded. “Understandable.” He looked around. Buckthorn was suddenly aware of how cramped and cluttered the space was, jammed floor to ceiling with shelves that were crammed with a variety of loose-leaf notebooks, manuals, guides, books and circulars. A similarly untidy pile of papers covered every inch of his desktop. His old desk chair was worn, a few rips patched with duct tape. “Nice place you got here,” Wolf said.

Buckthorn watched him carefully for signs of sarcasm, and saw none. Wolf noticed the wary look. “No, really,” he said. “This looks like a place where stuff gets done. Not...” he pointed to the ceiling, indicating the Sheriff's office directly above. He didn't finish the sentence. His look said everything Buckthorn needed to know about Wolf's opinion of Sheriff Stark.

“We try,” Buckthorn said. There was a brief uncomfortable silence. Janine broke in. “I've got that picture for you, sir.”

“Thank you, ma'am,” Wolf said. “My partner will be asking you to fill out some affidavits about chain of custody. Who's handled the photograph and...”

"I know what chain of custody forms are, young man," Janine said. "You're not in Mayberry."

"Yes, ma'am," Wolf said. "I realize that. Remember, I used to live here."

"Yes," she said. "Under another name." She turned and walked away.

Wolf turned to Buckthorn. "Sorry. I seem to have gotten off on the wrong foot with your girl."

"She hears you call her that," Buckthorn said, "you'll be even sorrier."

"Noted. So what do we know?"

Buckthorn took notice of the 'we' as he motioned Wolf to the single office chair across from him. "We know squat," he admitted. "A retired schoolteacher named Maddie Underhill was cleaning up storm debris with her son and grandson. Suddenly, all of this stuff started falling out of the sky. She saw some old photos and papers in the mess, remembered a story she'd seen about a similar incident, and started trying to get the debris organized."

Wolf looked puzzled. "Why?"

"Because that's the kind of person Maddie Underhill is," Buckthorn said. "A place for everything, and everything in its place."

"You know her, then," Wolf said, then held up a hand as Buckthorn began to reply. "I know," he said. "Everybody knows everybody here."

"Except you," Buckthorn said.

"Except me," Wolf agreed. "But let's try to let the past be past, okay?"

"So why did you get sent here," Buckthorn said, "except because of what happened two years ago?"

Wolf didn't speak for a moment. He got up and went to the glass wall of the office, where a half-closed floor to ceiling mini-blind gave partial privacy while allowing Buckthorn's people passing by to note that the boss was inside working. He looked out through the shade and fiddled with the pull. Finally, he said, "I volunteered."

"What?"

"I wanted to come back," he said. "I always liked this place."

Buckthorn didn't know what to say to that, so he blurted out the first thing that came to his mind. "It's a fine town."

"I know," Wolf said. "I'm sorry I never got to know it better than I did." He snapped the blind pull against the shade with an abrupt motion and turned back to Buckthorn. "So," he said, "can I see this picture?"

Buckthorn punched a button on his desk phone. "Janine," he said, "can you bring..." but she was already standing in the doorway, holding the Ziploc bag in one hand and a sheet of paper in the other. Wolf smiled. "Thank you, ma'am," he said as he reached for the bag.

"I'll need you to sign the chain of custody form," she said.

"Yes ma'am." He laid the bag gently on one of the few clear spaces on Buckthorn's desk. He looked at Buckthorn. "Do you have a pair of..." He stopped as he saw Janine holding out a pair of tweezers. "Thank you, ma'am," Wolf said again with elaborate courtesy. Gently, he worked the soggy photo out of the bag. The three of them gathered around the desktop and looked down at it as if expecting it to speak and reveal its secrets.

The girl's face looked back up at them. They couldn't see her body or much of anything below the chin, because someone was holding a folded newspaper directly below her face. They could clearly make out the headlines: PLANNING OFFICIAL INDICTED, one read. BRAVES SPLIT DOUBLEHEADER, a smaller one said.

"Okay," Wolf said. "Atlanta *Journal -Constitution.* Any idea from when?"

"Two days ago," Janine said. "I looked it up online. Those were the stories on the front page two days ago."

"Good." Wolf turned to Buckthorn. "Definitely a proof of life," he said. "But here's the thing. We did a search. There just aren't any open kidnapping for ransom cases on the Eastern seaboard right now."

"You're saying this hasn't been reported?"

Wolf nodded. "Exactly."

"But why?" Janine said. "Why wouldn't anyone call the police if their little girl went missing? Especially a pretty little thing like that?"

"Good question," Wolf said.

"The kidnapper ordered them not to," Buckthorn suggested.

"Maybe," Wolf said. "Or maybe it's the kind of thing the people involved want to settle privately."

"What's that supposed to mean?" Janine said.

"It means," Buckthorn said, "some kind of gang thing. Kidnapping for revenge."

"Or collateral," Wolf said. "Someone owes someone money, so they take the debtor's child as security."

"Dear Lord," Janine said. "That's awful."

"Yeah," Wolf said. "It is."

Chapter Nine

Lofton's phone rang as they were driving away from the house. They were in his truck, with Lofton at the wheel. He fumbled the bleating device out of his pocket and checked the number.

"Shit," he said. "It's Preston."

"Give me the phone," Donovan said. "You drive." Lofton hesitated, then handed the phone over.

"Yeah?" Donovan said. Then, "He's busy right now." There was a burst of agitated talking on the other end. "Who I am is none of your business. Have ya got Mr. Monroe's money?" Another stream of chatter. "We're runnin' out of patience, sunshine," Donovan said. "Give me a time frame here, unless you want your little girl coming back in a bunch of separate packages." He listened for another moment, then hung up. "He wanted to talk to her."

"If he starts thinking she's dead," Lofton said, "then he's got nothing to lose by going to the cops."

"True," Donovan said. "You realize how badly you've fucked this up, right?"

"Look, asshole," Lofton began, then his head slammed against the driver's side window as Donovan's left fist shot out and struck him in the side of the face. The truck slewed across the road, almost into the path of an oncoming SUV. The SUV's driver swerved and honked frantically.

"You crazy son of a bitch!" Lofton yelled, fighting the wheel to drag the big truck back into his lane. When he had the vehicle under control, he put his hand to the side of his head. It came away bloody. "Okay, motherfucker," he said in a low voice, and started to pull to the side.

"Don't," Donovan said. Lofton looked over. Donovan was leaned back against the passenger door, pointing an ugly black semiautomatic pistol at him.

"What the fuck?" Lofton said.

"Shut up," Donovan replied. "I got sent down here to clean up the mess you made, eejit. And if that includes burying you, the girl, and Preston in the same hole, then that's what I'll do."

Lofton tried to keep his voice steady. "Granddaddy on board with that?"

"He will be," Donovan said, "if it's necessary. So don't make it necessary. Right now, the only reason you're still breathing is because you're of use. I need you to help me get that girl out of that hole and shut her up. For good. Then we go take care of Preston. What I do with you after that depends on how well behaved you are from now till then. So, are you going to behave?"

Lofton didn't answer. His jaw was clenched in rage. *This ain't right,* he was thinking. *This son of a bitch ain't even family.*

"While you think about it," Donovan said, "consider this. Preston's not going to come up with that money. There was no way he was ever going to. I mean, Jesus, a hundred and fifty grand? To a guy with a gambling jones that bad? The guy's a loser, always has been. But you backed the loan. So, according to Mr. Monroe's rules, which you know as well as I do, you're responsible for it. Think about how you're going to cover that, if you want to get out of this alive. Now, I'm getting impatient. Are you going to behave, or do I just shoot you right now?"

"Okay," Lofton said through clenched teeth.

"Okay, what?"

Lofton's voice sounded like he was strangling on the words. "Okay, I'm going to behave."

"Good choice," Donovan said. "And if you're thinking of changing it, just keep in mind, you're on your Granddaddy's shit list right now. I can help get you off it, or you can go to number one on the list. Now drive."

***

Arthur Preston closed the phone. His face was pale and drawn, the dark circles under his eyes standing out prominently.

"Well?" his ex-wife said. "Did you talk to her? I didn't hear you talking to her. Was she okay?" Her voice held a high, thin edge of near hysteria.

"I don't know who it was I talked to," he said. His voice sounded faint, even in his own ears. "Someone I never heard before."

"What? What does that mean?"

"I don't know," he said. "He said I needed to come up with the money."

"That's it," she said. "I'm calling the police." She reached for her own phone on the coffee table.

"NO!" he crossed the room in a few long strides and grabbed her arm.

"Let go of me!" she screamed and struck at him with her free hand. Her nails caught his cheek and raked down. He screamed with pain and rage and caught her wrist. He slammed her back down against the couch. She thrashed under him like a wild animal, shrieking incoherently. He twisted just in time to catch her knee on his hip instead of his balls.

"LISTEN TO ME!" he roared, pinning her to the couch. She stopped struggling and stared up at him, her eyes filled with hatred.

He got his voice under control. "If we call the cops," he said, "they'll know. They've got people there. All over the place. They'll *know*, Myra. And they'll kill her."

"They've killed her already, you bastard," she said. "And it's *your fucking fault!*"

"No," he said. "They would have told me. They'd want me to know. Besides, that's not the way they do things. They'd..." he stopped. "They wouldn't do it all at once. They'd...they'd send me an ear. Or a finger. Something to let me know. Something to...motivate me. That's how these people work."

"Oh, now you're some sort of expert." She shook her head, then turned and spat, full in his face. He recoiled, releasing her arms. He stumbled backwards, landing on his ass on the floor.

She sat up, rubbing her wrists. "Do you have any idea how much I fucking hate you right now?"

"You mean more than usual?" he said bitterly. He got to his feet. "I can fix this."

"How?" she demanded. "You've never been able to fix anything. Ever. You fucking *loser*!"

It was such a familiar refrain, it amazed him to see how badly it could still wound him. "I can fix this. Don't call the police. She'll die if you do."

"Get out," she said. "And don't come back here without my daughter."

He didn't answer, just walked out the door of the house he'd once shared with her. He'd been there since he'd gotten the phone call from Lofton, letting him know he had Callie, that he was holding her for "security" on his debt.

He got into the car and sat there for a few moments, staring at the house but not seeing it. He'd known Monroe was getting antsy for his money, but he didn't have any idea he was ready to go that far. Not yet. He'd thought he'd have more time. Time to make it up. Time for one more score. Now, it looked like time had run out, and he had no idea what to do.

He opened the glove box of the old Buick and took the gun out. It was an old, battered .38 revolver that had belonged to his father. For a moment he thought of putting the gun in his mouth and pulling the trigger. But if he did that, Callie would definitely die. Right now, he'd welcome death, but only if he knew Callie was safe. He'd failed her so badly, in so many ways, he could do one last thing for her. Maybe she would remember him with something more than disappointment and hatred if he could do that. As those thoughts went round and round in his head, a plan began to take shape. He shoved the gun back into the glove box and started the car.

Chapter Ten

Wolf eased the picture back into the bag, then picked it up. "Okay," he said. "First thing we do is send the pic to the lab at Quantico. Run it for prints, which is a long shot. But we can also see if we can ID the printer."

"The what?" Janine asked.

"It's a digital photo," Wolf said. "Printed out on a computer printer. Different printer models have different signatures, a pattern of dots the manufacturer puts in. You can't see them on printed out documents, except under blue or in some cases UV light. We may be able to get a make on the printer."

"Wait a minute," Janine said. "You're telling me that printers have, like, fingerprints?"

Wolf nodded. "Yes, ma'am."

"Put on there by the people that make them?"

"Yes ma'am."

"And they don't tell us about this."

"No ma'am."

She tightened her lips. "Well, that doesn't seem right to me."

"Maybe not, ma'am. But if it helps us find the girl..."

She sighed. "Okay. We'll argue about this another day."

"Yes ma'am," Wolf said. "We'll also run the pic through biometrics. See if we get any hits."

"Do I want to know what that is?" Janine said.

"Facial recognition software," Buckthorn said. "It compares the face with others in a database."

"Including online ones," Wolf added. "If the girl has a Facebook or a Tumblr or a blog where she's put her pictures up, the computer might be able to match one of those with this, and we'll know who she is."

"I think I'm going to go home and put my computer in the trash bin," Janine said. "I'm going to feel like I'm being watched every time I send an e-mail." The two men didn't answer. She gave Buckthorn an exasperated look. "This is the part where y'all are supposed to tell me I don't have anything to worry about."

"You don't have anything to worry about," they said in ragged unison.

"Great."

"So," Buckthorn said, "you still like living in the twenty-first century?"

"I'm beginning to wonder."

Wolf chuckled. "Come on, Deputy, I want you to meet my partner."

"She's in the conference room," Janine said, "looking over the other papers."

Buckthorn looked over at Wolf. "She?"

Janine sighed. "Yes, Tim. She. There are female FBI agents these days, you know." She looked at Wolf. "You'll have to forgive Deputy Buckthorn," she said. "He still hasn't accepted the idea of women in law enforcement."

"I didn't say that," Buckthorn protested.

"I definitely wouldn't say it to Agent Dushane," Wolf said. He started down the hall.

Buckthorn felt his face reddening as he followed. "I don't have a problem with women officers!"

Janine, who'd fallen in beside him, snorted. "You just never hired any."

"We'll discuss the Department's gender discrimination problem later," Wolf said. They'd arrived at the door to the conference room.

"We don't have a..." he stopped himself as he saw the person bending over the conference table. "Um, hello," he said.

The woman looked up from the papers spread out in front of her like the pieces of a jigsaw puzzle. She was petite, only a little over five feet tall. She had a sharp-featured face with high, prominent cheekbones and dark, keen eyes. She looked as if she might have some Native

American ancestry. Her long dark hair was gathered in a braid that fell down her back.

"Don't have a what?" she said. Then she noticed Buckthorn and straightened up. "Oh, hi," she said. She walked over to him with a brisk, confident stride and stuck out her hand. "You must be Deputy Buckthorn," she said. "I'm Leila Dushane."

He took the hand. "Tim Buckthorn."

She gave his hand two quick, firm shakes, then let it go. "I've heard a lot about you." Then she smiled. She had a nice smile, Buckthorn thought. "All of it good."

He smiled back. "Glad to hear it."

"So what do we have, L.D.?" Wolf said.

The smile vanished and she shook her head. "We got *nada*, boss," she said. "Most of this stuff's so soggy it's turned to goop. Mrs. Porter," she gestured at Janine, "already got everything usable scanned in. We can go live with the Facebook page whenever you're ready. Then all we need to do is get the word out and hope people start recognizing their pics and calling in."

"Gaby called me," Wolf said. "She's on her way down with a cameraman. She thinks they can make the 11:00."

"Great," Dushane said tonelessly.

"Be nice, L.D." Wolf said.

She gave him a transparently phony smile. "I'm always nice, boss," she said.

"Uh-huh." Wolf turned to Buckthorn. "Agent Dushane doesn't like getting the media involved in cases. And she really doesn't approve of it when the reporter is my girlfriend."

"And Agent Wolf..." Dushane began, her voice harsh with anger. Then she cut herself off. Her lips tightened. There was a moment of uncomfortable silence, then Wolf spoke again.

"We need to get that picture up to Quantico," he said. "Quickly."

"I got a Fed Ex package ready to go," Janine said. "The guy'll be here in a half hour."

Wolf nodded at her. "Impressive."

She looked back at him impassively. "It's my job, Agent."

"I'm not underestimating you, Mrs. Porter," Wolf said. "Truly."

"Good thing."

"But I'm getting the feeling that's not the only problem you have with me."

Her expression didn't change. "I don't have a problem with you, Agent Wolf."

"Ma'am," Wolf said, "I don't think that's completely true."

She bristled. "Are you calling me a liar, young man?"

"See, that's what I mean. That tone, right there. No, ma'am, I'm not calling you a liar. I'm thinking you're too well brought up to let me know what you really think of me. Clearly you don't think much of me. But I'd like to know why."

"Why do you think, Agent Wolf?" she blurted out. "What did you ever bring this town but death and misery?"

"Janine," Buckthorn started, but Wolf waved him off.

"Mrs. Porter," he said gently, "I am as deeply sorry as a man can be about what happened here before. It wasn't anything I meant to do. I came here because it seemed like a safe place. I picked this place precisely because didn't expect the people who were looking for me to ever find me here. But they did. And when they came, I did everything I could to help defend this town."

She looked at him for a moment, then lowered her head and sighed. "I know, hon, I know. I'm not bein' fair to you. But Travis...one of the deputies that was killed...he was my nephew. My sister's boy."

"I'm sorry, ma'am," Wolf said.

"I know. I know you are. But just do us all a favor, all right? Get done with whatever it is you have to do, then go on. Go back to Charlotte, or Washington D.C, or wherever. Let us be."

"Yes ma'am," Wolf said. "I'll do my best."

Chapter Eleven

P reston sat in the parking lot of the Bojangles next to the bank and watched the cars going in and out of the lot. It was a small branch, on one of the outparcels of a good-sized shopping center in a nondescript suburb of Chattanooga. Preston had done the books for a couple of the smaller stores in the center. He knew that not only they, but the big-box stores, such as Best Buy and Target, made regular deposits there, as did most of the smaller stores. Plus, it was Friday, payday, so he figured the place would be flush with cash. Maybe not all the cash he needed, but maybe enough to placate Monroe and his grandson and get Callie back.

Preston had been in the place already and checked out the layout. He'd particularly noticed the overweight security guard who seemed to spend most of his time sitting down. When he did get up, he walked with a slight limp, as if he'd suffered some injury. Maybe a retired cop, long past his prime and put out to pasture.

Preston wiped his brow. The sleeve of the light-colored hooded sweatshirt he'd bought at the sporting goods store in the shopping center came away dark with sweat. It was hot in the car, and it wasn't going to get any cooler with him sitting here watching. Still, he hesitated. He'd never done anything criminal before. Well, the gambling. And the coke that made the gambling that much more of a thrill. But nothing *really* criminal. Nothing that involved holding people at gunpoint. He was forty-two years old. He was a *bookkeeper,* for God's sake. But now, here he was, back to the wall, with a gun lying on the seat next to him and nowhere else to turn. He looked at the dashboard clock of the aging car. 4:45. It'd be closing time soon, and by then it'd be too late. For everyone, but especially for his daughter. He took a deep breath and got out of the car, sticking the gun in his waistband and pulling the bottom of the hoodie over it. He stood looking at the bank for a moment, then walked with a fast, determined stride towards the front door, like a man walking to battle.

***

Sam Hough knew there was something hinky as soon as he looked up from filling out his deposit slip and saw the guy in the hoodie walk through the door. For one thing, it was hotter than the hinges of Hell outside, and who wore a sweatshirt in that kind of weather? Plus, the guy was no teenager. He looked to be in his mid-forties, although it looked like at least the last few had been hard, care-filled ones. But even without that, Hough would have known the guy was trouble. It was in the eyes. In seventeen years of law enforcement, he'd seen that look a few times, even in the quiet suburban department where he'd spent most of his career. It was the look of someone with absolutely nothing left to lose, the look of someone who just didn't give a fuck anymore.

"Psst," he whispered across the dark-wood standing desk where another officer, a young Latino named Mercado, was finishing his own deposit slip. He didn't know Mercado well; he was fairly new and they'd always worked on different shifts so far. But he knew Mercado's partner, Green, pretty well. He and Green had had a few beers down at their favorite sports bar, and Green never seemed to have any complaints.

Mercado looked up, puzzled. Hough jerked his chin at where Hoodie Guy was getting in the shortest of the three teller lines. Mercado clocked him immediately and looked back at Hough.

"You have got to be shitting me," he whispered. He'd figured things out right away. Good.

"Guess he's not from around here," Hough said, "Or he wouldn't have picked this bank."

"You got that right." Mercado looked at the security guard. "What about him?"

Hough smirked. "His job's to call us, right?"

"Hah. Right. So how do we…"

"I'll get in line behind him," Hough said. "You get next to him. He tries anything, we take his ass down, hard. I don't want any gunfire in here if we can help it." Mercado just nodded and moved to the teller line beside the one where Hoodie Guy was standing, hands in his pockets, looking down at the floor. The hood was pulled up and over his forehead.

This guy cannot be serious, Hough thought. He might as well have stuck a sign that said BANK ROBBER to his back. He moved in closer, got in the line just as it moved. Hough looked over at Mercado. Mercado glanced significantly to the door. Hough looked. He saw his own partner, Lee Curtis, walk in. Curtis was tall and thin, a former high school basketball star who'd kept his lanky, angular gracefulness even into middle age.

"Yo, Sammy," he called to Hough.

"Hey, Curt," Hough said. "C'mere a minute." Curtis ambled over, wearing his usual easy smile on a face that looked like it never left the farm. The smile slipped a bit when he caught sight of Hoodie Guy, who hadn't turned around at the exchange like some other people had. He raised an eyebrow at Hough, who nodded. Curtis got in line without another word. *And now we're three*, Hough thought. The line moved again.

***

Preston fumbled with the note in his pocket. He'd written it on a slip of soiled and creased scrap paper from the glove compartment, and now it felt damp with sweat. He found himself absurdly embarrassed at how shabby it probably looked. *Get a grip*, he told himself. *It's a robbery note, not a dinner invitation.* He fought down the hysterical laugh that threatened to bubble up out of his throat.

The line moved again. One more to go. He felt the weight of the gun in his waistband. His chest felt tight. He could feel the hammering of his heart and wondered why everyone in the bank couldn't hear it. Despite the heat of the sweatshirt, the sweat trickling down his back felt ice cold.

The line moved.

Preston pulled the note out of his pocket, shoved it across the counter, harder than he'd intended. It skittered across the smooth surface and onto the floor behind the counter. The young blonde female teller, obviously nettled, bent down to pick it up. She was looking at it as she came back up from behind the counter, her brow furrowed. He saw her eyes grow wide as the import of the note sank in. He reached for the gun...

Only to find his arms seized from behind and yanked up to the center of his back. He was propelled forward, into the edge of the counter, his breath coming out in an agonized whoosh as his sternum crashed into the hard unyielding surface. He cried out in shock and pain. Someone screamed, very near. Then he was on his face, on the floor, hands still wrenched painfully behind him. He heard the click of metal on metal and felt the cold rings of a pair of handcuffs encircling his wrists. Tears of frustration and rage sprang to his eyes as a harsh voice grated in one ear. He felt the steel of a gun barrel jammed hard and painfully into the other.

"Congratulations, genius," the voice said. "You just tried to rob the bank where half the cops in town come to deposit their paychecks. This is really not your lucky day."

It never is, he thought, as the cuffs clicked shut.

Chapter Twelve

"**T**hat's what I'm talking about," Donovan said.

The loader squatted at one edge of a large rectangle of torn-up earth, turned to mud by the recent storms and churned into a chaotic series of rills and gullies by the comings and goings of tons of equipment. The land had been marked off with strings attached to small, upright bits of wood, showing where the foundations of a house would soon be poured. The front of the machine was a deep scoop, its once-bright yellow paint scratched and abraded off from repeatedly gouging into the thick, rocky soil. Clumps of muddy soil mixed with stones still clung to the front blade. A jointed backhoe arced up from behind the open driver's seat like the leg of a giant insect.

"Great," Lofton said. "Now all we have to do is drive it ten miles back to my house with no one noticing."

Donovan pointed to the low-slung black trailer parked on the other side of the building site. "No, numb-nuts," he said, "we hook that up to this truck, hot-wire the loader if we have to, and haul the fucker back. It's the weekend. No one'll notice the thing gone till Monday."

As it turns out, they didn't need to hot-wire the loader; the operator had left the keys under the seat. It took them less than a half hour before they were pulling away, the big truck grumbling under the unaccustomed load of the trailer banging and squeaking behind them. "You ever run one of these things before?" Lofton asked.

Donovan shook his head. "You?"

"Naw. Too much like work."

Donovan shrugged. "How hard can it be?"

"We're just as likely to kill that girl tryin' to dig her out of there." Lofton squinted at the sun, lowering behind the trees. "Especially in the dark."

"Saves us having to do it later," Donovan said. "Important thing is to get her out of there before someone digs the body out of *your* cellar." The emphasis on the word *your* made it clear that Donovan still blamed Lofton for the mess. Lofton seethed inside, but kept his mouth shut. *I'll deal with him later*, he thought. *See if I don't.*

***

Gabriella Torrijos looked unhappy. "It's the best part of the story, Tony," she said. "No, scratch that. It *is* the story."

"I know," Wolf replied. "And you'll be the first one I tell it to. On camera. I promise. But if you run with it now, whoever's holding her might kill her to cover his tracks. We can't let him know we know about this."

She stared at the ground, her anger apparent in the tension of her shoulders. "My producer told me I shouldn't take this story," she said. "Conflict of interest, he told me. You shouldn't cover a story involving someone you're...emotionally involved with." He noticed she didn't say *love*. She never did. But now wasn't the time or place to go through that again.

"But I told him you trusted me," she went on. "I told him you wouldn't talk to anyone else."

"Which is true."

"But now you tell me I can't use the biggest part of the story. That I've got to make this another puff piece. I don't do puff pieces any more, Tony."

"It's just till we find her."

"If you do," she said. She looked up at him, hurt in her wide dark eyes. "I've got to tell you, Tony, I'm feeling a little used right now."

He tried to contain his own anger. "I think you're missing the big picture here, Gaby. There's a girl out there we need to find. And I need your help."

She sighed. "I know, I know." She gestured to her cameraman, a middle-aged black man with thinning gray hair standing a few feet away. He shouldered his camera and made his way over to them, a wary expression on his face.

"Howard," Wolf said.

"Agent Wolf," Howard Jessup replied.

"Been a while."

"That it has. Everything okay?"

"Yeah," Wolf said. "Just had to set some parameters for the story."

"Parameters," Howard said. He looked at Gaby quizzically. She was looking away, her jaw set. "Okay," he said. "Where we setting up?"

"I'll be over here," Wolf said. Gaby didn't answer. She began talking to Howard in a low, tense voice. Wolf walked over to where Leila Dushane was waiting.

"Trouble in paradise, Boss?" she said.

Wolf glared at her. "L.D.," he began.

"Shutting up, sir," she answered briskly.

They watched as Howard set up the camera and aligned the shot to put the bulky concrete structure of the Gibson County governmental center behind Gaby, the words "Sheriff's Department" on the sign behind her arching over her head. When he was done, he turned on the recorder. He counted down from five with one outstretched hand, folding his fingers one by one. When he reached zero, Gaby's face lit up in a professional but warm smile, all trace of her earlier anger gone.

"Bob, we're here in the Gibson County town of Pine Lake, where a mystery seems to have literally fallen from the sky..."

"I hope this works," Buckthorn's voice came from behind them. Wolf and Dushane turned. He was standing there, in uniform, his hat in his hands.

"Me, too," Wolf said.

"When do you expect the results from the lab?" Buckthorn asked.

"Don't know," Dushane said. "I'm already getting a lot of whining about how backed up they are. I may need to get on the phone and kick some asses."

"You do that," Buckthorn said. "That girl needs all the help she can get. She's probably scared out of her mind."

Wolf nodded, studying Buckthorn's face carefully. He saw the same determination to protect the innocent that had driven him into the Crimes Against Children Unit as a young agent, then into undercover work against exploiters of children and teenagers. "We'll get her," he said.

"And the bastard who took her," Dushane added.

Buckthorn just nodded. "Call me if you hear anything." He turned and walked towards his patrol car, putting his hat on as he went.

"Man," Dushane said, "did you see his eyes? And have you noticed the way he grinds his teeth?"

"Yeah," said Wolf. "I did. And I have."

"That guy's intense."

"He's a good cop," Wolf said.

"You don't think he's wound a little too tight?"

"That's what makes him a good cop," Wolf said.

"You're not worried he might snap?"

"Not really. No more that I am about me. Or you."

"Me?" she said. "I'm a goddamn poster child for mental health." She watched Gaby winding up her story. "Okay. I'm going to go see if I can get the lab rats motivated. You and the missus can have some alone time."

Wolf let the jibe go. "I'm going to call Steadman first," he said, referring to the current Deputy Director who'd run the operation that had gone terribly wrong, causing Wolf to go to ground in Pine Lake.

"Pat Steadman?" Dushane asked.

"Yeah," Wolf said. "He might be able to bring some pressure from above."

"Couldn't hurt." She pulled out her cell phone. "They going to let us use the conference room?"

"For the time being. It's as good a place to run this investigation as any, until we get some idea of where the girl is."

"You really think she's alive, boss?"

"I have to," Wolf said.

***

Callie awoke to the sound of a rumbling engine. She raised her head and listened, straining her ears in the darkness. Some kind of truck, or heavy equipment. "Hey," she tried to call out. "Hey! Down here!" her voice came out as a weak croak, barely audible even to her. She slumped in despair. But as the sound of the engine grew, her hope grew with it. Someone was coming for her. Someone would get her out. Maybe it was even her dad. All she had to do was hang on.

Chapter Thirteen

"Good damn it," Donovan said.

Clouds had been gathering, swollen and menacing with the promise of more rain, dark and heavy enough to bring on the summer twilight a good hour and a half before the usual time. They'd gotten started moving some of the debris from the spot over where Lofton said the girl had been stashed. It took him a while to figure out the controls, and even longer to get the hang of working the articulated back arm with the scoop on the end. Donovan had leaned against the truck watching, a smirk on his face as Lofton struggled with the machine. More than once, Lofton considered steering the loader over there and running the son of a bitch down with it. He was about to do it at one point, but then he saw Donovan talking on his cell phone. Something told Lofton he was talking to Granddaddy, telling him what was going on. Donovan was Granddaddy's emissary in this. Lofton would be deeper in the shit if he messed with him. But when this was over, and he was back in Granddaddy's good graces—well, that'd be different, wouldn't it?

Then it started to rain. It started tentatively, a few fat, heavy drops that rang like tiny hammers on the metal nose of the loader. Lofton shut the engine down.

"The fuck are ya doin'?" Donovan called over. "Ya afraid you'll melt?" Before Lofton could reply, there was a flash of light, followed a few seconds later by a sharp crack, then a long, loud rumble of thunder that rattled the ground and filled the air with a bass vibration Lofton could feel in his chest.

"Fuck you," he called back. "I ain't stayin' out here to get struck by fuckin' lightnin'."

Donovan shook his head in disgust and yanked the door of the truck open. He climbed in as Lofton hopped down off the loader and jogged to the truck. When he got there, it was raining in earnest, the big drops filling the air so that running was like dashing through a waterfall. When he got to the truck, Donovan was already in the driver's side, lighting a cigarette. Lofton growled deep in his throat and ran to the other side.

The door was locked. Donovan was looking at him, his mouth open in laughter. The sound was drowned out by the drumming of the rain on the roof.

Lofton slammed his hand against the metal of the door. "God damn it," he shouted, "Open the motherfuckin' door, Donovan!" It was coming down in sheets now. Lofton's shirt and pants clung heavily to him. Donovan laughed again and gave him the finger. Lofton pounded on the door. "You asshole!" he screamed. Donovan just laughed harder. If Lofton had had his gun at that moment, he would have blasted the window open and put a round right into Donovan's laughing mouth. But all he could do was keep pounding on the door and screaming incoherently as Donovan's muffled laughter filtered through the glass. Finally, Donovan relented, leaned over and opened the door. Lofton yanked it open and scrambled inside. The air conditioning was up full blast, and the sudden outwash of frigid air was like being dunked in ice water.

"Ya look like a drowned dog," Donovan said, still choking with laughter. It was all Lofton could do not to leap across the seat, wrap his hands around Donovan's throat, and choke the life right out of him. But Donovan had picked his gun up off the dashboard as Lofton had clambered in, and he held it loosely in his right hand as he took a drag off the cigarette held in his left. He laughed again, a sharp, mean sound. "That was feckin' hilarious," he said.

"Fuck you," Lofton said, which just set Donovan off again. Lofton looked at the gun, calculating his chances of taking it away and blowing Donovan's brains out. Not good, he decided. The man was notoriously quick. Lofton was going to have to bide his time. He clenched his jaw and stared straight ahead at the rain pouring down the windshield.

"Ahhh, come on," Donovan said in a voice dripping with phony solicitude. "You're not mad, are ya? Are ya gonna cry, little girl? Huh?"

Lofton didn't look at him. "What are we going to do?" he said. "We can't do anything until this rain lets up."

"We wait," Donovan said. "It's just a summer thunderstorm. It'll blow over."

But it didn't. Just as soon as it would start to die down, another squall blew up in its place. It went on till past dark, as they sat there. Donovan had eventually run dry of laughter, and now sat fuming, watching another storm build in intensity around them.

"Fuck this," he said, "it's too dark. We've got no work lights. We're gonna have to come back in the morning."

"And leave the loader here?" Lofton said. "Somebody's gonna be looking for it."

"It's Friday night," Donovan said. "Driver's probably out gettin' drunk. No one'll miss this thing till Monday."

"I don't know," Lofton said.

"You got any other ideas?"

Lofton shook his head. "Guess not."

"Come on," Donovan said. "Let's go get a drink ourselves."

Lotfon didn't want to spend any more time with Donovan than he had to, but it looked like they were stuck together, at least for the moment. "Yeah," he said. "Okay."

***

Callie only half heard the rumble of the engine as it pulled away. She'd been drifting in and out of consciousness, her mind fogged with pain and fatigue. She could hear the trickle of water near her head becoming stronger, as if someone had turned the handle on a faucet. A sudden crack of thunder shocked her awake. *It's storming again*, she thought. She felt a sudden brief stab of panic at the thought of the basement filling with water, rising slowly, inexorably, higher and higher until it covered her mouth and nose and drowned her. A soft whimper escaped her throat. A second explosion, seeming to come from right above her, made her jump. Her head felt suddenly clearer. She realized how thirsty she was, and leaned her head over to where she could hear the water flowing. She felt it run over her face, warm and strangely soothing. Opening her mouth, she drank. *It's going to be okay*, she thought. *It's going to be okay.* She was having more and more trouble convincing herself.

Chapter Fourteen

Buckthorn rolled over and looked at the clock on his bedside table. 3:43 AM. He sighed. Sleep just wasn't going to come. Every time he closed his eyes, he saw the eyes of that terrified girl in the picture.

Well, if I can't sleep, he thought, *I might as well get some work done.* He dressed quickly and drove to the Sheriff's department. On the way, he turned up his radio, listening to the chatter. It was a quiet night in Pine Lake and the even smaller hamlets that made up Gibson County. Every now and then, a bored voice would come crackling over the radio, reporting the location of one or the other of the deputies on night patrol. One of the newer guys pulled a car over for weaving, a possible DWI. Anyone driving at this time of night was more likely than not to be making his or her way home from one of the local roadhouses or, if they were feeling particularly adventurous, from the notorious Rancho Deluxe Club over in Blainesville.

Buckthorn reached for the mike button to offer backup, but two other patrol cars had already responded. Buckthorn let his hand drop with a sigh. He drove through the streets of the little town, eyes automatically scanning the darkened storefronts and parking lots. The lights of the lower floor of the government building glowed through the darkness up ahead. He parked the car in his reserved spot and walked through the glass doors. The lights were on in Dispatch, and he waved at Monica, the night dispatcher, who was talking into her headset. She waved back and kept talking.

Buckthorn was about to go into his own office when he saw the lights on in the conference room. His brow furrowed with annoyance.

He'd told everyone that they needed to be turning lights off in unused rooms, to save the county money. Most of them had listened. He walked down the hall and looked inside.

Leila Dushane was seated in one of the rickety chairs, her feet up on the table. She was typing something on a laptop computer propped up on her legs. She looked up as Buckthorn entered.

"Hey," she said. "You know, the Wi-Fi in here sucks."

"Sorry," he said. "We weren't expecting company."

"You're here early," she said.

"I could say the same thing about you."

She sat up, placing the laptop on the conference room table. "I'll tell you a secret about me," she said. "I'm kind of a freak. I only need a couple, maybe three hours of sleep a night. Always have. Since I was a baby."

"Your parents must have loved that."

She laughed. "You have no idea. But it came in handy in school. And for work, of course. What's your excuse?"

He shrugged. "Couldn't sleep."

She stood up and stretched. "Thinking about that girl?" she asked. Buckthorn just nodded.

"She's probably not even in your jurisdiction," she said.

"Doesn't matter."

"No," she said, looking at him appraisingly, "I guess not."

"You get anything from the lab?"

She shook her head. "No, not yet, but Tony...Agent Wolf...got the Deputy Director to give them a little extra motivation. We should get something soon. Meantime, I've been chatting online with a lonely guy at NOAA."

"The weather guys?"

"Yeah. The weather guys. I was asking about this kind of phenomenon. How many miles can papers blow, how do they get picked up, that sort of thing."

"And he just told you?"

"Here's a tip, Lieutenant. You want to find out anything and everything about a particular subject, go online, find a geek who knows the subject, then tell him you're a girl who's interested in what he does.

If you can, imply you've got big tits. Between the lame come-ons and cheesy jokes, you'll get all the info you ever wanted and more."

"I'll keep it in mind," Buckthorn said. "So what did the weather guy tell you?"

"Basically, we got a lot of ground to cover. That system was a big bastard, with some serious winds. I could tell you a lot about updrafts and windshear and stuff like that, but the condensed version is, we could be talking about a search area from here to Northeastern Alabama and as far west as Nashville. Maybe even further."

Buckthorn gritted his teeth. "Damn it," he said, with a little more vehemence than he'd intended.

"Take some deep breaths, cowboy," she said. "We get a hit from that Facebook page, we'll narrow it down."

"Anything from that yet?"

"No. But the phone number your assistant set up runs right to dispatch, and Monica in there's got me on speed dial." She looked at Buckthorn. "You got some motivated people here, Lieutenant," she said. "They'd walk through fire for you. All I had to do was mention this was something you'd like done and they snapped right to it. My compliments."

"They're good folks," he said.

She looked at her watch. "So," she said, "I don't suppose there's any place to eat around here at 4 AM on a Saturday morning?"

"Lulu's," Buckthorn said. "They open at 5, but the owner'll be there already, making the biscuits. It's probably a little more countrified than you're used to."

"Honey," she said in an exaggerated drawl, "you're talkin' to a coon-ass gal from La-fay-ette, Louisiane. Biscuits at Lulu's sounds like just the ticket. How's the coffee?"

"Strong enough to strip the enamel off your teeth, if you get it from Lulu's personal pot."

"And she'll share?"

"Lulu's a he. And yeah."

"Well, lead on, then, sheriff. Lead me to the promised land. I always wanted to meet a guy named Lulu."

Chapter Fifteen

Lulu's was a low, broad building with a huge gravel parking in front. The big plate glass windows in the front were darkened, but when they peered through, they could see light behind the kitchen doors behind the lunch counter. A black sign with white letters hung from a suction cup stuck to the inside of one of the double glass doors: CLOSED. Buckthorn ignored it and rattled the door. There was no response, so he rattled it again.

The door to the kitchen burst open and a short, plump Asian man in a white apron over a red polo shirt and khaki pants stormed out, looking annoyed. The angry look turned into a wide grin as he spotted Buckthorn. He fumbled beneath the counter for a moment, then came up with a set of keys.

"Hey, Tim!" the man said in heavily accented but fluent English as he opened the door. "How's it hangin'? Who's your friend?"

"This is Agent Leila Dushane," Buckthorn said. "She's with the FBI. Agent Dushane, this is Lu Liu."

"Lulu's," Dushane said, extending a hand. "I get it."

Liu took the hand. A worried look crossed his face. "Nice to meet you, Agent. I tell you, I got no problems here. All my cooks and busboys got their green cards. I checked."

She laughed. "Not that kind of agent, Mr. Liu," she said. "And the name is Leila."

He looked relieved as he released the hand. "Okay, good. You two want coffee? First batch of biscuits is about ready."

"Thanks, Liu," Buckthorn said.

In a few moments, they were seated in a booth with worn vinyl seats and a Formica tabletop. Liu plopped down two big mugs of steaming coffee in front of them. "Biscuits in a jiffy," he said. Dushane picked up her mug with both hands and brought the mug to her nose for a long sniff, like a wine connoisseur savoring the bouquet of a fine Cabernet. "Mmmmm..." she murmured, her eyes closed. Then she took a sip. Her eyes popped open. She took a longer drink, then put the cup down with a satisfied sigh.

"Now THAT," she said, "is a fine cup of coffee." And she meant it. Buckthorn hadn't been lying. The stuff was strong, all right. A couple more cups, and she might not even need that two hours of sleep for a week.

Liu appeared with two plates, each one holding a pair of biscuits the size of a man's fist. There was a thick slice of ham in the middle of each.

"You want to wait, I can cook up some eggs," he offered.

"This'll do me fine," Dushane said.

"Thanks, Liu," Buckthorn said.

"So," Dushane asked as Liu bustled away. "You grew up around here?" She took a bite of biscuit. The ham was sizzling hot, heavily salted, the juice thick and tasting of hickory smoke. It was delicious.

"Yeah," Buckthorn said. "Lived here all my life. Except a couple years when I went away to college."

"Where'd you go?"

"North Carolina State. You?"

"LSU for undergrad. Tulane for law school."

"Huh," Buckthorn said. "You're a lawyer?"

"No need to be insulting, Lieutenant," she said, then grinned. "I got recruited by the Bureau right out of law school. You'd be amazed at how many agents are law school grads. Only thing we have more of is accountants."

"Guess it makes sense," he said. "All those complicated financial crimes."

"Exactly."

"Too rich for my blood."

"Mmm. So why'd you only stay two years?"

He looked down at his plate. "Came home to take care of my mom and my little sister."

There's a story there, Dushane thought. He'd been starting to relax while they'd sat at the booth, but something in that memory had shut him down. Part of her knew she should just let it go, but there was something about Buckthorn that intrigued her. With that thinning sandy hair and the weathered lines on his face that made him look older than he probably was, Lord knows he was no Brad Pitt in the looks department. But the intensity she'd remarked about to Wolf struck a chord in her. It was very much like her own. So she pressed on. "What, did your mom get sick?"

"Something like that," Buckthorn said. "How you like those biscuits?"

"They're awesome," she said, and she meant that, too. "But there's no way I can eat both of these."

"I usually wrap one up and take it to work with me."

"I'll do that," she said. And with that, the opportunity to ask any more about him passed. She was surprised to find that that disappointed her. She was mulling that over when her phone beeped. Buckthorn's went off at the same time. They pulled them out and checked them.

"We've got a hit from the Facebook..." Dushane said.

"Monica just got a call from..." Buckthorn began at the same time. They stopped, each motioning the other to finish, neither one willing to do it. Finally Buckthorn chuckled. "Let's go."

Liu came out of the kitchen as they got up to leave. "You guys leaving already?"

"Got a call," Buckthorn said, reaching for his wallet.

Liu waved him off. "On the house."

"Liu," Buckthorn said impatiently, "You know better than that. I got to go." He pulled out his wallet and handed Liu a ten dollar bill. "Keep the change. Thanks for opening up for us."

Liu smiled and the bill disappeared into his apron pocket. "Okay, Tim. Have a good day. Nice meeting you, Leila."

"You too," Dushane said, jogging to catch up with Buckthorn as he strode out the door. She pulled out her phone and hit the speed dial as she got to the patrol car.

Chapter Sixteen

Wolf rolled over and picked the buzzing cell phone off the nightstand in his motel room. "Yeah?" he said.

"Boss," Dushane said, "We got a hit on the Facebook page. Someone recognized one of those pictures. Buckthorn and I are on our way back to the Sheriff's department."

"A hit? From where?" Wolf said. Then, as the import of what she'd just said began to sink in, he said "Wait? What? You and Buckthorn? Back from where?"

Dushane sounded annoyed. "From breakfast, boss. I know I woke you up, but try to focus."

"Oh. Okay." He sat up and rubbed his eyes. He could hear the shower running. "Who was it that called? What's the location?"

"Don't know. All we got's a text."

"Okay. On my way." As he crossed to the room's tiny closet, the door opened and Gabriella Torrijos walked out, wrapped in a large, fluffy orange towel. She always brought her own towels to hotels. Her hair was wet from the shower. The sight of her, and the memory of the night they'd just spent, stirred his desire. He started for her. Then he realized the phone was still in his hand and what that meant. He sighed. She looked quizzically at him, then noticed the phone and his expression. Her face went blank.

"Back to work," she said. "If you ever really left."

He felt a flash of anger. "We were just together. Did it look like I was working?"

"Hey," she said with a shrug, "You're the master of undercover. How do I know?"

"Are we going to start this again? If you didn't want to do the story, you could have just told me. Or sent someone else." He turned to the closet and began looking for a clean shirt. "We'll talk about this later."

"But we don't talk, Tony. Later never comes. We spend a night together, we have a few laughs, we have great sex, then you're off again, chasing bad guys."

"I could say the same thing about you."

She sat down on the bed. Her voice trembled a little as she said, "This isn't working, Tony."

He pulled a dress shirt on, selected a pair of pants. "We need to get away for a while. After this case. I swear it."

She shook her head. "No. Because you're right. If it's not you chasing bad guys, it's me chasing another story. It's never going to end. Until one of us gives it up. And we both know that's not going to happen. " She took a deep breath, the shudder in it betraying the sob she was holding back. "You never really break cover."

The accusation cut him. *And you never stop probing*, he wanted to lash out. *You never stop* pushing. *You never*...his thoughts were interrupted by the chime of her phone, which had been resting on the bedside table next to his. She picked it up. "Hello? Yeah. I'm still in Pine Lake. Yeah. On my way." She set the phone back down and looked at it, then at him. "Not that tie," she said. "The blue one with the squares."

"Okay," he said, pulling the tie she'd described off the hanger. "I hate wearing these damn things," he muttered.

"And that's the other problem," she said. "It's not that you hate a suit. It's that you loved undercover. It nearly got you killed, but you loved it. And now you can't do it anymore. I outed you in a big way when I put your face all over the news. You can't do what you loved any more. And I feel like you blame me."

"I don't," he said.

"So you say. Now. But..." her phone chimed again. She looked at it balefully, then sighed and answered. "Hello?" Then, "I'll ask." She looked at Wolf. "Any hits from the Facebook page?"

"Uh, yeah," Wolf said. "I was going back to the sheriff's office. They've got something. I don't know from where yet."

She spoke into the phone. "Yeah. They've got a hit. Just found out. No, I don't know from where." She listened for a moment, then closed her eyes. "Yeah Yeah, I'm still here. Okay. Bye." She shut off the phone. "Looks like I'm here a little while longer," she said.

"Gaby..."

"You need to go. And I need to get ready. Will you be available to interview?"

"I don't know. Probably not. Not yet."

"Okay. Let me know when you're ready." She went into the bathroom and shut the door behind her. He stared at it. He started for it, then his own phone went off, the soft double tone that indicated an incoming text. He looked down at the screen.

SOMETIME TODAY, BOSS?

He sighed, finished dressing, and left without another word.

Chapter Seventeen

"The hell you mean, you ain't got her?" Monroe said.

Donovan's tone stayed level. "We got rained out," he said.

"God damn it," Monroe said, his thin, reedy voice rising with anger. "You can't work in rain? What kinda pussy are you? How much longer you think it's gonna be before someone starts snoopin' around?"

"We're getting ready to start when it gets light. We'll get her out. One way or another."

"Listen here, you..." the words trailed off into a spasm of coughing. The hacking and wheezing grew worse until Monroe was doubled over in the wheelchair, racked by the spasms until he was gasping for breath. Patience crouched at his side, holding his oxygen mask. Every time she tried to put it over his mouth and nose, however, he batted her hand away stubbornly with the hand holding the cell phone. Finally, weakened by lack of oxygen, he subsided into semi-consciousness and she slipped the mask over his face, deftly taking the phone from his hand as she did so. He slumped in the chair, taking long gulps of the oxygen. Patience stood up and put the phone to her ear, walking into the next room as quietly and cat-footed as she could.

"Sean?" she said. "You still there?"

"Yeah," he said. "I'm here. He still alive?"

"For the moment," she said. "How's it going, really?"

"Lofton'll be starting at first light," he said. "If I can get him sobered up."

"What?"

"We got rained out last night. Ended up in some bar in a strip mall somewhere in this god-forsaken 'burb."

"This is serious, Sean," Patience said. "Maybe it's time for you to cut our losses."

"When we get rid of the evidence," Donovan said. "Then I get rid of Lofton. And you do what you have to do."

"Gal?" the weak croak came from the living room. "Where you at, gal?"

"Coming, hon," she called back. "I've got to get back to work, baby," she whispered into the phone.

"Me, too," he said.

"I miss you. I can't wait till we're together again." She made her voice low and smoky with supposed passion. "I can't wait to feel your hands on me. I can't wait to feel you...inside me."

"I can't wait for that, either," he said.

"Bye." She closed the line and took a deep breath. The time was getting close. She could feel it. With Lofton gone and Monroe dead, Donovan would have a clear shot at running the whole operation. And she had a clear shot at running Donovan. Or did she? She gnawed at her lip uncertainly. Would he get tired of her? Find someone younger? She knew she was still attractive and young enough, but a man who'd assumed the kind of clout Lamp Monroe wielded might decide to trade up to a newer model. She needed something, some iron handle on Donovan.

"Gal?" the querulous voice came again.

"I have a name, damn it," she muttered. "On the way, hon," she called out. She took a deep breath and put her worries away for the moment. She had work to do, and something would come up. It always did.

***

"Bartlett, Tennessee?" Wolf said. "Where's that?"

They were crowded into the department's communications center—Wolf, Dushane, and Buckthorn—looking at one of the bank of computer screens that formed a broad semicircular wall around the crescent-shaped dispatch desk. Monica, the dispatcher, had put the Facebook page with the message on it onto the screen.

"Suburb of Chattanooga," Monica said. She reached out and clicked the mouse. The Facebook page disappeared, to be replaced by a Google Map. "Place was a little country crossroads fifteen years ago. Now it's got a population a little over 5,000. Mostly commuters." She clicked, typed, then clicked again. A website came up with a banner for a local TV station. TORNADOES SMASH INTO AREA, a headline blazed. Monica clicked on a picture and a video began playing, a blonde female reporter earnestly describing the damage caused by a pair of tornadoes that had touched down near Bartlett.

"So who's our contact?"

"Retired Presbyterian minister," Monica said. "Insomniac, from the sound of it. My kind of guy. Up all night surfing the 'net, saw the page, recognized a couple of people he knew. Their house got blown down. He called them, they messaged us, then called. Wanted to know how they get their pictures back."

"Anyone else from the area see anything that ended up here?" Dushane said.

Monica shook her head. "Just this guy and his family. The Nutters."

"Nice name," Dushane said.

"So we know some of the debris comes from this place," Buckthorn said. "Does that mean it all came from there?"

"Maybe not," Dushane said. "My source at NOAA said it could be a mix from all along the storm track. But it's more likely that our pic came from the same area."

"Okay," Buckthorn said. "Chattanooga. That's which office?"

"Knoxville," Dushane said. "I'll call them."

"Great. Now all we have to do is get there." He grimaced. "It'd be a good time to have a plane."

"The Bureau can get us one," Dushane offered.

"That'll take a while."

"I can get us a plane," Buckthorn said.

Wolf looked surprised. "You can?"

"Us?" Dushane said.

"Yeah. I think."

"You got an airport around here?" Dushane said.

"No. Private plane. Private airstrip."

"Who do you know with a plane?" Wolf asked.

"My brother-in-law."

"And he'd fly us to Chattanooga?" Dushane said.

"Probably. Or if this Bartlett place has an airport, he can get us right there."

"Okay," Wolf said. "Thanks. Think you can arrange it?"

Buckthorn looked at his watch. "Yeah. They should be up." He looked up at the picture taped to the wall. The girl's frightened eyes looked back at him. *If anyone's going to help that girl,* Mrs. Underhill had said, *the Lord means for it to be you.* "One condition."

"You get to go along," Wolf said.

Buckthorn nodded.

"No," Dushane said. "No way."

"Not your decision, L.D.," Wolf said. "Okay. We'll call you a consultant."

Buckthorn smiled slightly. "Thanks."

"Boss..." Dushane began.

He looked pointedly at her. "Don't you have some phone calls to make, L.D.?"

"Yes, boss," she said. She was muttering to herself as she walked away.

"I've got some calls to make myself," Buckthorn said.

***

"You're going *where*?" Janine said.

"Bartlett, Tennessee," Buckthorn replied. He was sitting behind his desk, his phone receiver in one hand. Janine was standing in the doorway. "It's just for a day or so."

"What in the world for?"

"We think that's where the pictures and letters came from. Including the one of the kidnapped girl."

"That's not our case, Tim," she said. "It's Agent Wolf's."

"I want to see how this plays out," Buckthorn said.

"That man's nothing but trouble. And I don't much care for his partner, either. She's got a smart mouth."

Buckthorn grinned. "Pot, meet kettle."

"Hmph. And how are we supposed to run things with you gone?"

"Duane can handle it."

"Duane's too young."

"He's the best deputy we have. All the other guys look up to him. Why is this such a problem for you, Janine?"

"I don't know," she said. "I just have a feeling this isn't going to turn out well."

"It'll be fine, Janine."

"You tell Sheriff Stark about this?"

"No. And you're not going to, either."

"If this is such a great idea, why won't you tell the Sheriff about it? He is your boss, you know."

"And I'm yours." He regretted the words as soon as he'd said them, even before he saw the wounded look cross her face.

"Well. I guess you told *me*," she said. She turned and walked out.

"Janine," he said to the empty doorway. But she was gone. He started to get up, but his sister picked up the phone on the other end of the line. "Hello?"

"Loretta. It's Tim."

"Hey, stranger!" his sister said. "Where you been hidin' out?"

"You know. Working."

"That's our Tim. When you gonna come out and see the boys? They've been askin' after you."

Buckthorn felt a quick pang of guilt. "Soon," he said. "Look, is Brubaker around? I need to ask a favor."

"Wow. That's a switch."

"Don't start, Loretta."

"I'm not startin' a thing, hon. It's just you never wanted his help before. Even when he offered it."

"Can we not do this now? I've got kind of a situation here."

"You okay, Tim?"

He could almost see her, standing in her immaculate kitchen, a line of worry between her perfectly plucked and shaped eyebrows. "Yeah. I'm fine, sis. Really. But there's...there's an investigation going on, and I need to see if we can use Bru's plane."

"Sure, hon. He's in his office." She raised her voice, the sound muffled by a hand over the receiver. "BRU! PHONE! IT'S TIM!" Her voice returned to normal as she came back on the line. "Let's get together soon, Tim. We can cook out. Bru got a new gas grill."

"That'd be good." There was a click on the line and Brubaker Starnes' voice replaced Loretta's. "Tim! How you doin', hoss?"

Something about Bru's constant hail-fellow-well-met demeanor always made Buckthorn wary. Loretta had scolded him more than once for his standoffishness. "He's just a happy guy," she'd said. "It's why I married him. Lord knows I was tired of feelin' bad all the time." It was the closest she ever came to acknowledging the situation with their mother.

There was no denying that Brubaker Starnes adored his wife and their two boys. But Tim knew too much about the people he'd destroyed on his way to becoming Gibson County's richest man to ever trust him. He knew deep in his heart that if it advanced the cause of Brubaker Starnes, that hand slapping his back might have a knife in it one day. And his brother-in-law wouldn't lose a night's sleep.

"Hey, Bru," Buckthorn said. "I need kind of a big favor."

"Sure, Tim," Bru said. "What can I do for you?"

"I need to get me and two other people to a little town in Tennessee. A place called Bartlett. It's near Chattanooga."

"How soon?"

"Immediately."

"Huh," Bru said. "So you want me to fly you?"

Buckthorn took a deep breath. "Yeah. It's important."

"This a police thing?"

"Yeah. The FBI's involved."

"The FBI? Good God, Tim, what have you got yourself mixed up in?" Despite the words, Buckthorn heard interest in Bru's voice.

"I can explain when I get there. Can you do it?"

"Sure. I had a couple things planned, but nothin' I can't reschedule. You comin' out right now?"

"Yeah. We need to go ASAP."

"Awright. I'll need to gas up and check the weather. We'll go VFR, so I don't have to file a flight plan."

Buckthorn had no idea what that meant. "Whatever's quickest," he said. "Thanks, Bru. I owe you one."

"I know." Brubaker hung up. Buckthorn knew he meant it. He was in his brother-in-law's debt now, and he didn't like it a bit. But the thought of the girl's face drove him on.

Chapter Eighteen

"T his is a bad idea, boss," Dushane said.

"Maybe," said Wolf. "Wouldn't be the first time."

"I mean, don't get me wrong. I agree with what you said earlier. He's a good cop. But he's not one of us."

"He's the one who found the picture. It's as much his case as ours."

"No. It isn't. It really isn't." She looked at him skeptically. "What's really going on here, Tony?"

"Maybe I feel like I owe the guy."

"Owe him what? Sheriff Tim's big adventure?"

"I just…" they were interrupted as Buckthorn re-entered the conference room."It's all set," he said. "I can drive us to the house."

"This isn't going to be some kind of crop duster, is it?" Dushane said.

"No," Buckthorn said. "Twin engine. I think it's a…Beechcraft? That sound right?"

"Sure," Wolf said.

"Those are pretty upscale," Dushane observed. "Your brother-in-law must be loaded."

"Yeah," Buckthorn said. "Pretty much." His face got that "I don't want to talk about it" look that Dushane was starting to recognize. "Let's go," he said.

They left Pine Lake in Buckthorn's cruiser, stopping by the motel so each of the agents could pack a small overnight bag . The next stop was Buckthorn's small house, where he threw a change of clothes and some toiletries into an old gym bag before setting off for the Starnes house.

Outside of town, the landscape turned to gently rolling hills. Here and there, rough fences marked off farms where cows looked up with mild interest as they passed by. Some of the farms looked as if they were going to ruin, the fences sagging, the empty fields overgrown. From time to time they passed new-looking developments, single-family homes on tiny lots. The developments had names like Woodridge and Deerefield Farms, and the fences enclosing them were newer and looked recently painted. "Bru...my brother-in-law...built most of these," Buckthorn said.

"Now I get how he can afford the plane," Dushane said.

Five miles outside of town, Buckthorn turned off the road onto a clay driveway that passed between two large stone posts on either side of the entrance. The driveway quickly passed into a stand of pine trees that lined the road. As they came out of the trees, Dushane spotted the house.

"Wow," she said.

The Starnes house was a sprawling structure of redwood and glass that would have looked more at home in the Hollywood hills than the North Carolina Piedmont. It spread across a low rise, surrounded by trees on three sides. On the fourth, the land sloped gently down to a wide field with knee-high grass waving gently in the morning breeze. A long strip of concrete ran the length of the field, with a two-engine plane sitting at one end, in front of a metal hangar. Dushane could see a tall man walking beside the aircraft, looking it over, bending down from time to time to look at the undercarriage. The man spotted the car and waved. Buckthorn stopped the car next to the house. He didn't get out immediately, but instead sat behind the wheel for a moment. Dushane was about to ask him if he was going to get out, but he took a deep breath like someone about to pull out a splinter and opened the door.

"Tim!" a voice came from the house. A woman came out a side door. She was tall, slender, with dark hair. She was dressed in perfectly creased designer jeans and a white silk blouse. She ran up to Buckthorn with a girlish squeal and threw her arms around him, pressing her cheek to his. He grinned and hugged her back. It was the most relaxed Dushane had seen him, and she marveled at the transformation in him when he smiled. "It's so good to see you," the woman said. She broke the hug and looked at Wolf and Dushane getting out of the car. "You'll have to excuse me, y'all," she said. "I haven't seen this one in seems like forever."

"It's been, like, a month," Buckthorn protested.

"Like I said." She held out a hand. "I'm Loretta Starnes," she said with a wide smile.

Dushane took the hand, noting the perfectly coiffed dark hair and the wide, dark brown eyes. "Special Agent Leila Dushane. This is my partner, Special Agent Tony Wolf."

"Leila. What a pretty name," Loretta said. Dushane was usually wary of compliments, but the woman seemed sincere, and her good humor was so infectious, she couldn't help but smile back. "Thanks."

"Y'all want to come in for a glass of ice tea?" Loretta said.

"Thanks, Ma'am," Wolf replied, "but we need to get moving."

"Right," Loretta said. "Some kind of mysterious police business." She made air quotes with crooked fingers on the last two words.

"Yes, ma'am," Dushane said. "We appreciate the loan of the plane."

"Ain't my plane, hon," Loretta said with a grimace. "That's Brubaker's toy. And if you're brave enough to go up in that little bitty thing, believe me, you are welcome to it."

The side door burst open again and two young boys came pelting out. "Uncle Tim!" one yelled. He looked to be about ten years old, the other one a year younger. They had the same light blond hair and their mother's dark eyes. They barreled into Buckthorn's legs, yelling. He laughed and scooped the younger one up, the smile on his face getting even bigger. The boys both began talking at once, with their mother adding her voice into the cacophony, scolding them to let their uncle be.

A tall, lean man in khaki pants and a polo shirt walked up. Dushane recognized the man who had been tending to the plane. He had the kind of tan that comes from years of working and playing outdoors, and his thick hair was silver-gray.

"Daddy!" one of the boys said. "Uncle Tim says y'all are going in the plane. Can we come? Can we? Please?"

"Sorry, guys," the man said. "This is business."

"Awwwwwww..." the two boys said in unison. The man nodded at Buckthorn. "Tim."

Buckthorn nodded back. "Bru." He turned to introduce the man, but he'd already stepped forward and extended a hand to Wolf. "Brubaker Starnes," he said. "My friends call me Bru."

"Tony Wolf," Wolf said, taking the hand and giving it a quick, firm shake.

Starnes turned to Dushane. "And who might this little lady be?" he asked, his eyes running up and down her body appraisingly.

I might be the one that's going to put a boot up your ass if you call me 'little lady' again, she thought, but she smiled a tight professional smile and extended her hand. "Special Agent Leila Dushane."

"Leila," he said, taking the hand. "Like the song."

Strike two, you smarmy fuck, Dushane thought. Over the years, she had come to truly detest Derek and the Dominos' classic rock song "Layla," not because she thought it was a bad song, but because every douchebag she ever met thought it would impress her if they mentioned it. God knows why. Some, especially the drunk ones, even tried to sing it to her.

"Different spelling," she said, never letting the smile drop. "Thanks a lot for playing chauffeur."

He'd been holding on to her hand just a beat too long, but now he let it drop. "I've got the plane gassed up," he said, clearly nettled at the word "chauffeur".

"Let's get going, then," Wolf said. Starnes turned and walked away without another word. Wolf gave Dushane a warning glance. She looked back at him with exaggerated innocence. He shook his head.

They fell in behind him, Buckthorn pausing a moment to give his sister and nephews a last hug before jogging to catch up. He fell in beside Starnes as they walked to the plane.

It was a Beechcraft King Air, sleek and fast-looking, with round porthole windows. Inside, the passenger compartment was lush, with comfortable leather seats. Buckthorn clambered up to the copilot's seat while Dushane and Wolf took their places in the back. Buckthorn and Starnes took the front.

Dushane leaned across to Wolf, her voice pitched low. "Did you see it?"

"What?"

"Buckthorn's sister."

"What about her?"

"The hair. The eyes."

"What are you talking about..." he stopped. "Ah," he said.

"You saw it too, right?"

"Now I do."

Loretta Starnes had the same color hair and wide dark eyes as the girl in the photograph—not close enough to be even a family resemblance, but definitely the same physical type.

"Still think it's a bad idea to bring him?" Wolf asked.

"Even worse now." But as she thought about Buckthorn, relaxed and chatting with his nephews, she found herself beginning to warm to the idea of having him along. This was a different man than the tense, stiff, worried deputy she'd seen so far. She realized with a start that Wolf was still talking.

"You think you could manage to avoid pissing our pilot off at least until we get there?" he said. "And if you say 'yes, boss', I'm putting you in for a transfer to Anchorage."

"What better place for someone who can't sleep?" Dushane said.

"I'm serious, L.D.," Wolf said.

"Okay. But if he makes a move on me, I'm shutting his ass down. With extreme prejudice."

"Come on now," Wolf said. "Our host and pilot is a happily married man." Dushane didn't answer, just looked at Wolf levelly. Finally, he sighed. "Okay. You're right. You need me to back you up?"

"Thanks, boss," she said. "I can handle him."

"Okay. And Buckthorn?"

"What about him?"

"You think you can handle *him*?"

"What are you saying, boss?"

"Nothing," Wolf said. "Forget I ever said anything."

"I'll try," Dushane said, her voice frosty.

The engines coughed, then roared to life, the heavy drone putting an end to anything but half-shouted conversation. Dushane was a little disturbed by how relieved she felt about that.

Chapter Nineteen

They'd begun work again at first light, Lofton using the backhoe to attack the mound of debris that used to be his home. He worked without finesse or skill, clawing away, moving the rubble to one place, then realizing it would be in the way and having to move it again. Donovan sat in the truck, smoking cigarettes and fuming. This was taking forever. He considered just shooting Lofton and taking over the operation himself, but something in him rebelled. When it came to the heavy work, he was already beginning to see himself as the one who told others what to do. Plus, for all his clumsiness, Lofton was farther along in learning how to run the machine that he was. So he sat and smoked and thought of Patience.

As he'd risen through the ranks of Lamp Monroe's organization, he'd had the opportunity to sample more than the usual man's share of female flesh. He'd certainly had women who were prettier, many who were younger. None of them had gotten under his skin the way Patience had. None had had the capacity to make him wake up, hot and sweaty, in the middle of the night, aching for her when she wasn't there. He'd started working for Monroe to advance his own ambition, but now he'd met someone whose ambitions were equal to, if not greater than, his own, and he was surprised to find that irresistible. The realization had been coming came upon him slowly, then it burst all at once, like a storm you didn't see coming until the sudden blast of cool wind and the first roar of thunder split the sky: he was meant to be king, and Patience was meant to be his queen. And nothing... *nothing*...was going to stand in the way of that. Least of all Lampton's dumb-ass grandson.

Donovan stubbed out the cigarette in the already brimming ash-tray. He picked the Glock up off the seat beside him and opened the truck door. He stuck the pistol in his waistband as he walked to where Lofton was wrestling with the backhoe.

***

They rose up out of the emerald-green fields, into a landscape of puffy white and bright blue, the mounded clouds scattered here and there along and adjacent to their path. Buckthorn looked down and to his left, where the town where he'd spent most of his life lay below him. He saw the glittering jewel of the lake that gave the town its name, the early morning sunlight reflecting off the water. Not far away, so close as to make the distance seem negligible, the town itself stood in its neat, tree-lined rows. From the air, it looked like a town from a train set, a place where nothing bad could ever happen. Buckthorn knew better. Evil had come there, and been defeated, and it wasn't coming back. Not if he had anything to say about it.

He'd left the place as a young man, never intending to return. But circumstance had drawn him back. Circumstance and the need to pro-tect what he loved. And he'd never left, because he'd never lost that need. It had just expanded to encompass the whole town, the whole county he knew would always be home. Leaving now had felt strange, unnatural. But there was someone else who needed protecting. Her eyes called to him, pulling him on. *I'll be back*, he promised as the town fell away behind him.

"Beechcraft eight, Charlie, papa," Buckthorn heard Brubaker's con-fident voice over the headset he'd put on. Buckthorn had put on a similar rig at Bru's suggestion. "Request VFR flight following to Chatanooga." In a moment, the reply came back. "Beechcraft eight Charlie Papa, roger, squawk one, two, zero, zero."

"Roger," Bru said, and reached down to arrange a set of dials on the complicated dashboard of the small plane. That task done, he relaxed back into his seat, but keeping his hands on the wheel.

"So, Tim," he said easily, his voice coming through the headset, "you seem pretty tight with the FBI."

He looked back at where Wolf and Dushane were sitting. "Don't worry," Bru said, "they can't hear a thing over the engines. Not without these on."

Buckthorn turned back and faced the front. "Okay."

"Mind telling me what's going on?"

Buckthorn hesitated. "There's been a kidnapping," he said finally. "Some evidence turned up in Pine Lake. We're following that."

"Huh. You're hittin' the big time."

"I guess."

"So," Bru said after a pause, "you thought any more about what we talked about?"

Buckthorn knew it was coming, and his answer hadn't changed. "I'm not a politician, Bru."

"Hell, Tim, you don't think I know that?" Bru said. "It's why the voting public in Gibson County will just fall all over themselves for you. You're a real honest to God lawman, not that damn empty suit sittin' on his fat ass in the Sheriff's office. Hell, after that whole biker thing, you're a damn hero."

Buckthorn's mind sheered away from thinking about that day. "Why do I feel like it's not law enforcement that's really on your mind, Bru?" he said. He saw his brother-in-law stiffen with anger, then get control of himself.

"Fine," Bru said. "You want me to say it? I will. Yeah, I think it'd be good for business to have a relative of mine as Sheriff. Even one who doesn't like me very much, God knows why."

"I like you fine, Bru..."

Bru went on as if he hadn't spoken. "Not because I think you'll let me get away with anything, because I know damn well how much of a tight-ass you are. But I'm not worried about anything I've done, Tim. I got nothin' to be ashamed of."

"That's good."

"I just think it'd open doors. You wouldn't even have to ask for them to be open. People will just naturally want to be nice to the brother-in-law of the Sheriff. The fact that you'd be good at the job is just icing on the cake as far as I'm concerned."

Buckthorn looked out the window and didn't answer.

"Hell, Tim, don't I at least get points for honesty?"

That brought a slight smile to Buckthorn's face. He turned back and looked at Bru. "Yeah," he said, "But I never did think it was altruism on your part."

"I don't believe in altruism, Tim," Bru said. "I believe in what you'd call enlightened self-interest. What's good for Gibson County is good for me and my family. And vice versa. I do what I do because I want my family to be safe. I think you'd keep the county safe as Sheriff, Tim. And I can put you there."

He'd always heard that the Devil tempted you by offering you the thing you wanted most. Not that he thought Bru was the Devil. He just bargained like one. And with every bargain you made with the Devil, there was always a catch, a hidden hook. The fact that Bru had dangled one hook in the open meant there was probably another. Still, he knew Sheriff Stark was considering retirement. If he was going to make the move, now would be the time. Stark left him pretty much alone to carry out the law enforcement in Gibson County the way he thought it ought to be done. Someone else might not be as hands-off.

He turned to Bru. "Okay," he said. "Let's talk more when we get back."

"Well," Bru said with evident satisfaction, "that's progress."

Chapter Twenty

Donovan had almost reached the rubble pile where Lofton was working. The roar and scrape of the big backhoe had covered the sound of his approach, and Lofton was so intent on his unaccustomed task, he wouldn't have noticed a company of soldiers approaching. His face was screwed up tight in concentration, his tongue protruding absurdly from one corner of his mouth like the tongue of a kid lining up a difficult marble shot. *He'll never know what hit him*, Donovan was thinking. He was reaching for the gun when he felt the vibration of the phone in the pocket of his suit jacket. He considered ignoring it, but habit made him pull it out and look at the screen. He swore under his breath when he recognized the number. He pushed the button and put it to his ear. "Yeah?"

He heard the grating wheeze of Lamp Monroe's voice on the other end, but the noise of the big machine was making comprehension impossible. "Hang on," he said. He backed away from the rubble pile, back towards the truck, keeping Lofton in his sight. When he reached the truck, he opened the door and slid inside. The big, sturdy doors cut the noise to a low growl.

"Sorry," he said. "Noisy as fuck out here. Say again?"

"I said we got a change in plans. Preston got hisself picked up by the cops."

"What? How?"

"Dumb sumbitch tried to rob a bank for the money. Went about as well as you'd expect."

"No shit." Donovan was impressed in spite of himself. "From what Lofton says, I didn't think he had it in him."

"Don't look like he did," Monroe said. "But he's got what you might call an incentive to give someone up to save his own ass. We need to give him an incentive not to."

"What do you mean?" But Lofton knew what it was as soon as he said it.

"The fuck you think I mean? We need the girl alive. And we need to let him know she stays that way as long as he keeps his mouth shut an' takes his medicine like a good boy."

God damn it. Donovan mouthed the words silently. Then he spoke. "I don't know if she's still alive. And the way your grandson's shoveling shit around, the odds aren't good for her even if she is."

"Then get over there and dig her out yourself, damn it!" Monroe's voice trailed off to a ghastly choking sound. *Jesus,* Donovan thought, *here he goes.* But after a few more hacks and gurgles, Monroe's voice came back stronger. "She dies, he's got no reason not to let the cops know about him and Lofton. And Lofton leads him to me. And you."

"How do you know he's not talking already?"

"We got somebody sittin' on him. One of our lawyers."

"How long you think that'll last?"

"Till he gets to a lockup where we can work a more permanent solution."

The old bastard's got tentacles everywhere, Donovan thought. "I like it," he said.

"Imagine how good that makes me feel," Monroe said. "Now go do your damn job." He killed the line.

Donovan stared at the phone for a moment in impotent fury before struggling to get himself under control. He had never looked forward more to the day when he could see Lampton Monroe dead and rotting in the ground instead of slowly rotting above it. But it wasn't the time yet. *Patience,* he thought. He smiled, well aware of the double meaning. She'd make it all worth the wait.

He looked over to where Lofton was still bumbling around with the loader on the rubble pile and frowned. Damn fool would probably cut the girl in half with the loader blade if he kept that shit up. He opened the door and leaped out of the truck, breaking into a run as he approached the loader. "Hey!" he yelled. "HEY!"

Lofton finally noticed him and stopped what he was doing. He dropped the blade to the ground and looked at Donovan quizzically. Donovan made a slashing motion across his throat. *Cut it off.* Lofton looked annoyed, but reached down and turned the key. The motor died, leaving a huge and echoing silence behind it.

"What the fuck?" Lofton said.

"We got new orders," Donovan said. "We need the bitch alive."

Lofton glanced towards the rubble pile. "I think that horse has done left the barn, cuz," he said.

"You better hope not. The cops have Preston. We need his daughter for leverage."

Lofton slammed his hand against the loader's dash in in frustration. "FUCK!" he screamed.

"We don't have time to cry about our troubles," Donovan said. "How close are you to the last place you had the girl?"

Lofton looked over his shoulder at the rubble pile. "I was right over it, I think. I was getting ready to start digging down."

"Well, we can't do that with the loader," Donovan said. "We'll need shovels." He looked at the slowly climbing sun. "We need to go find a hardware store."

"Fuck," Lofton said, more softly. He looked at the rubble pile, at the space he'd cleared right above where he thought the girl might be. He climbed down from the loader and walked over to the cleared area.

"You down there, little girl?" he called out. "You down there?"

There was no answer.

Chapter Twenty-one

Two agents met them on the tarmac at General Aviation, standing side by side next to a black Ford Taurus sedan. One was white, one African-American, but they were dressed in nearly identical dark suits and sunglasses, arms crossed in front of them as the small plane taxied toward them. Bru pulled the plane to a stop a short distance away and began shutting down the engines. They clambered out, stretching to relieve stiff muscles. The agents walked over, the black one in the lead. He was tall and broad-shouldered, his greying hair cut close to his scalp. His partner was tall as well, with an almost identical haircut, but he was a good bit younger.

"Agent Wolf?" the older agent said, holding out his hand. "Special Agent in Charge Alton Watson." He turned slightly to indicate the other man. "Special Agent Braswell."

"Thanks for meeting us," Wolf said. "This is my partner, Special Agent Leila Dushane."

"I know Agent Braswell," Dushane said. "We were at the Academy together." She nodded to him. "What's up, Fireball?"

Braswell nodded stiffly. "I'm fine, Agent Dushane."

She turned to Wolf. "You see where he got the nickname."

"Not now, L.D.," Wolf said.

Watson was looking at Buckthorn and Starnes, standing a few feet behind Wolf. "And who are these people?" His tone indicated he didn't expect to be happy with the answer.

"Lieutenant Tim Buckthorn," Wolf said. "Gibson County, North Carolina, Sheriff's Department. He found the initial POL. He's consulting with us on this."

"Consulting," Watson said, as if he'd never heard the word.

"Yeah," Dushane said. "Consulting."

Buckthorn looked at her in surprise. She looked back without expression.

"And this is...?" Watson was looking at Starnes, who took the opportunity to step forward, hand outstretched, grinning broadly. "Brubaker Starnes," he said. "I'm the one who flew these boys here. And the little lady, of course," he said, smirking at Dushane. "Pleased to meet you fellows."

"Thank you for your help, Mr. Starnes," Watson said. "But I'm afraid this is as far as you go."

The smile vanished. "Wait. What?"

"This is an official investigation," Watson said. "No civilians. Sorry."

Starnes turned to Buckthorn. "Tim," he said.

"Sorry, Bru," Buckthorn said. "I'm just a consultant myself."

Wolf gestured to the small terminal at one edge of the field, where a sign advertised Hertz Car rentals. "Maybe you can rent a car," he said. "Go into town."

"Do some shopping," Dushane offered.

"Shopping?!" Bru's face was getting red. Buckthorn stole a look at Dushane. She looked back at him, still no expression on her face. Then, so fast he'd he almost missed it, she winked. *She's enjoying this*, he thought.

"We need to get going," Braswell said. "There's been a development." He and Watson were moving to the car, Wolf and Dushane following. Buckthorn looked at Starnes and spread his hands as if there was nothing he could do.

They climbed into the Taurus, Watson and Braswell taking the front, Wolf, Buckthorn and Dushane squeezing into the back with Dushane squashed in the middle. Despite the obviously uncomfortable position, she didn't complain. Buckthorn was aware of the warm pressure of her thigh against his. He looked at her as if to apologize for the uninvited contact. She didn't seem to notice.

"So..." Wolf began.

"What's the news?" Dushane spoke over him. Wolf looked briefly annoyed.

"Local PD picked up a guy trying to rob a bank," Braswell said. "This idiot was a candidate for one of those 'World's Dumbest Criminals' shows. Tried to knock over the branch down the street from the police station. The place where the local cops deposit their paychecks."

"Whoops," Dushane said.

"Three cops jumped him as soon as he got the note out. Place was federally insured, so they called in the Bureau. It was pretty small stuff and there wasn't really much investigating to do, so we were going to let the local yokels have it. But one of them overheard the guy muttering something in the back of the patrol car." He paused, obviously for dramatic effect.

"Well?" Dushane said.

"Preston...that's the guy's name, Art Preston...was crying like a baby, snot running everywhere, and pretty incoherent, but the cop said he's sure he heard him say 'they're gonna kill her.'"

Buckthorn felt his heart rate pick up. "He say anything else?"

Braswell glanced at him in the rearview, then turned slightly to look back at him over the seat. "Who did you say you were again?"

"Just answer his question," Dushane said.

"Listen, Dushane," Watson broke in.

Wolf overrode him. "I'd like an answer to that myself."

Braswell gave Buckthorn a hard look, then deliberately turned to make it obvious he was answering Wolf and not the interloper. "No," he said. "He clammed up. Then he lawyered up."

"That fast?" Wolf said.

"Yeah. Within a couple hours, actually. Some guy I never heard of named Renfro. Supposed to be pretty high powered talent from Atlanta. Got there around midnight."

"This Preston guy doesn't sound like any kind of pro," Dushane said. "So how'd he rate a hitter like that?"

"Especially since he hadn't even called this Renfro," Watson said. "Or anyone else for that matter."

"Someone knew Preston had been taken," Dushane said.

"And they found out quickly," Wolf said. "Whoever's behind this Renfro character has someone on the inside. Either of the local force or the Bureau."

"The Bureau?" Watson was offended. "That's impossible."

"Not in my experience," Wolf said.

"Not in my office," Watson said. "I can guarantee you that."

"I can't be sure of that," Wolf said.

"You want to walk into town?" Watson snapped at him. "Because if you're going to start right off..."

Buckthorn had had enough. He'd felt the quickening excitement, the feeling that they were getting somewhere, and now these people were bickering and keeping him from that. It sounded like the kind of turf war he'd always despised, the kind he ruthlessly quashed back in his own office. "Can we keep our eyes on the goddamn ball here?" he snapped.

Everyone fell silent for a second. Dushane was staring at him as if he'd suddenly grown horns. "There's a kidnap victim, a young girl, still out there," Buckthorn went on doggedly. "If she's still alive, she's probably scared to death. And the clock's ticking. We need to keep going forward, not get sidetracked."

"Listen, whoever the hell you are..." Braswell started.

"He's right," Watson said. "So put a sock in it for the moment, okay, Dave?" He ignored Braswell's stunned look and glanced in the rearview at Wolf. "Agent Wolf," he said, "I'm one hundred percent sure that if there's a leak, it's not in my office. I've worked with most of these people for years. Been to their homes. My kids played baseball and soccer with some of theirs. But if you think we need to firewall this, I'll do what I can."

"I'll take your word and put that on hold for the time being," Wolf said. "But Lieutenant Buckthorn's right. We need to get ahead of this thing. We have anything on this Renfro character? Any persons of your particular interest in his client roster?"

"Already got a call in to Atlanta to check up on that," Watson said.

Wolf nodded. "We get any local connections with his clientele that look like heavies, we start there."

"That could take time that we don't have," Dushane said. "What about the wife?"

"Preston's wife?" Braswell said.

"Yeah," Dushane said. "She missing a daughter?"

There was another brief silence. "Jesus," Dushane said, "No one's talked to the wife yet?"

"We're not even sure if he's married," Braswell said.

"We only just got this information," Watson added.

"Like what, last night?" Dushane said. "Jesus." She took a deep breath. "Okay. Whatever. What's the wife's name?" Still no answer. She gritted her teeth and pulled out her phone. "What are you doing?" Buckthorn said.

"Seeing if the county puts their marriage license or divorce records on line," she said.

"Places do that?"

"Some do. You'd be amazed at how much info some places put out there." She tapped away. "But not Hamilton County. Shit. Okay." She leaned over the front seat. "The locals still have him?"

"Yeah," Watson said. "Waiting for the paperwork to take him to the Federal lockup."

"Tell them to look in his wallet. Find the emergency contact numbers."

Braswell pulled out his own cell phone. "What if the guy's divorced?"

"Then we hope he's one of those guys who never bothers to clean the old cards out of his wallet." Braswell nodded and began punching in numbers. As he began speaking, Dushane leaned back and closed her eyes. When she opened them, she turned her head to look at Buckthorn. She grinned. "Thanks for the kick in the ass, cowboy. We needed that." She reached down and gave his knee a quick squeeze. He felt the blood rush to his cheeks as she leaned forward again.

Braswell was talking to someone. "Okay. Myra Preston. Gimme the address." He had a small notebook out and was scribbling in it as he listened. "Great. Thanks." He shut off the phone. "607 Grampian Way," he said to Dushane.

"Well?" she said impatiently. No one answered. She looked over at Wolf, who was smiling sardonically. "Oh," she said, abashed. "Um. Yeah. Sorry, sir."

Wolf shook his head and chuckled. "Not a problem, L.D.," he said. "I'd sooner walk into a threshing machine than get in your way when you've got the bit between your teeth. And now you've got Buckthorn to back you up, I might as well go home."

Dushane's face turned bright red. "I didn't mean...I mean..."

He patted her on the shoulder like a fond uncle. "It's okay, L.D.," he said. "I like initiative. Next time, though, don't charge till I sound the bugle, okay?" For once, she seemed speechless.

Wolf turned to Watson. "Can we split up?" he said. "You take the lawyer, we go talk to the wife? We'll need a car."

"We can do that," Watson said. He sounded relieved.

Chapter Twenty-two

6 07 Grampian was an undistinguished brick ranch-style house, very much like every other house on every other tree-lined suburban street. The only thing that stood out were the two large, gleaming Harley motorcycles that sat in the driveway behind an older model Ford Explorer.

"Well, there's a sight to bring back bad memories," Wolf murmured. He was behind the wheel of another Ford Taurus they'd borrowed from the local FBI office.

"Yeah," Buckthorn said. The big bikes raised their own set of evil associations for him. He reached down to where his sidearm still rode in its holster on his belt, as if to reassure himself it was still there. The feel of the grip under his fingertips calmed him somewhat.

"Looks like Mrs. Preston has company," Dushane said from the back seat.

"Well," Wolf said, "let's go see what's what." He turned to Buckthorn. "I'm going to have to ask you to stay here for the moment, Lieutenant," he said.

His back stiffened. "What? Why?"

"Don't get your feathers in an uproar, cowboy," Dushane said. "It's just that Agent Wolf and I do this together all the time. We've got it down by now. We know each other's moves. A third party in the mix might throw us off. And, if any shit starts, I know you'll come running. And I like having you at our backs."

"Thanks," Buckthorn said. "I think."

"Don't worry, Tim," Wolf said. "When we find the girl, you'll be in the mix. I promise."

Buckthorn took a deep breath, willed his heart to slow down. "Okay," he said. "I guess I get it."

Wolf nodded. He and Dushane got out of the car and advanced on the door. Buckthorn could see the tension in their backs and shoulders. They knew as well as he did that something here was seriously off. It was a matter of the instinct they all shared. The day was beginning to heat up, promising a blistering afternoon. He opened the passenger side door a crack, to let some air in. *And in case I have to come running*, he thought.

***

"You thinking what I'm thinking, L.D.?" Wolf said.

"Yeah," Dushane replied, "if what you're thinking is that those two big shovelhead Harleys look as out of place in this neighborhood as a priest at a bar mitzvah."

"Cute."

"Thanks. I got a bunch of those."

"I'll bet."

The door opened just as they reached it, before Wolf had a chance to knock. The man standing there was broad and squat, with a shaved head, small piggy eyes, and a pair of neck tattoos that looked like they'd been done in prison, probably by someone with serious vision problems.

"Whatever it is," he said in a low growl, "we ain't buyin'."

Wolf had his badge case out. He showed it to the bald man. "I'm with the FBI," he said. "Special Agent Tony Wolf. My partner's Agent Dushane. We'd like to talk to Mrs. Preston."

"She ain't home," the man said.

"Really," Wolf said. He gestured at the Explorer. "That her car?"

"Yeah," the man said. "But she ain't here."

"You know when she'll be back?" Dushane asked.

"She didn't say," the bald man said. He noticed Wolf looking over his shoulder into the house and closed the door slightly. "Leave a card. I'll have her call."

"You mind if we ask who you are?" Wolf said.

The man gave back a nasty grin that showed a mouthful of yellowed and crooked teeth. "I don't mind you askin,'" he said, "but I ain't answering."

"And why not?" Dushane asked.

"Because fuck off, that's why not," the man said. He slammed the door shut.

"Well, that was rude," Dushane said.

"Totally," Wolf said.

"We should kick his ass."

"In a little bit, maybe. But there's at least one more guy in there, and we don't have enough to go busting in."

"I hate it when you get all bogged down in legalities. You know he's lying, right? About Mrs. Preston being in there?"

"Of course. I didn't say we were leaving. Right now, let's see if we can run the plates on those Harleys and get some idea who we're dealing with here. We may also want to get the local agents back here for backup."

"Okay." They turned to walk back to the car. "Boss," Dushane said, "do you notice something?"

"Other than Buckthorn being gone?"

"That was what I was talking about, yes."

"Damn it," Wolf said.

"I told you bringing him was going to be a bad idea."

***

Buckthorn had started moving as soon as he saw the tattooed man answer the door. There was no use trying to sit still. The man was an apparition right out of the nightmares that still troubled Buckthorn's sleep, a dead ringer for the bikers that had terrorized him and his town when the outlaw biker gang known as The Brotherhood had come to Pine Lake looking for Wolf two years ago. Everything about him was *wrong*, and Buckthorn needed to do something about it.

He moved down the driveway, unnoticed by the man who was focusing all his attention on Wolf and Dushane. He slipped around the side of the house, down the length of a narrow side yard formed by a waist-high line of shrubbery hugging the side of the building on his left and a chain-link fence that marked the property line on his right. The side yard opened onto a back yard that ran the length of the house, but was only about twenty feet deep. A tall wooden fence shielded the back of the property from the house that undoubtedly backed up to it from the next street over. A sudden sound from inside the house made Buckthorn jump. He recognized the rattling of pots and pans. He rounded the side of the house carefully, walking as light-footed as he could manage.

There was a small concrete patio at the rear of the house, furnished with a pair of rusty metal patio chairs and a matching glass topped table. There was a gas grill pushed up against the house. The table top was dull and cloudy with dirt and some kind of greenish mold. The gas grill was covered with spider webs. No one sat back here, at least not any more. A set of sliding glass doors led indoors from the patio. The curtains were drawn across them. As Buckthorn drew closer, he heard the sound of pots and pans rattling again, but this time, he heard something else, a low, rhythmic sobbing. The sound of a woman weeping.

"What the *fuck* are you doing?" Dushane whispered behind him. He whirled, drawing his pistol as he did. Dushane flinched backwards, one hand raised defensively, reaching inside her suit coat for her own weapon with the other.

"Listen," he hissed. She did, cocking her head slightly to hear better. Wolf sidled up next to her, walking as carefully as Buckthorn just had. "Hear that, boss?" Dushane whispered.

Wolf listened. There was the sound of a male voice, pitched too low for them to hear, then a short, sharp cry of pain. The sobbing redoubled.

"Sounds like probable cause to me, Agent Dushane," Wolf said.

"I agree, Agent Wolf. With exigent circumstances, even."

"Go back up. Cover the front. They may try to get out that way. And call Watson and Braswell. Tell them we've got a possible hostage situation." Dushane looked like she was about ready to argue, but then nodded and slipped off down the side yard again, her weapon drawn.

Buckthorn advanced on the door. "Hey," Wolf said. Buckthorn ignored him. He reached for the handle of the door and applied gentle pressure. The door moved aside slightly. Buckthorn turned to Wolf. *It's not locked*, he mouthed silently.

I know, Wolf mouthed back.

Slowly, so as not to make a sound, Buckthorn eased the sliding glass door open an inch, then another. The sound of voices inside grew louder.

"Please," a female voice, thick with tears. "Just leave me alone."

A male voice replied, a high tenor with a thick country accent. "Don't worry, sugar," the voice said, "Once the two of us get you broke in, you're gonna love it. They always do. Me an' Beano, we done this lots of times. An' we got all day an' night."

Buckthorn's jaw tightened. He moved the curtain aside an inch with the barrel of his pistol and peered through the narrow opening.

A high counter stood a few feet away across a strip of tile floor. A pair of tall chairs, like barstools with brass backs, faced away from him. On the other side of the counter was the kitchen. It was a cramped space. The appliances looked old, the laminate counter-tops worn and chipped.

A woman was pressed back against the stove, crowded back by a man in faded jeans and a ragged t-shirt. The man was rail-thin, but with knotted muscle showing beneath his sleeves. His hair was cut in a mullet that hadn't seen a barber's shears in a while. The woman was in her late forties, still slender, with thick black hair. She had her hand on the man's chest as if to push him away, but she wasn't pushing hard, despite the fact that he had his left hand on her breast, squeezing none too gently. The gun in the man's right hand explained why.

Buckthorn turned back to Wolf. He pointed at his eyes. *I see.* He held up his index finger, then put the hand to his throat. *One hostage.* He placed a hand on his chest, palm open. *Female.* He held up the finger again, put the hand on his forearm, then brought it back to his face, moving it up and down his cheek as if stroking an imaginary beard. *One suspect. Male.* He pointed at his pistol. *Handgun.*

Wolf remembered that Buckthorn and his department had had hostage rescue and SWAT training. He nodded, held up a fist. *Understood.* He pointed at Buckthorn. *You're in the lead.*

Buckthorn pointed at his own chest, then to his right. He pointed at Wolf, then straight through the door. *I go right, you go straight.*

Wolf nodded. Buckthorn looked back through the curtain. The man was pressed against the woman, his face buried in her neck. She was sobbing openly now. Buckthorn couldn't see the gun or the man's right hand. He weighed that for a moment. He really wanted to know where that gun was. Then the woman gave a low wail of pain and despair, followed by a gloating chuckle from the man. Buckthorn reacted without thinking, yanking the sliding glass door open so hard it rattled in its tracks. He charged though, gun held in front of him with both hands.

"POLICE!" he shouted. "DON'T MOVE!"

Chapter Twenty-three

They'd found a Home Depot and used Lofton's credit card to purchase shovels, an axe, a chainsaw and a pair of crowbars. They'd also bought some light coveralls, hard hats and heavy boots. Now, toiling under the broiling sun, they looked like any other construction workers. Donovan was fuming. This was beneath him, and he hated Lofton for the slowness and ineptitude that made it necessary for him to have to join in and sweat like a common laborer.

They'd located the space above where the girl had been. Lofton had moved much of the bigger debris away with the backhoe, but there was still a considerable pile of fractured lumber, drywall and brick. They dug where they could, stopped and moved brick where they had to, used the chainsaw to cut through where a pair of ceiling joists had fallen together in a rough "v", their ends trapped under a larger pile of rubble off to one side, making it impossible to move.

"Are you sure this is the right place?" Donovan said finally.

"Yeah," Lofton said. Donovan noticed he was looking a little green. He wasn't used to hard work, either, and the hangover didn't help. "Southwest corner of the basement. Under the kitchen stairs."

"The whole fuckin' thing has fallen in," Donovan said. "She's been crushed. We'll be taking her out of there in pieces."

"She survived for a while. We both heard her. That means there has to be some kind of space under there."

Donovan threw his shovel down in disgust. "I need a drink of water." They'd purchased a pallet of bottled water that was sitting in the front passenger seat of the truck. Donovan grabbed a bottle, twisted the cap off with a savage motion, and tipped it up, his foot on the running board. The water was hot from sitting in the truck cab, and gave no relief. He swished it around in his mouth to at least cut the dust, then spit it out. He looked over the hood of the truck and froze.

A blue and white police car was cruising slowly up the street towards the house. Donovan could see two officers in the front seat. The car pulled up to a stop next to the truck. Donovan instinctively looked over at where he'd left his pistol on the seat. He reached in and shoved the gun beneath the cardboard pallet of water bottles.

A young officer was getting out of the car, ostentatiously sliding his baton into its loop on his belt. The cop was slender and bony, the skin of his face drawn tight across his skull. He had his cap pulled down so it was hard for Donovan to see his eyes.

"Mornin' sir," the cop said in a thick Tennessee drawl. He leaned on the hood of the driver's side and looked over at Donovan. "Ever'one all right?"

"Yes, sir," Donovan said. "No one hurt, thank Christ. Hell of a mess to clean up, though."

"Yes sir," the cop said. "I'm gonna have to ask you to leave, though."

"What? Why?" Donovan said.

"Area hasn't been secured. There's still power lines down. Maybe gas leaks. And you ain't got a permit for debris removal."

"Ain't no gas here," Lofton said. He'd walked over, a shovel still in his hand. "Everything's electric, and it's shut down. I got a propane tank for the grill, but who knows where that is."

The cop never changed expression. "I said you need to leave, sir."

"Since when do I need permission to clean up my own damn property?"

Eejit, Donovan thought. *We do not need you escalating the damn situation right now.* But Lofton seemed determined to do just that.

"I need to see some I.D., sir," the cop was telling Lofton.

Donovan glanced over to where the butt of the gun peeked from beneath the pallet of water bottles. He could yank the pistol out, drop the cop where he stood. Taking his partner out would be a little more of a problem, but Donovan knew he was fast enough. But suppose he killed both men. What then? They'd certainly called the stop in to headquarters. The cop was looking at Lofton's license. He looked up and noticed the backhoe parked on the adjoining lot.

"That your backhoe, sir?" he asked.

Lofton was looking sick. "Ah, yeah," he said. "I mean, no. It's, you know, rented."

Donovan cursed inwardly. His hand inched towards the gun. The cop stared at the backhoe. "You got the rental paperwork?"

"Let me look," Donovan said. He slid into the passenger seat and fumbled at the door to the glove compartment with his left hand. He crossed his right over and eased the gun out, keeping it low. He saw the cop passing by the front grille. He was coming around the truck to the passenger side. Donovan put his finger on the trigger.

***

Mullethead sprang backwards, away from the woman, his mouth open and slack with surprise. Buckthorn saw to his relief that his right hand was empty. He'd laid the gun on the counter. Buckthorn saw him glance towards it.

"Don't make me kill you, son," Buckthorn said in a low voice. "Because I am powerfully tempted to shoot you down, even with your hands empty." He stepped to his right to let Wolf come up beside him, his own gun steady. "I think this here FBI agent might feel the same way."

"I do," Wolf said. "So you best get the fuck down on your knees, Bubba, and put your hands behind your head." The man didn't move.

"NOW, GOD DAMN IT!" Buckthorn shouted.

At that moment, the bald man came through the door that led to the rest of the house. He was holding a 12-gauge shotgun. As he raised the weapon, both Wolf and Buckthorn swiveled and fired. Both shots went wide, the heavy slugs splintering the plywood door behind the man. It was enough to spoil his aim, however. The tight pattern of double-ought buckshot impacted in the ceiling above Buckthorn's head. Bits of the popcorn ceiling rained down on him like snow. He fired again, but the bald man lurched backwards out the kitchen door and disappeared.

"Look out, Tim!" Wolf called out. Buckthorn saw Mullethead turning towards him with the gun in his hand. He'd scooped it up off the counter while Buckthorn had been distracted by Baldy. The woman was between Wolf and Mullethead, spoiling his shot. The man turned towards Buckthorn, raising the gun and grinning with triumph. He had the clear shot that Buckthorn didn't.

***

When Dushane heard the shots, she began pounding the front door in frustration, caught up in a frenzy of indecision about what to do. She couldn't get through the door, and if she ran back around the house, she'd not only be disobeying Wolf's order, she'd probably be too late to do anything. So she did what she was most used to doing when frustrated or scared: she yelled and hit things.

"FEDERAL AGENT!" she shouted, beating the door with the flat of one hand while holding her weapon in the other. "OPEN THE GODDAMN DOOR!"

To her shock, the door actually did burst open. The bald man she'd seen earlier barreled through the opening and ran blindly into her, nearly knocking her down. He was holding a shotgun in one hand. She was pushed back, the two of them tangled together, until he shoved her away with his free hand. As she stumbled backward, she brought her gun up. When she'd recovered her balance, she was in perfect shooting stance, knees slightly bent, gripping the weapon in both hands, arms locked. Baldy was only halfway through the motion of bringing the shotgun to bear, the barrel still pointed at an angle away from her as he registered the fact that the barrel of her .40 caliber pistol was trained squarely on his center of mass.

"Don't move," Dushane said in a flat, deadly voice that was so far divorced from her earlier loud bellowing that the sudden contrast shocked him into immobility. "Drop the weapon," she said. He hesitated. "*Now*," she added. He let the shotgun drop, then slip from his hand. The look on his face, however, warned her he was still calculating. It pissed her off. She just knew this lowlife wouldn't still be trying to figure a way to take down a man.

"On the ground, scumbag," she growled, reaching into her pocket for a pair of zip cuffs. Baldy bent over, as if he was going to lie down on the grassy lawn. Then he made his move. He lunged straight for Dushane, reaching for her wrist with one hand while swinging a wild haymaker with the other. The fist connected with her head, and every-thing went dark-red for a moment.

***

In the kitchen, the woman shrieked with rage. She snatched a carving knife out of a block on the kitchen counter and buried it to the hilt in Mullethead's left shoulder.

"Ah, FUCK!" Mullethead screamed. He didn't drop the gun in his right hand, however; he tried to turn it on the woman. She used the knife still buried in the meat of his shoulder like a handle to turn him away from her. He let out a howl of agony.

"Lady, get DOWN!" Buckthorn shouted. She heard him and dropped, letting go of the knife. Buckthorn's and Wolf's guns roared at the same time, and these shots hit home, knocking Mullethead back against the sink. They fired again and again, the impact of the bullets jerking Mullethead back upright every time he tried to fall. Finally, the slide popped back on Wolf's pistol, followed by Buckthorn's. The shocked silence that followed was broken only by the dead-weight thump of Mullethead's body hitting the floor and the woman's soft whimpers of terror.

Buckthorn moved around the counter and knelt by the woman. She was curled up in the fetal position on the floor, not seeming to notice that she was lying in a slowly spreading pool of Mullethead's blood. He reached out to put a comforting hand on her shoulder, and she gave a twisting, convulsive leap that brought her to her knees, her arms wrapped around him as if she was drowning. Her voice rose in a ban-shee wail that trailed off into convulsive, wracking sobs. He wrapped his own free hand around her shoulders. "It's okay," he said in as soothing a voice as he could muster. "It's okay." She only cried harder. Buckthorn heard another sound, this one seeming to come from out-side the house. It sounded like a woman shouting, not in fear or pain, but in what sounded like anger. He looked up at Wolf.

"It's Dushane," Wolf said. "I'll go check. You secure the hostage."

Even if Buckthorn had wanted to, he didn't think he'd be able to break the woman's grip long enough to get up. "Go," he said to Wolf, and held the woman tighter against him.

Wolf went.

***

As the cop approached the truck door, Donovan stepped out of the truck, keeping the door between himself and the cop. He held the gun low, out of sight.

"Sorry," he said. "Must have left the paperwork on the kitchen table."

The young cop looked at him steadily for a moment, as if trying to intimidate a confession out of him. Donovan fought down the impulse to laugh out loud. He'd stared down badder men than this at the age of 16. Finally the cop looked away.

"Okay," he said. "Just get out of here." He reached into the breast pocket of his uniform shirt and handed Donovan a card. "Call this number. It's the Emergency Management Center. They've got people in from FEMA and from the State. They'll tell you when it's clear to come back and start debris removal. And I hear the FEMA people can help reimburse you for the cost. Includin' what it cost to rent the backhoe."

Donovan reached out with his left hand and took the card. "Thanks." The cop just nodded.

"Come on," Donovan said to Lofton. "Let's go." He slid the gun back under the seat.

Chapter Twenty-four

Wolf entered the living room from the splintered kitchen door. He saw the open front door, heard Dushane's voice raised. There was another voice, a male one. It sounded like...

It sounded like the man was crying.

Wolf exited the door into the front yard. The bald man who'd greeted them earlier was lying on the ground, his hands secured behind him with plastic zip cuffs. He was writhing in obvious pain. Wolf saw the shotgun lying a few feet away in the grass.

Dushane was standing over him, looking down, shouting at the top of her lungs. She was holding her own weapon in her right hand, down at her side. She was pointing at the bald man with her left, using her extended index finger to emphasize her words.

"You have the RIGHT to remain SILENT, you bald-headed COCKSUCKER!" she screamed. "Which you MAY want to DO, so people don't find out you got your BUTT kicked by a GIRL!"

"L.D.," Wolf said.

"You have the right to whatever piece of shit DEFENSE Attorney you can get to REPRESENT your sorry redneck ASS."

"L.D.," Wolf said, louder this time.

"If, and this seems likely, you cannot scrape up enough spare change to get even some bottom of the barrel SHYSTER to stand up for you, one will, God help you, be APPOINTED to hold your hand as the JUDGE sends you off to the FEDERAL motherfucking PENITENTIARY!"

"L.D.!" Wolf shouted it this time.

She looked up, her eyes blazing. "Kinda busy here, boss."

"I can see that. Stick to the script, if you would. Or better yet, go help Deputy Buckthorn secure the scene indoors."

"Damn it," she said. "This son of a bitch tried to..."

Wolf could hear sirens approaching. "Just do it, L.D."

She sighed. "Yes, boss." She looked down at the bald man, who was looking up at her, fear in his eyes, like a rabbit hypnotized by a snake. He turned to Wolf. "Keep that bitch away from me," he said in a high, pleading voice. "She's fucking crazy."

"Believe it, motherfucker," she snarled. She stomped past Wolf into the house.

"She kicked me in my fucking knee," the man whimpered. "I think she broke it."

"You want to know why she did that?" Wolf said.

The man looked baffled.

"Because fuck off, that's why." As the first police car roared to a stop in the driveway, lights flashing and siren wailing, Wolf stood over the bald man.

"You're under arrest for kidnapping and for assaulting a federal officer," he said. "For starters. You have the right to remain silent..."

***

Dushane walked back into the living room, still shaking a little from adrenaline. Baldy had been faster than she'd anticipated, and she was rattled at how close he'd come to disarming her before she'd delivered a vicious side kick to the man's kneecap. That was the move she privately called "The Equalizer." No matter how big someone was, it only took eight pounds of pressure to shatter their knee. She'd never met anyone who could keep fighting after that. She hoped she never would.

She looked towards the kitchen as she entered. There was blood on the counters and floor, and she saw Mullethead in a bloody heap next to the refrigerator.

She saw Buckthorn, perched on the end of the couch. The dark-haired woman was lying there, face down, sobbing into a pillow. Buckthorn was speaking softly to her, so low that she couldn't make out the words. He wasn't touching her, but he had his arm braced on the back of the couch, held over her protectively like an angel's wing. As she drew closer, Dushane could make out the words.

"It's okay," he was saying. His voice was deep and soothing. "It's all right. Nothing is going to hurt you. You're safe. You're safe. They're gone. I promise, they're gone. It's okay." She stopped, struck by the look on his face. It was fierce, intense, and she had the distinct feeling this wasn't the first time he'd done this. He looked up at her, eyes blazing, as if she was a threat.

"Hey," she said softly. "We've got people on the way."

"Tell them if they have a sexual assault unit, they need to get them here. Or meet us at the station."

"Was she..." Dushane trailed off.

"They were getting ready to," Buckthorn said. "But before...they'd been messing with her for hours. Terrorizing her. Telling her what they were going to do to her. Bastards."

"Can I talk to her?" Dushane said. He looked hesitant, but then nodded.

She got down on one knee. "Ma'am?" she said softly. The woman had stopped crying, but she still lay face down, like a child, taking in long shuddering breaths. "Mrs. Preston?" Dushane said, a little louder.

The woman turned her head. Her haunted eyes were bloodshot, her face streaked with tears, but Dushane had seen those eyes before. They were the same ones as the girl in the photo. A strand of black hair hung down over her face. Dushane reached out to brush it out of the way, and the woman recoiled.

"Sorry. Sorry," Dushane muttered. "My name's Leila Dushane. I'm with the FBI, and I need to tell you something. Can you hear me?"

After a moment, the woman nodded.

Dushane looked back over her shoulder to the kitchen. "That guy that was touching you? With the bad haircut? He's dead. He's got so many goddamn bullets in him he'd have died of lead poisoning if he hadn't bled out. And that other son of a bitch? Bald, with tattoos? He's lying in the grass outside, crying for his mama because I broke his fucking knee. And let me tell you, ma'am, it felt *gooood*. You want me to, I'll go back out there and break his other one. I never liked this job all that much anyway."

The woman gave her a slight smile, then a laugh that turned into another sob. But she got back under control quickly.

Dushane went on. "Here's what you've got to keep in mind. Neither of those guys is going to hurt you anymore. Ever. One's dead, and I swear to you, me and my partner are going to get creative in thinking up ways to extend the other one's stretch in federal prison to the point where if he walks out those prison gates at all, he'll need a goddamn walker to do it. That suit you?"

The woman nodded.

"But here's what I need you to do for me," Dushane went on. "I need you to tell me why those guys were here."

The woman's voice was an agonized whisper. "I can't. I *can't.*"

Buckthorn stood up. He walked across the room to a wall where several pictures were hanging. He reached out and took one off the wall, carefully lifting it off its hook. He walked back over to the couch and sat back down. "Ma'am," he said softly, "is this your daughter?" Dushane got a look at the picture. It was a class photograph, a young girl posed against a backdrop that looked like silver and blue clouds. The woman burst into tears again.

"Mrs. Preston," Dushane said. "If we don't get to her in time, they're going to kill her."

"If...if I tell you...tell you anything..." she choked the words out between sobs, "they'll do worse."

Chapter Twenty-five

"You and your partner here caught yourself a couple of real winners here, Agent Wolf," Watson said. They were crammed into a conference room in the local police station. Wolf and Dushane were seated. Dushane had her feet up on the conference table. Buckthorn leaned against the wall.

"Your dead guy is one John Metcalf," Watson went on. "AKA Flatline."

"Someone must have had the gift of prophecy," Dushane said.

"The nickname, we're told by the gang enforcement unit, had to do with Mr. Metcalf's, shall we say, lack of cognitive skills."

"Guess he won't have to worry about anyone making fun of him anymore," Wolf said.

Watson shot him a look, then went on. "His buddy's name is Mark Sledz, with a 'Z'. AKA Beano."

"Beano?" Buckthorn said.

Watson nodded. "Seems that his former comrades in the Outlaws motorcycle organization hung that one on him because of one or more episodes of uncontrollable flatulence."

"I did notice a certain odor about him," Dushane said.

"Bikers?" Buckthorn said.

"Former," Watson said. "Seems that Sledz and Metcalf were asked to leave the Outlaws organization after being caught *in flagrante*. With one another."

Dushane made a face. "Euuw."

"Tolerance, Agent Dushane," Wolf said.

"I am tolerant. But eeeeuuuw."

"So what were two former bikers doing at the Preston house?"

"Here's where it gets interesting. After leaving the Outlaws, Sledz and Metcalf started doing a little freelance work for a guy named Sean Donovan."

"Doesn't ring any bells," Wolf said.

"Donovan's a piece of work. Irish national. Former member of the Provisional IRA. When they declared the cease fire in '97, he did what a lot of those guys did who'd never done anything but hold a gun. He went into robbery, extortion, anything to turn a buck. Got into some kind of dispute with the leadership in 2000 and fled to the States. Rumor is a woman was involved."

"So what's he doing hanging out with outlaw bikers?" Dushane said.

"Like I said, Donovan's never been anything but a gunman, but he's good at it. He landed in Miami, not New York like most of those guys. He must *really* have pissed off someone back home, to not want any association with anyone he'd known. Eventually, he drifted over to Mississippi, got hooked up with a local boss known as Lampton Monroe, AKA the Lizard King."

"The who?" Wolf said.

Braswell spoke up for the first time. "He was big in the Dixie Mafia, back in the day. Weed, pills, gambling, but especially prostitution. He saw how much ass was being sold at truck stops by hookers working independent. Forty bucks for a quick bang in the sleeper cab or a BJ in the front seat. The working girls are known as 'lot lizards.'"

"Charming," Dushane said.

"You get a look at some of the girls," Braswell said, "you'd know where the name comes from. But Monroe saw profit in all those horny truckers moving up and down the Interstate. He moved in, and before long, all the girls were paying out to him. Or dead."

Buckthorn thought of Mrs. Preston's desperate statement, "If I tell you anything, they'll do worse" than killing her daughter. He'd suspected what she meant. Now he knew.

Watson spoke up. "Monroe has a semi-legit organization, a 'private security company.' It's called Dixie Security. Rent-a-cops. Their specialty is working lot security for these big truck stops."

"They're the pimps," Dushane said.

"Exactly. Once Monroe controlled the parking lots, we think he started recruiting truckers to move product for him. Weed, heroin, methamphetamine, you name it."

"And the money just rolled in," Wolf said. "So why is this Lampton Monroe guy not in jail?"

"Believe me, we've tried. We've had our eye on this bastard since the late 70's. When the whole Dixie Mafia thing fell apart, he seems to have peeled some of the businesses off with him, particularly the prostitution. But no one ever seems to live long enough to testify against him. Some of the people we've tried to recruit disappear, then turn up a couple years later in pieces in a swamp in Georgia or Louisiana."

"Late 70's?" Buckthorn said. "How old is this guy?"

"Old," Braswell said. "And he's got about a half-dozen health problems, any one of which is going to do him in any day now. Or so we've heard. But the old bastard's just too mean to die. He's holed up in a big-ass mansion, an old plantation house, if you can believe it, outside of Biloxi."

"So you think this Donovan's the one running the show?" Wolf said.

"Well, the heir apparent is Lamp Monroe's grandson Lofton," Watson said. "Lofton's been seen more and more, flashing money around in places like Atlanta, Nashville, New Orleans. But he's apparently a guy who wants to make his own mark, not just take over the family business. He decided a few years ago to develop some of the neglected areas, like gambling and loan sharking. He moved up to Chattanooga to put some distance between him and the old man."

"Which brings us back to the unfortunate Mister Preston," Braswell said.

"Let me guess," Wolf said. "Mr. Preston's into Lofton Monroe for a hefty chunk of change. I bet the wife can confirm it."

"She's still not talking," Dushane said. "And now the doctors have her under sedation."

Braswell grimaced. "We're trying to get his financials. The bank's giving us some static."

"Be a lot easier if he had an Arab name," Watson said.

"The picture we saw in the house," Buckthorn said. "That's the girl from the photograph we found. Isn't that enough?"

"Enough so that they're sending a CARD team," Wolf said, referring to the FBI teams with particular expertise in child abduction cases. "One's in the air right now."

"Glad someone's finally taking this seriously," Buckthorn said. "I hope it's not too late."

Braswell's face reddened. "Now, listen, Mister Buckthorn..."

"Lieutenant," Buckthorn interrupted him.

"What?"

"It's Lieutenant Buckthorn. Just so you know."

"He's right," Dushane said.

Braswell turned on her. "Are you seriously taking his side in this?"

"We're on the same side," Wolf broke in. "Let's try to keep that in mind."

"Yeah," Watson said, his voice hard. "We are. But we do need to address the problem of Lieutenant Buckthorn here."

"What problem?" Buckthorn said.

"We've got an officer-related shooting involving an FBI field agent, which comes under the scrutiny of the Office of Professional Responsibility..."

Wolf groaned. "You have *got* to be kidding."

Watson went on as if he hadn't heard. "As well as involving a person whose status is, to put it mildly, ambiguous. That would be you, Lieutenant."

"I'm a sworn law enforcement officer," Buckthorn said.

"Not here, you're not," Watson said. "Normally, the Tennessee Bureau of Investigation investigates officer-related shootings to determine if they were justified. But you're not an officer in Tennessee. They want nothing to do with you, and neither does our OPR."

"So where's the problem?" Buckthorn said.

There was a stunned silence.

"Yeah," Dushane said. "From where I sit, Lieutenant Buckthorn's the luckiest guy in the room right now. He doesn't have anyone looking over his shoulder."

"Looked at another way," Watson said, "he's basically a civilian, and we should let the locals handle him."

"Oh, HELL no," Dushane said.

"Not your call, Agent Dushane," Watson said.

"This man saved my life," Wolf said. "More than once, in fact. We are *not* throwing him to the locals."

He and Watson stared at one another, neither willing to back down. Watson was the first one who spoke.

"Okay, that's it," he said. "I was trying to decide how to handle this, and you three just made up my mind for me." He sat down. "The CARD team's on its way to take over the kidnapping angle. OPR's also looking at the shooting. I'm the Special Agent in Charge in this field office. And I say you three are out of this."

Dushane leaped to her feet. "What!?"

"I tried to work with you people," he said, "even though the word was that Agent Wolf is nothing but trouble. That's probably why he's still a field agent after so many years in. But what's the first thing you lunatics do? You get in a damn gunfight. Without even waiting for backup. Believe me, that's also going to be of interest to OPR. We're going to handle this from now on, Agents. And *Lieutenant*. And we're going to follow procedure. Starting with putting the two of you on administrative leave while OPR looks over the shooting."

"While you wait for the CARD team," Wolf said, "that girl could die."

"She has a name," Buckthorn said. "It's Callie. Callie Preston."

"We know, Lieutenant," Watson said. "Thank you. You can go home now. I'm sure your brother-in-law is anxious to get back."

"Agent Watson..." Wolf said.

"We're done here," Watson said. "Go home, people. It's our case now."

***

"Damn it," Dushane said. She kicked the tire of the borrowed Taurus. "Damn it to HELL!" She kicked it again.

Wolf was leaning on the car, his cell phone to his ear. "We need to talk about your anger management problem, L.D."

"I'm managing my fucking *anger* just fucking *fine*, thank you very fucking *much*," she snarled, smacking her hand on the hood of the car.

"Who are you calling?" Buckthorn said.

"Steadman," Wolf replied. "Damn it. Voice mail." He raised his voice slightly. "Pat, this is Tony Wolf. I need you to call me back. ASAP."

"Pat Steadman?" Buckthorn said.

"Yeah," Wolf said. "He's always backed me up. Saved my ass after that little dust-up in your hometown."

"That why you're still a field agent?" Buckthorn said.

"Yeah. Well, it's not like the guy's a miracle worker. I can't see myself being a good bureaucrat, anyway."

Buckthorn felt his phone buzz in its holster on his utility belt. He pulled it out and looked at the screen. "Well, our day just got better."

"Great," Dushane said. "How?"

"It's a text from Bru." He held the phone up. They gathered to look. SCREW THIS. GOING HOME.

"Hey, Buckthorn, have I mentioned that your brother-in-law's kind of an asshole?" Dushane said.

Buckthorn smiled slightly. "No, but I had a feeling you felt that way." He shrugged. "Family. What are you going to do?"

"Okay, I take your point," Dushane said. "But what *are* you going to do?"

Buckthorn rubbed his jaw. "Well, I guess that's a good question."

"We'll get you home, Tim," Wolf said. "I owe you that."

"But, in the meantime..." Dushane said, a sly look on her face. She let the words hang.

"What are you thinking of, L.D.?" Wolf said.

"I mean, it's not like they said we couldn't still use the car. While we're, you know, trying to figure a way back home. And while Watson and Fireball up there are sitting around playing pinochle waiting for the CARD team."

"You're not really being fair to them, L.D.," Wolf said. "It *is* Watson's territory."

"Boss—and I'm calling you that because I know it's the boss talking, not the legendary bad-ass Tony Wolf who I idolize and who I begged to get teamed up with—boss, fuck 'fair.' 'Fair' can kiss my petite Cajun ass. We've got a little girl who's gonna die if we don't get something done right now."

"She's right," Buckthorn said. "You know how this works. Every second is precious."

Wolf shook his head, but he was clearly weakening. "OPR's going to have kittens."

"Come on," Dushane said. "You're turning into an old man right in front of my eyes here. It's heartbreaking." She looked at Buckthorn.

He nodded. "Tragic, even."

"It's not just my career that's on the line here, L.D.," Wolf said. "You've got a lot more to lose than me."

"But if it was just you, you'd go, right?" Buckthorn said. "You'd keep investigating. You'd do whatever it took to save that child. Right?"

Wolf dodged the question. "You guys are ganging up on me."

"Refer to my previous comment about fairness," Dushane said. "Thanks for worrying about me. But I'm a big girl. I take my own chances."

"Besides, this Deputy Director Steadman'll back you up, won't he?" Buckthorn said. "This might be one of those 'ask forgiveness, not permission' moments."

Wolf sighed and threw up his hands in surrender. "Okay, okay. So what do we do?"

"We find a Starbuck's," Dushane said.

Wolf was incredulous. "You want coffee?"

"That, too. But what I mainly want is a wi-fi connection."

***

It was the thirst that awakened her. The scant trickles of water that had been sustaining her were gone, and the summer sun that she only barely believed in any more had turned the tiny space around her into an oven. Her tongue felt so swollen that it threatened to bulge from her mouth, and her throat was a dry, dusty path of flame down into her cramping belly. She strained for the sound of the machines she'd heard earlier, the ones she hoped were digging her out. She heard only silence.

Callie knew then she was going to die. No one was coming. They'd given up looking. They'd given up looking, and she was going to die here, in this dark and cramped place, *buried alive*. Her body shook as she began to sob, but there were no tears. It wasn't fair. She'd tried to keep hope alive for what seemed like a geological age, and it was just *not fair* that it should come to nothing like this. The brief flame of anger at the sheer injustice of it all that welled up inside her burned out as quickly as it had flared, guttering and dying, along with her hope. It left her empty and hollowed out, feeling as if she was filled with ashes. She wasn't even afraid any more. She closed her eyes and waited to die.

Chapter Twenty-six

"Okay," Dushane said as she opened her laptop on the table. They hadn't found a Starbuck's, but the local coffee shop they'd found advertised "Free Wi-Fi". The place was small, with large overstuffed chairs scattered about and a couple of tables. The rich aroma of coffee filled the air. It was almost empty, and they'd had no problem finding a table. Wolf had gone to the service counter, where a bored-looking wannabe hipster, complete with goatee and thick-framed glasses, lounged against the wooden counter.

"What are you looking for?" Buckthorn asked.

"Register of Deeds," Dushane said. "See if our Mr. Monroe or his granddaddy have any property listed in their names nearby."

"Would it be under their own names?"

"Maybe. Probably not. But we start with the easy stuff, and sometimes we get lucky. Or they get dumb. Or both."

"I hear you." Buckthorn watched her, fascinated by the intensity on her face as she tapped away at the keys.

"Stop staring at me," she muttered. "It makes me nervous."

"Sorry," he said, his face reddening. She looked up.

"It's okay...Jesus, you're blushing, aren't you?"

"No, I'm not."

She chuckled and went back to work. "Yeah, you kinda are." The smile left her face. "Huh." She sat back, scowling.

"What?"

"Seems the local registrar of deeds requires you set up an account with them before you can search property records. And accounts can only be set up on weekdays, during regular business hours. What the hell is the point of that?"

"Keep people from nosing around?"

"They're public records," she said. "In any case, can't look that way. Let's try the tax office...and...hah!"

Wolf had come to the table, carrying three large black coffees. "Something?"

"Monroe, Lofton S., has three parcels of land listed for taxes in this fine county. And here are the addresses." She looked up. "One appears to be a residence, two are commercial."

"You think he's keeping the girl at one of those?" Buckthorn said.

"I say we pay him a visit," Wolf said, "and ask."

Dushane took one of the coffees. "I think that's a hell of an idea."

***

"If we go back," Lofton said, "we're going to get arrested."

They were sitting in a McDonald's on a busy street near Bartlett's downtown area. Both of them had cups of coffee in front of them. Lofton's was untouched, Donovan's half full.

"We don't go back," Donovan replied, "someone digs that girl's body out of your house, and everything goes to shit." He took a sip of his coffee. "For all of us."

"What do we do if the cops come back?"

Donovan shrugged, trying and failing to hide his irritation. "We deal with it."

"How? Shoot it out with the fuckers? That's the problem with you, Donovan. You think a gun solves everything. This ain't fuckin' Belfast."

"I'm from Derry, you cunt," Donovan said, his voice rising.

"Jesus, keep it down," Lofton said.

"You keep pushing me, Lofton, and you'll see what a gun can solve. That's a promise." The two men stared at one another. It was Lofton who looked away first.

"This isn't getting us anywhere," he said. "I need to call Granddaddy and ask him what to do."

"And what is it exactly that you think he'll tell you, fuckwit?" Donovan said. "He'll tell you to handle it. Like we're doing." He tossed down the last swallow of coffee. "Now if you're not going to drink that, we'll be on our way." He stood up, leaving his coffee cup on the table. Lofton didn't get up.

"You coming or not?" Donovan said. "Makes no difference to me." He walked off towards the door, not looking back. He'd almost reached the truck before he realized that Lofton had the keys. He slowed, then stopped, cursing inwardly. If he had to go back and demand the keys, Lofton might refuse. He'd either have to start a fight right there in public or back down. The first would probably get them arrested and set them back even further, the second was unthinkable. He turned. Lofton was hurrying out the door, a contrite look on his face.

Donovan smiled.

***

"I do believe we're getting closer," Dushane said.

The neighborhood they were driving through had been upscale, large houses sitting on spacious wooded lots. But the storm hadn't taken any more notice of the affluence than it had of the trailer parks a scant few miles away to which it had also laid waste. There were signs of damage everywhere: downed trees, piles of fractured lumber next to houses with gaping holes facing the street, blue tarps covering gaps in roofs torn open by ferocious winds. Wolf was at the wheel, moving slowly so as to better survey the area. Dushane rolled a window down. The whine of machinery and the jagged roar of chainsaws cut through the thick, humid air.

Dushane looked down at her phone. "Turn right here." Wolf took the right turn. Here there were more trees down, more and even bigger houses with stripped shingles and damaged outbuildings. Then...

"Mother of God," Dushane said.

Where the tornado had actually touched down, the devastation was total. There didn't seem to be any place where one brick was left atop another. Million-dollar houses were scattered across the ravaged landscape as if picked up and tossed in the air by a giant hand. Unlike the place they'd just left, there was no one working in the ruins. They passed a man and woman standing beside a Mercedes SUV next to a lot that looked less like a residence than it did a dump for construction waste. The man was staring at the pile, the woman's head buried in his shoulder. Her shoulders shook. As they passed by slowly, the man turned to look at them. His face was blank with incomprehension.

"Left here," Dushane said, her voice hushed.

"This looks like a driveway," Wolf said.

"It is. It's Monroe's address."

The road led through what had once been a stand of trees that had shielded the house from the view of the neighborhood. The few trees that were left were stripped of foliage. Some were twisted into a corkscrew shape, like green sticks. Others were tumbled into untidy piles, their roots exposed like the tentacles of some dead undersea creature. The driveway ended in front of a mound of rubble where a house had once stood.

"I don't think anyone's home," Dushane said.

Wolf pulled the car to a stop and killed the engine. "If she was in there," he said quietly, "she's dead."

"You don't know that," Buckthorn said. He got out of the back seat. Dushane and Wolf looked at each other. Wolf shrugged. They got out as well.

"Look," Buckthorn said. He was pointing off to the side of the property, where a yellow front-end loader with a backhoe was sitting. He walked over to the pile. Wolf and Dushane followed him. "Someone's been moving this stuff around," he said. He pointed. "There's a cleared space there."

"And...shovels," Dushane said.

"Where...oh." Wolf said. He saw them, standing upright, stuck in the soil of the back yard. An axe lay in the grass next to them.

Buckthorn walked over to the cleared area. Debris had been moved aside, leaving an area of intact flooring. Piping and electrical conduit stuck up raggedly at the edge like the dangling nerves and veins of a severed limb. "This is the place they were interested in," Buckthorn said. "Like they knew something was here."

"Or someone," Wolf said.

"But there's nobody here," Dushane said.

"Not above ground," Buckthorn said. He stomped on the floorboard, hard. "CALLIE!" he shouted. "CALLIE PRESTON!"

Silence.

Buckthorn stomped again, harder. "CALLIE! YOU DOWN THERE, GIRL?"

"There's nothing there, Tim," Wolf said.

Buckthorn ignored him. "COME ON, CALLIE! GIVE US A SIGN! SOMETHING! ANYTHING!" He paused.

"This is getting..." Dushane began.

"Shhhh..." Buckthorn said. He bent over, listening, then got down on his hands and knees on the exposed floorboard. "I hear something."

"Tim," Dushane said. "Come on, man, it's not..." She stopped as he held up his hand. Then she heard it.

From beneath the floorboard, a slow, faint, but distinct tap. Then another, louder one. Then a third.

Then silence.

***

When she first heard the voice, she thought she must be dreaming. Then she thought maybe it was the voice of God, calling her home. But why would God be asking her for a sign? Wasn't He the one that showed people signs? She snapped to sudden awareness. There was someone up there, but it wasn't God, and the voice wasn't coming from Heaven. Someone was looking for her. Someone who knew her name. *Dad*? She thought, but it didn't sound like him. She had to let them know she was down here. She tried to cry out, but all that came out was a dry croak. She tried again. Nothing. She groped frantically around in the dark for something, anything she might use to make noise with. He hand closed around a piece of wood that had fallen into the tiny void where she was trapped. She grasped it in her cuffed hands and reached up, trying to strike the ceiling above her head. She couldn't get her hands up high enough. She heard another voice, fainter. It sounded like a woman. She stretched, stood on her tiptoes. She felt the hunk of wood brush against the ceiling. Summoning what felt like the last of her energy, she jumped upward . It rapped against the boards above her head. She jumped again. It struck the ceiling again, harder, sending a shock up her weakened arm. The third jump knocked the piece of wood from her hand. She sank down again, exhausted. After a moment, she began groping for the hunk of wood. She couldn't find it. She flailed her hands in frustration against the darkness, as if it was something she could beat down. They were there. They were so close. They had to have heard her.

Chapter Twenty-seven

"You heard that, right?" Dushane said.

"Yeah," Wolf replied.

Buckthorn was already moving towards the tools he'd seen, particularly the axe lying in the grass. He thought about his own patrol car, its trunk crammed full of rescue and survival gear from rain ponchos to flares to chainsaws. He had no idea what the FBI carried around in their cars, but it was worth a shot.

"Tony, Leila," he called back, "Check the trunk of the car for tools. Someone call EMS. Tell 'em we've got someone trapped in rubble." He reached the axe, looked back. Dushane was in a dead run towards the car. Wolf had his cell phone to his ear, talking quickly. Buckthorn felt a strange sensation of warmth and satisfaction spread through him. He spent so much time worrying and fretting and planning for the worst to happen, driving the men and women under him without mercy, training constantly so they'd be ready when it did. But when the balloon actually went up and the crisis began, he felt calm. He recalled the first time he'd met Wolf, back in Pine Lake, when Wolf had taken the TV reporter and her cameraman hostage. He'd been frustrated when Wolf had gotten away, but before that, there'd been a part of him, deep in his core, that had felt perfectly at home. It was where he was meant to be, in the middle of the crisis, with people who knew their jobs and who'd get them done or die trying. And now, here he was, with the man he'd tried to capture, on the same team. And Dushane rounded out the mix perfectly. They weren't *his* team, but they were a team, and they'd get this done. He was actually grinning as he shouldered the axe and headed back to the rubble pile.

Wolf was snapping the phone shut as Buckthorn reached him. "ETA seven minutes," he said. Dushane came running up, a disgusted expression on her face. "Nothing in the trunk but someone's gym bag. Someone who really needs to rinse out some things."

"Okay," Buckthorn said. He leaned over. "CALLIE," he yelled. "HANG ON, SWEETHEART. WE'RE COMING IN TO GET YOU." He straightened up and looked at the other two. "Stand back," he said. He raised the axe over his head and brought down onto the wood flooring, as heard as he could. The heavy forged steel blade bit deep, burying itself in the wood with a heavy *thunk* that shook the floor beneath their feet.

"Don't you want to wait..." Wolf began. Buckthorn looked up at him as he wrenched the axe free. "Never mind," Wolf said. "Let me know when you want me to take a turn."

"Hey," Dushane said. "Someone's coming."

Buckthorn paused and looked. A large black truck was cruising slowly up the driveway.

***

"Fuck. Me," Donovan said.

"We're both fucked," Lofton said. He was behind the wheel. "The guy with the axe is a cop."

"Not a local," Donovan said. "The uniform's different."

"Not a state cop, either," Lofton said. "I got a couple on the payroll, and that ain't their uniform."

"Beats me, but unless I miss my guess," Donovan said, "the other two are cops as well."

"What the fuck are we going to do?"

Donovan reached for his gun. "We take care of this."

"Don't be an idiot," Lofton said. "Look at what they're doing. You think that guy's trying to lay in some wood for the fireplace? They've found the girl."

"How?" Donovan demanded.

"Who gives a damn how? They did. And you know they've called for backup. We need to get out of here."

Donovan was silent, his jaw working furiously. He hated the idea of running. Anything but forward motion felt like surrender. He was from a long line of people who'd starve themselves to death before they'd surrender. Anyway, where could he run to? Lofton wasn't waiting for a suggestion. He was backing the truck up, swinging it around for a three- point turn.

***

"You thinking what I'm thinking?" Dushane said. The truck was backing up, starting to turn around.

"Yeah," Buckthorn replied. He started to drop the axe, then stopped and held it out to Wolf. "Your turn."

Wolf hesitated. "You don't have any jurisdiction here, Lieutenant."

Buckthorn let the axe drop. It landed on the floorboards with a deep thump. I don't care," he said. He started towards the FBI car. He felt rather than saw Dushane trotting alongside. "You stay here," he said.

"Like hell I will," she shot back. "That's an FBI vehicle, cowboy, even if we don't strictly have authorization to use it."

"Those guys might be dangerous."

"Probably. But I have a gun. More to the point, I have the keys."

Buckthorn drew up short as they reached the car and looked at her. "Give them to me."

She stared back, her jaw set. "No."

"Damn it, Leila," he started, but Wolf interrupted him. "Get moving, you two!" he shouted.

Buckthorn looked down the driveway. The truck had completed the turn and was accelerating away. He could hear the sound of sirens approaching. "Fine," he snarled. He ran to the passenger side and slid in. The engine roared and the acceleration pushed him back in the seat as he fumbled for the seat belt.

"I saw two people in the front seat," she said. "I'd be really surprised if they weren't armed. Get on the radio and see if you can get us some backup." She hit a switch and a siren began to wail. The big black truck in front of them was accelerating. Dushane pressed harder on the gas and the big car responded smoothly, closing the gap. An ambulance passed them going in the other direction, lights flashing, siren wailing as if in answer to their own, dropping suddenly and dramatically in pitch as they streaked past each other. They passed the couple they'd seen earlier, still standing outside their ruined house. They were moving fast enough that the figures were nothing but a blur, but Buckthorn registered a brief glimpse of mouths hanging wide open in surprise. He turned his attention back to the unfamiliar dashboard. He studied the radio for a moment, then picked up the mike and pressed what he hoped were the right buttons. "All units, all units, this is FBI car number..." he paused. "What the hell number are we, anyway?"

"Damned if I know," Dushane muttered. "I'm a stranger here myself." She gave a grunt of surprise and yanked the wheel to the left as a compact car came out of a driveway to their left, almost into their path. The car swerved sickeningly for a moment, then Dushane got it back under control.

"FBI car," Buckthorn said awkwardly. "We're on..." he looked around. "All the street signs are down."

"Look at the GPS," she said. Her teeth were gritted, in concentration rather than irritation. They were coming out of the zone of total devastation, into a more heavily traveled area. Her eyes darted from side to side, looking for hazards, before fixing again on their quarry. They were gaining on the black pickup.

"Woodlawn Drive," Buckthorn spoke into the microphone, squinting at the tiny screen of the GPS bolted to the dash.

A voice came back, tinny with static and harsh with irritation. "Who is this? This is a secure channel. Identify yourself."

"I thought I just did," Buckthorn muttered. He jammed his hand against the headliner above him to brace himself as Dushane slewed the Crown Vic around a curve. There was a sharp popping sound and a hole appeared in the windshield, cracks spreading around it like a sunburst. Buckthorn heard a second shot hit the front of the car like the blow of a hammer on the bumper.

"Oh, you did NOT just shoot at a federal agent," Dushane said, her voice high and nearly breaking with outrage. "Buckthorn, see if you can discourage that shit, would you?" Buckthorn already had his weapon out and was pressing the button to lower his window. He chambered a round and raised up on the seat to lean out. The wind roared in his ears, blew back his hair and made his eyes water. Another shot from the truck struck the car roof at a shallow angle and skipped away. Buckthorn raised his weapon and took aim. Then he hesitated. They were in a neighborhood now, the houses apparently undamaged by the storms. There were people on the sidewalks, staring at the vehicles rushing by. The car rocked and weaved with Dushane's maneuvering, making the car an unstable platform. Buckthorn clenched his teeth and slid back into the car.

"Civilians," Dushane said.

"Yeah."

The people in the truck had no such scruples. Another thump shook the car, this one appearing to come from up front. "If that asshole hit the radiator," Dushane said, "we're in trouble."

Buckthorn just nodded.

***

Donovan drew back inside the car. "I think I hit the radiator," he said.

Lofton muscled the truck around another sharp curve. "Good," he said.

Donovan looked out the window at the peaceful streets and well-manicured lawns zipping past. "You got any idea where the hell we are?" he said. "Or where we're going?"

Lofton laughed, a little hysterically. "I lost track of where we were after the second or third turn," he said.

Donovan looked back. The cop car showed no signs of slowing. He cursed under his breath. "Get us to some open road," he said. "We're getting nowhere like FUCK!"

Lofton had made another turn down another unfamiliar street in the suburban grid. But this street ended abruptly in a fence of orange and white traffic barriers, topped with flashing amber lights. The pavement ended a dozen yards beyond the barrier, next to a large sign, black letters on rough white boards, that identified the large, plowed-up area of gray and brown earth beyond as FUTURE SITE OF ST. MARY OF THE ANGELS CATHOLIC SCHOOL. The road turned to dirt and clay beyond the sign and ended at a massive pile of dirt. Lofton and

Donovan both screamed as the truck plowed through the barrier. Lofton stomped the brakes as hard as he could and the truck skidded on the dirt, threatening to go sideways and roll, until he brought it under control and got it going straight again.

Directly aimed at the mound of earth.

***

Dushane sucked in her breath as she saw the truck plow into the dirt pile like a plane crashing into the side of a mountain. She stepped on the brakes, wrestling against the car's attempt to skid, then slid to a stop a dozen feet behind the truck. Both she and Buckthorn bailed out of the car at the same time, Dushane drawing her weapon as her feet hit the ground, Buckthorn's already aimed. Both took cover behind the open car doors and began shouting at the same time.

"FEDERAL AGENT! OUT OF THE TRUCK AND GET ON THE GROUND!"

"POLICE! OUT OF THE VEHICLE! NOW!"

There was no response at first, then the doors of the truck flew open and two men fell out, one on each side, stumbling and nearly going to their knees before recovering. Both were dressed in coveralls, like construction workers. Each one had a gun in his hand.

"DROP THE WEAPON!" Buckthorn yelled, his voice a hoarse bellow. He could hear Dushane shouting as well. The one on his side responded by raising his gun and firing, so fast Buckthorn barely had time to register the movement before the window next to him shattered. He flinched and fired back, the report and the vibration traveling up his arm feeling all too familiar. The shot had no effect. The man turned and ran. Buckthorn heard another sharp bang and looked over at Dushane. She had ducked down behind the door. He looked over to where the man on her side was walking towards them, his pistol held out in a sideways grip he'd probably seen in a movie somewhere, firing as he went and shouting. Buckthorn braced his arms atop the car and took aim. Out of the corner of his eye he saw Dushane pop back up. The two of them fired simultaneously. Both shots struck the advancing man. The impact stopped him in his tracks and rocked him back. His gun hand flew up in the air, the weapon spinning from his grasp.

He fell backwards to the ground with a thump they could hear clearly from where they stood. In the sudden silence that followed, Buckthorn could hear approaching sirens. Dushane and Buckthorn moved cautiously towards the fallen man, weapons still held out in front of them. "Where's the other one?" Dushane called out.

Buckthorn looked around. There was no sign of the other man. He'd vanished around the side of the mound of dirt.

"He's gone into the construction site," he said. "Stay here."

She knelt by the man on the ground, felt for a pulse in his neck. "You're not going in without backup."

"Then come on." He started sprinting towards the site. "Wait," Dushane said as she stood up. The sirens were almost upon them. "We should..." she was interrupted as a white patrol car with red stripes roared down the street towards them, siren howling. The officer behind the wheel spotted them and stood on the brakes. The patrol car slid on the pavement, then hit the soft sand and skidded to a stop, throwing up a spray of dirt and mud, halting just inches from their rear bumper. An officer leaped from the car, gun drawn. "DROP YOUR WEAPONS!" he yelled. "GET ON THE GROUND!"

"I'm a cop!" Buckthorn called back.

"FBI!" Dushane yelled. The officer didn't seem to hear them over his own voice, which had climbed almost to the point of breaking.

"There's s suspect getting away, asshole!" Dushane yelled. Another red and white pulled up, adding the screaming of its siren to the chaos. Another officer jumped out, his own weapon drawn, shouting as well.

"Oh, for God's SAKE!" Dushane said. She knelt and laid her weapon on the ground, then went prone in the dirt, hands behind her head. Buckthorn clenched his teeth and did the same, a couple of feet away. The two local officers charged forward, guns at the ready. One stopped a few feet away, holding his gun on them, while the other holstered his and produced a pair of zip cuffs. "Hands behind you," he barked as he walked to where Buckthorn was lying.

"Son," Buckthorn said through clenched teeth, "does this uniform I'm wearing look familiar? At all?"

The officer slowed, stopped. "Wait. You're a law enforcement officer?"

"No, genius," Dushane snarled. "He's the goddamn UPS man."

"You need to be quiet, ma'am," the officer said, but some of the steel had left his voice. His face was beginning to show doubt.

"Yeah," Buckthorn said. "I'm a sheriff's deputy."

The officer looked stricken. "Jason," he called back. "This guy's a deputy sheriff."

"Not from around here," the other one called back.

"No," Buckthorn said. "Not from around here. I'm from North Carolina. And this lady here's an FBI agent I'm helping on a case. You mind if I sit up?"

The other officer had come up to join the first one. "Oh. Oh, shit."

"Yeah," the first one said. "Sorry, um…"

"Buckthorn," he said as he sat up. "Lieutenant Tim Buckthorn. Gibson County, North Carolina." He began brushing the dirt off. "This is Special Agent Leila Dushane, FBI."

"Charmed, I'm sure," she said sourly, sitting up and brushing off her own dark pantsuit. "Goddammit," she muttered. "This thing is ruined." Buckthorn noticed a look of disapproval cross the first officer's face at the language. "Mind if we see some I.D., ma'am?"

She sighed and reached into her jacket pocket.

"You've got an armed subject back behind us in that construction site," Buckthorn said. "He's wanted in a kidnapping case. And you can add ADW on a law enforcement officer and a federal agent while you're at it."

The two officers looked at each other. "You two can stand up now," the first one said.

They got to their feet. "You going to call that in?" Buckthorn said. He looked at the first officer's nametag. "Officer DeSalvo?"

"Yeah," DeSalvo said. He headed over to his car at a trot. Buckthorn shook his head.

"Asshole's probably halfway to Kentucky by now," Dushane said.

"Who's the guy we just…" Buckthorn said. He stopped as the enormity of the unspoken word brought home to him what he'd just done. Again. He felt a twisting in his gut, and a feeling like a huge weight suddenly pressing down on his shoulders.

"Defended ourselves against?" Dushane said. She reached up and ran a hand through her hair to brush the dirt out. He could see her clearly, as if she'd come into sharper focus. He saw that her hand was trembling. "You okay?"

"Yeah," she said. "Fine. You?"

"A little shook," he said.

"Shaken," she said absently.

"What?"

"Shaken. Not shook."

The absurdity of it made him laugh. She looked over at him, scowling, and then she laughed, too. She wiped her eyes with the back of her hand. "We need to get back," she said. "See if the girl's all right."

"Yeah," he said. They started walking back towards the car.

"Hey," the second officer said, "You guys need to stay here."

"No we don't," the two of them said in unison, and that started them laughing again. There was an edge to the laughter, something right on the brink of hysteria.

DeSalvo hurried up. "We need you to give a statement," he said. He reached out as if to restrain Buckthorn. He stopped at the look on Buckthorn's face, his hand raised in the air as if frozen.

"Son," Buckthorn said as gently as he could, "we are still in the middle of a federal investigation in which a young girl's life is at stake. We just located her—we think—but she needs rescuing and medical help. We'll be glad to come in when it's done and give you all the statements you need. But if you try to interfere with said investigation, this young lady will place you in federal custody, which is not somewhere you want to be. And, son, I don't want to be rude, but I have already had a hard day. I am far from home, I've been shot at—twice—and I have gone without my lunch, which always makes me irritable. What this is leading up to is that if you put that hand on me, I'll break it off and put it in my pocket. So. We clear?"

DeSalvo's hand dropped to his side. "Yes sir," he said.

"Good." They got in the car. Dushane started it up. "Not bad, cowboy."

He suddenly felt very tired. "Thanks."

"When this is over," she said as she pulled off, "I am going to buy you a drink. Maybe several."

"As long as you don't try and correct my grammar."

"I'll do what I can."

The followed the trail of steadily worsening damage back to the site. They saw the flashing red and blue lights of the emergency and police vehicles from two blocks away. When they pulled up, the long drive-way was clogged with a collection of fire trucks, patrol cars, and an ambulance. People in a variety of uniforms milled about, faces set with grim purpose. As they got out of the car, they could hear the high grat-ing whine of a chain saw. People were gathered around the spot where they'd heard the tapping. A trio of people dressed in orange coveralls with the six-armed blue star of EMS workers stood by a white-sheeted gurney resting on the ground. Tony Wolf stood a few feet away, watch-ing. The only sign of nervousness he showed was the constant jiggling of his right leg. He spotted them approaching and raised a hand in greeting.

"What's the word?" Buckthorn shouted over the noise of the saw.

"They're cutting through," Wolf replied. "We haven't heard anything from down there since you left." He looked Dushane and Buckthorn up and down, noting the dirt and mud on the front of their clothing. "What the hell happened to you two?"

"We had a little trouble," Dushane said. "We..." her voice broke.

Wolf's brow furrowed with concern. He motioned for them to follow him. They walked away from the site, far enough from the noise to be able to converse without shouting. "You okay, L.D.?"

"I'm fine," she said, but her voice was hoarse.

"What happened?" Wolf asked Buckthorn.

"The truck crashed. The driver and the passenger drew on us."

Wolf rubbed a hand across his face. "How bad?"

"One dead. The other got away when the locals pulled up and mis-took us for the subjects."

Wolf grimaced. "Shit. Who did the shooting?"

"Both of us."

"L.D., tell me the truth. How are you?"

She cleared her throat. Her voice was steadier when she spoke. "Holding it together, boss. For now."

Wolf nodded. "Glad you're honest about the 'for now'. We'll talk later about what you need to do to get past this. Right now," he nodded over their shoulders, "things are about to get ugly."

Buckthorn looked back. Watson and Braswell were striding across the lot towards them. Watson's face was stormy. Braswell had a smug little smile on his.

"Special Agent Anthony Wolf," Watson said. "Special Agent Leila Dushane. Timothy Buckthorn. The three of you are under arrest for theft of government property and for interference with a federal investigation. You have the right to remain silent..." Braswell was taking a set of plastic zip cuffs out of his pocket, his smile getting broader as he did it. Dushane started to speak, but Wolf held up his hand and she fell silent. He listened patiently while Watson read off the Miranda warnings. "Now turn around," Watson ordered.

"Sure," Wolf said. "As soon as we get done here."

Braswell's face went blank with surprise. Watson's scowl deepened. "What did you just say to me?"

Wolf gestured at the knot of workers. The saw had stopped and they were prying at the boards with a long crowbar. "I said, as soon as we find out if the girl's okay, we'll come with you."

Braswell had recovered from the shock and his scowl now matched Watson's. "You'll come us now, you son of a bitch," he said in a low, savage, voice. "Or I'll..."

"You'll do what, Fireball?" Dushane snapped. "Shoot us? Granted, this might be the only range you wouldn't miss at, but you really think you're going to pull the trigger on a couple of fellow agents and a uniformed cop, out here in broad daylight, in the middle of a crime scene?"

Watson stared at Wolf in frustration, his jaw working in fury. There was a shout from the rubble pile. "EMS, over here!" The EMS workers were moving towards the group standing around a newly-made hole in the wood flooring. Buckthorn started walking towards them. "Hey," Braswell said. Buckthorn ignored him. His concentration was fixed on the scene in front of him. He vaguely heard Dushane say, "I wouldn't do that if I were you, Fireball." He reached the hole with no one interfering with him. "Excuse me," he said. One of the rescue workers, a slender blonde woman with her hair cut short, looked at him, annoyed, but moved aside when she saw the sheriff's uniform. Then she did a quick double take. "You're not with the county," she said.

"No," Buckthorn said. He knelt at the edge of the hole and looked down.

The girl was there, about five feet down, surrounded by a jumble of debris. Workers were hauling out every board, chunk of concrete and piece of drywall they could reach, starting at the top, leaving the girl looking as if she was at the bottom of a cone of construction trash. She was slumped on a sturdy-looking wooden chair, her head lolling to one side. One leg was cuffed to a thick metal chain that disappeared into the mess around her. Beneath the matted and tangled raven hair, her face looked as pale and bloodless as if she was carved from bone. There were scrapes and scratches on her face that made her look as if she'd an unpleasant encounter with a large and angry animal. She was covered with dirt and concrete dust, but she was unquestionably the girl from the picture Maddie Underhill had found, what seemed like ages ago. He couldn't tell if she was breathing. He felt his own breath stop, his heart pounding in his chest. She couldn't be dead. Not after all this. Not after they'd gotten this close.

"Callie?" he called down to her. "Callie? C'mon, girl, wake up. You're almost home." There was no response. His voice rose. "Callie? Wake up. Come on, your Mama's worried about you. You need to wake up. Please." He heard his voice crack on the last word, felt the hot tears stinging his eyes. He wiped them away. "Callie," he whispered.

"Sir," a voice said, "you need to move aside." He felt a hand on his shoulder, brushed it away savagely.

"Come on, Tim," Dushane said. She was kneeling beside him. She put her arm around his shoulder. "Let these people work."

He looked up. Two of the EMS workers were setting the gurney down. Another, a tiny woman with short red hair and freckles, was standing behind Buckthorn, stethoscope around her neck. She looked like a teenager, but the determined expression on her face showed she wasn't someone to underestimate. Buckthorn stood up and stepped aside. The woman sat at the edge of the hole, her legs dangling over, then gently levered herself down onto the scrambled pile of wreckage. A board moved as she put her foot on it.

"Careful," someone said. "It's still unstable."

"I know," the woman replied through clenched teeth. She leaned down, picked up the board, and held it up. Buckthorn leaned over, took it, and tossed it behind him. The woman repeated the process, with the people around the hole taking the pieces she handed up, until she had widened and deepened the cleared area. Buckthorn saw Watson and Braswell taking chunks of debris and carrying them out of the way. Finally, the woman was able to slide down beside the girl in the chair, so close they were touching. She placed two fingers on the girl's neck, then stuck the stethoscope in her ears and bent down to listen. Buckthorn held his breath again.

"There's a pulse," the woman called up. "But it's weak. Somebody hand me down the bolt cutters. And get the lift set up." The group burst into a flurry of activity. A firefighter handed the EMS worker down a pair of long-handled metal cutters. A trio of other firefighters had already begun constructing a complex-looking tripod which they moved over the hole after attaching a heavy pulley system from which descended a yellow web harness. In minutes, the girl was ascending out of the hole, hanging limp in the harness. The EMS worker climbed out of the hole after her colleagues had taken the girl, detached her, and laid her on the gurney.

"Tell me," Buckthorn asked, "is she going to be all right?"

"You the father?" the woman said, cocking her head quizzically, taking in his soiled and wrinkled uniform.

"No," he said. "She's..." he hesitated, realizing that she wouldn't tell a stranger anything. "My little sister," he said.

Dushane was standing a few feet away. "Wait, what?"

The EMS worker didn't seem to notice. "She's got some nasty scrapes and bruises, and some lacerations, but doesn't look like there's any life-threatening blood loss. She's severely dehydrated and in shock, but there's no sign of spinal damage. At least not now. We're taking her to the trauma center at Erlanger, to be on the safe side. But I think she's in good shape, considering. You want to ride the ambulance with us?"

Buckthorn looked over to where Watson and Braswell were fastening Wolf's hands behind him with the zip cuffs. "No," he said. "Thanks. I'll meet up with her there later." *Maybe much later*, he thought as he began walking over to them.

Chapter Twenty-eight

Patience saw the look of shock cross Lamp Monroe's face and saw the cell phone slip from his grasp as he began to fall forwards. She rushed to him, reaching him just in time to keep him from slipping out of the chair and sliding to the floor. His shoulders were shaking, and his breath came in gasps. "What?" she asked. "What's wrong?" The gasps turned to convulsive coughing that shivered the old man's body as if he were in the throes of a seizure. She grabbed the oxygen tank by the bed and pressed the mask to his nose. He struggled against her, but he was too weak to break her grip. In a moment, he quieted. He slumped back into the chair, semiconscious, his eyes half closed. She studied him for a moment to make sure the immediate crisis had passed, then picked the phone up from off the floor. "Sean?"

"Jesus," Donovan said, "did the old fucker die?"

"He's resting. But something gave him a hell of a shock. What the hell happened?"

"Lofton's dead. Cops shot him."

"Oh, my God. Are you all right?"

"I'm fine. Some locals showed up and the stupid bastards got in each other's way. I got out clean."

"That's good," she said. Her mind was racing ahead. This was opportunity, if she could figure out how to use it.

He went on. "But I think the cops have found the girl. The ones who shot at us were at the site when we got back."

She started to speak, but Lampton was awake and pulling at her arm to get at the cell phone. "Be safe," she said as she handed the phone back to him. Lampton pulled the mask away. The face beneath it was contorted with rage. "Get back here," he croaked into the phone. "Now." There was a pause. "I'll deal with that. Just get your ass back here. I don't care how." He broke the connection and slumped back in the chair, his eyes closed, breathing heavily.

"I'm sorry about your grandson," she said.

"He din't have sense enough to pour piss out of a boot if you printed the instructions on the heel." The words were harsh, but his voice lacked its usual force. It was as if he was reciting the words by rote. *I'll be damned,* she thought. *The old man cared about his grandson after all. Wish I'd known that earlier.*

Monroe opened his eyes. Patience had to restrain herself from taking a step back at the vehement rage smoldering in them. "He was a damn fool," he said, "but he was family. You don't kill my family without payin' for it."

"What are you going to do?" she asked.

"That ain't none o'your business, gal," he said. He picked up the phone and started to press buttons. "Now leave me be for a bit. I got some calls to make."

"Yes, sir," she murmured. She kept her eyes down as she left the bedroom, closing the door behind her. When she heard the click of the closing door, she put her ear to it. She could hear clearly; the old man's voice was stronger than she'd heard it in months.

"It's time," he was saying. Then: "Good. You ain't gonna hear from me for a while. But you'll be took care of." Then there was silence.

She stood up. With Lofton dead, there was no heir apparent to Monroe's business except Donovan. And she had Donovan under control. For the moment. She considered going back into the bedroom and holding a pillow over the old man's face until he stopped struggling. Or diluting or even poisoning his medications. He wouldn't last long without them. She'd greet Donovan as the new king when he returned. He'd be grateful. He'd make her the queen. But then what? She thought. He'd know what she'd done to put him on top, and that knowledge would give him power over her. He'd own her. She had no desire to be owned. Not ever again. But if the positions were reversed...and with that a plan began to form in her mind. She put her ear back to the door. At first, all she heard was more silence. Then she heard the sound of weeping. She thought for a moment, then walked back down the hall to her own room and picked up her own cell phone. She dialed a number she knew by heart. A bright, cheerful voice answered. "Law Offices of Suddreth and Blanco."

"This is Patience Matthews," she said. "I need to speak with Mr. Suddreth. He'll know what it's about."

***

The FBI agents had driven the three of them to the local police station, where they'd separated them immediately. Braswell had stuck Buckthorn in an interview room and left without speaking. That had been over three hours ago. Buckthorn supposed it was better than a cell. The interview room was like the ones in his own department back home: bleak and sparsely furnished with just a table and two chairs. There was a mirror on the wall that was almost surely one-way with an observation area behind it. Leaving a subject alone for a long time was a time-honored tactic; Buckthorn had used it himself on occasion. He wondered if Braswell and Watson knew that. Of course, it was possible that they were leaving him alone because they didn't know what to do about him. He wondered if they'd try to interrogate him. *Maybe they'll let me take notes on their technique*, he thought wryly.

He was worried about Dushane. The man at the construction site was almost certainly the first man she'd ever killed. He remembered the shock of that, the sickening knowledge that you'd taken another human life. The fact that you'd had no choice, that it was him or you at the time, softened the impact, but only slightly. It was still a psychological blow. He was feeling it himself. It gave him an odd sense of relief that he could still feel something. He hoped it would never become routine to him. He wished he could be there for Dushane to help her through it.

That thought made him pause. He'd tried very hard for years not to mix his professional and personal lives, with the result that he hadn't had much of a personal life to speak of. He thought about her statement that she was going to buy him a drink, maybe several. He found himself liking the idea very much. Except that he'd buy, of course. He smiled at the thought. Then he looked around the room and the smile vanished. First, he had to get out of here.

The door opened and he took a deep breath. He figured Braswell or Watson, or maybe some local cop, would yell at him, jerk him around, probably threaten him. But he knew in his heart it had been a justified shooting. He had nothing to be worried about. *If I can keep telling myself that*, he thought, *maybe I'll believe it.*

Watson came in, holding a file folder, his seemingly permanent scowl in place. He was followed by a man Buckthorn didn't recognize. The new arrival had a fringe of greasy hair around his bald head, and the red face of someone with poorly controlled high blood pressure. His belly overlapped the waistline of this cheap suit. He didn't look happy either.

"This is Detective Rivers," Watson said. "From the Bartlett PD."

Wolf stood up and offered his hand to Rivers. "Lieutenant Tim Buckthorn," he said. "Gibson County Sheriff's Department."

Rivers looked confused for a moment. He obviously wasn't used to a suspect standing up and introducing himself. He took the offered hand automatically. Buckthorn shook it firmly and sat down.

Watson's scowl deepened. "This isn't a courtesy visit, Buckthorn. You may think you're King Shit back home, but here, you're in trouble. Deep trouble."

"I'm a sworn law enforcement officer," Buckthorn said, "and I was assisting two federal officers in the performance of their duties. Those duties involved locating a kidnap victim and pursuing the subjects responsible for said kidnapping. Are you going to write this down, Agent Watson? Detective Rivers? Because this is the only statement you're going to get from me."

Rivers spoke up. "Now you listen here..."

Buckthorn went on as if Rivers hadn't spoken. "Agent Leila Dushane of the Federal Bureau of Investigation and myself were engaged in a vehicle pursuit of two subjects believed to be the kidnappers. At one point, they wrecked their vehicle and attempted to flee on foot, ignoring orders to stop. One subject produced a firearm and began firing at me and Agent Dushane. We engaged said subject with our own weapons."

"What you did was..." Watson said. Buckthorn raised his voice over Watson's and went on. "I believe the subject was struck by at least two shots and was dead at the scene." He looked at Rivers. "Uniformed officers of the Bartlett PD arrived on the scene at this point and apparently mistook Agent Dushane and I for subjects. In the confusion, the other subject made his escape." He dropped the formal tone. "So did your folks get him?" he asked Rivers. Before he could answer, he turned to Watson. "And if you say 'we're asking the questions here,' I promise you, I will laugh straight in your face."

"No," Rivers said. "We didn't get him."

Buckthorn grimaced. "So who was the man we shot? Lofton Monroe or Sean Donovan?"

"That's on a need to know basis," Watson said.

"You have got to be kidding me," Buckthorn snapped. "Damn it, Agent Watson, I'm trying to help you people here. And you're not even going to show me photos of the possible suspects so I can tell you if they were the people who shot at us?"

Watson glanced down at the file folder on the table in front of him. Buckthorn sighed. "Are the pictures in there? May I?" he reached for the folder. Watson snatched it away. Buckthorn's teeth clenched involuntarily in frustration. "Do you want me to say please? Okay, please."

Watson took two photographs out of the folder and laid them on the table, not meeting Buckthorn's eyes. Buckthorn slid them towards him.

The first was a police mug shot. It showed a young man with dark hair and a cocky sneer on his face. The name and booking number that would normally appear across the bottom had been obscured with marker.

Buckthorn tapped the picture. "That's the guy we shot," he said. He looked at the other picture. This one was some kind of surveillance photo, grainy and blurred, and apparently taken from long range. It showed a stocky man in a dark suit, getting out of a BMW convertible. Buckthorn could make out a prominent jaw and dark hair cut short, but that was all. He shook his head. "This guy, I don't know. He could be anyone."

"That's the only photo we have of Sean Donovan," Watson said.

Buckthorn looked again. "Sorry." He looked up. "So can I go now?"

Watson didn't answer. He gathered up the photographs and slid them into the file folder.

"Wait," Buckthorn said as they stood up. "What about the girl? Is she okay?" They didn't answer as they moved towards the door. "Look,"

Buckthorn said a little desperately, "I know we stepped on some toes here, but can we at least keep in mind that this was all about that young girl?"

Watson left without answering, but Rivers paused at the door.

"She's in ICU," he said softly. "Last I heard, her condition's stable. She's going to live."

"Thank you," Buckthorn said. "I really appreciate you telling me." Rivers just nodded and walked out. Buckthorn heard the lock click again. He shook his head and addressed the mirror. "Right now," he said, "I can't say I'm real impressed with the local FBI." He didn't know if there was anyone behind the mirror, but it made him feel better to say it out loud.

Another hour went by before the door opened again. But it wasn't Watson or Braswell this time. It was Tony Wolf. Dushane was standing behind him.

"Come on," he said. "We're leaving."

Buckthorn stood up. "Just like that?"

"Well, sort of. We need to stick around for a while in case the locals have more questions. But we're not under arrest."

"Okay. Well..." he looked down at his uniform. The mud had dried to a crust, and he knew he probably smelled like he'd just crawled out of a swamp. "I need someplace to get cleaned up and change clothes."

"We'll get a hotel," Dushane said. "Courtesy of the FBI. And then, those drinks I promised you."

"Sounds like a deal," Buckthorn said.

As they walked out of the police station, Buckthorn said,"I'm not looking a gift horse in the mouth or anything..."

"But you want to know how I swung this?" Wolf said. " You can thank our old friend Deputy Director Steadman. He remembers you. And likes you, apparently."

Buckthorn thought back to the dry, emotionless senior FBI agent who'd come to Pine Lake in search of his long-missing agent, Tony Wolf. "I barely know him."

"Well, he was so pissed at me, he was going to let the two of us twist in the wind. But when I mentioned you were wrapped up in this, too, he made a few phone calls. After cussing me for a bit, of course. We're still going to have to go in front of OPR, but I'll worry about that when it happens."

"Huh," Buckthorn said. He stopped and looked around. They were standing on the sidewalk outside the station. It was starting to get dark. "So, do we have a car here, or what?"

"I thought asking for another FBI car would probably be pushing it," Wolf said, "so I called a rental place. And unless I miss my guess..." A Ford Fusion was pulling up to the curb, a large van bearing the logo of a national rental company right behind it. A young African-American man in a white shirt and tie got out of the Fusion, holding a clipboard. "You the one called for a car, sir?"

"Right." Wolf walked over and the two started going over the paperwork.

"This on the FBI, too?" Buckthorn asked Dushane.

"Nah," she said. "The boss is picking this one up."

He reached for his wallet. "Let me get some of it."

She waved him away. "You can get dinner."

"And the drinks we talked about."

She shook her head. "I told you, I got those."

"No, really. It wouldn't feel right. A lady paying, I mean."

She cocked an eyebrow at him. "You're kidding, right?" Then she laughed. "What am I saying? You don't kid, do you?"

He smiled. "Not often, no."

"We'll have to work on that," she said. She shook her head and chuckled again. "Are you for real, Tim Buckthorn?"

"Yeah," he said. "I am."

She gave him a long appraising look, then smiled. "Yeah," she said, "I guess you are."

"Let's go," Wolf called out.

"You got shotgun," Dushane said. "But don't get used to it."

The hotel was a chain place near the airport; nothing fancy, but the room was clean and the bed looked comfortable. Buckthorn looked at it longingly, realizing how tired he was. He considered just stripping off his dirty uniform, crawling between the sheets, and sleeping for the next year. But he needed a shower and his stomach was growling.

The shower revived him somewhat, and by the time he was dried off and clothed in the jeans and workshirt he'd brought from home,

Dushane was knocking on his door. He opened it to find her standing there, dressed in black pants, a red silk blouse, and boots. She looked gorgeous.

"C'mon, cowboy," she said, "let's go eat." It sounded like she'd already gotten a couple of drinks in ahead of him.

Wolf was standing beside the rental car in the parking lot, his cell phone held to his ear. His brow was furrowed in worry. As they approached, he was apparently finishing his call: "Look, be careful, all right? Okay. Love you." He put the phone in the pocket of his shirt.

"Trouble?" Buckthorn said.

"It's Gaby," Wolf replied. "She's on a story. Some kind of hostage situation. In your neck of the woods."

That got Buckthorn's attention. "Say what?"

"Don't worry, it's the next county over. I think. Place called Blainesville. Some guy's holding a bunch of people in the local newspaper office."

"Damn," Buckthorn said. He pulled his own phone out, tried to turn it on. It was dead. He thought about asking Wolf if he could borrow his phone. If Blaine County needed assistance, they'd call his department. *And if they do, exactly what are you going to do from here?* He asked himself. He took a deep breath and tried to relax. Duane and Janine would handle anything that needed handling.

"You okay?" Dushane said.

"Yeah," he said. "Let's eat."

They took a busy six-lane road from the hotel. As they drove, Buckthorn reflected on how alike most cities looked once you got outside of the downtowns. Same hotels, same fast-food places, same oil and tire changers. The thought made him even more homesick for Pine Lake and the places he knew, and where people knew him.

"Chili's okay?" Wolf said.

"Yeah, whatever," Buckthorn said.

"Long as I can get a drink," Dushane said. Buckthorn and Wolf looked at each other. "Okay," Wolf said as he pulled into the parking lot.

As it turned out, Dushane had several double bourbons with dinner, and her voice got louder with each one. Several times Buckthorn and Wolf reminded her to keep her voice down. She'd laugh at them, calling them a "couple of old guys," then order another drink. At one point, she got up and went to the restroom, weaving slightly in the aisle.

"It's the shock of what happened," Buckthorn said.

"Yeah. I know."

"She needs some help dealing with it."

"Yeah, Buckthorn. I know. I'm on it, okay?"

"Sorry," he said.

Wolf sighed. "Don't be. Sorry. I didn't mean to snap at you. How about you? How you holding up?"

Buckthorn took a sip of his beer. It was his second of the night. "I'll be okay," he said. "As soon as I get home."

"You really love that place, don't you?" Wolf said.

Buckthorn shrugged. "Sometimes. Sometimes, not so much. You know the best thing about living in a small town?"

"What?"

"Everybody knows you. Knows all about you. You know the worst thing about living in a small town?"

Wolf smiled. "Everybody knows you and knows all about you?"

"You got it. Still. It's home."

"Must be nice," Wolf said. "Having a place to call home like that."

"Well, your old place is still for rent," Buckthorn said.

"Really?"

"Yeah. The realtor says people are scared of it. They still think the whole house is wired to explode."

Wolf laughed. "Sorry about that."

Buckthorn joined him in the laughter. "You could probably get it back cheap."

"I'll think about it." Dushane came back, stumbling a little as she rejoined them in the booth. "Whass so funny?" she said.

"Wolf's talking about moving back to Pine Lake," Buckthorn said.

She nodded. "Nice town. Nice people." She patted Buckthorn on the shoulder. "Nice people."

"Come on, L.D.," Wolf said. "We need to get you to bed."

She squinted at him, a lopsided grin on her face. "You sexually harassin' me, boss?" She turned to Buckthorn. "You're my witness. My superior just prepositioned me. Proposition. Whatever." She raised her voice. "Help! I'm bein' harassed!" She started giggling. People at the tables around them were falling silent and starting to stare. The waitress hurried over, a look of concern on her pretty face. "Is everything okay?"

"Yeah," Buckthorn said. "Just get us the check."

"You better not mess with me," Dushane said to Wolf, shaking a finger in his face. "I killed a guy today." She turned to the waitress. "I did. I killed a guy. Shot him dead." She formed her thumb and forefinger into the shape of a gun. "Bang!" she said. The wide-eyed girl jumped as if she'd actually been hit. The tables around them had fallen silent, leaving only the noise of the rock music over the sound system and the baseball game on TV. Dushane noticed the drop in the decibel level and looked around, squinting as if she'd just now noticed the other people in the restaurant. She turned back to Wolf. "I think. I need to go," she said with as much dignity as she could muster.

"I think you're right," Wolf said.

Buckthorn reached for his wallet. "Get her to the car. I'll get the check."

"Okay. Come on, L.D." She leaned on Wolf as he led her to the door. The waitress stared at her, then turned back to Buckthorn. "Did she really kill someone today?"

"Can I just have the check?" Buckthorn said.

The girl didn't move. "Are you guys cops?"

"Yes, ma'am," Buckthorn said. "The check?"

The girl fished in the pockets of her apron. "I thought you might be. But the other guy, I wasn't so sure of. And that drunk girl...so, really, did she kill someone?" She handed him the check.

He looked down at the bill and his heart sank. Dushane had had even more to drink than he'd thought. And she'd ordered the good stuff. This was really going to put a dent in his bank account. "Yeah," he said. He pulled out his debit card and handed it to her.

"Wow," the girl said. "Were you there? Did you shoot anybody?"

She was young, no more than twenty, and her eyes shone with an eagerness that shocked him. It made him feel a little queasy. "I'd really rather not talk about it," he said, "if you don't mind."

She looked disappointed, then brightened as she realized that his not wanting to talk about it probably meant the answer to her question was "yes." She took the card from him. "I'll be right back."

Buckthorn sat down at the table and rubbed his hands over his face. His earlier fatigue was back, redoubled. He began to wonder if he was going to be able to get back up.

When the girl came back, she surprised him by sliding into the booth seat opposite. As he started to fill out the slip, she murmured, "I'm off in about an hour and a half. If you want to come back and, you know, talk about it. It might do you some good."

He looked up in shock. She still had that bright, eager look in her eyes. The proposition couldn't have been more explicit if she'd rented a billboard.

"Thanks," he said, "but I've got to get up early."

She pouted. "Well, if you change your mind..."

Buckthorn wanted nothing more on earth at that moment to be somewhere else. "Thanks," he murmured. He signed the slip and passed it across the table to her. Then he got up and walked swiftly to the door without looking back.

Wolf was waiting in the car near the door with the motor running as he came out. As he slid into the passenger seat, he looked into the back. Dushane was looking out the window, not speaking. Buckthorn looked at Wolf. *She okay?* he mouthed without speaking. Wolf nodded. "Sorry to stick you with the check," he said. "We'll settle up later."

"Don't worry about it," Buckthorn said. He lapsed into silence as Wolf pulled out of the parking lot.

The waitress's reaction to the thought that he might have killed someone that day had left him shaken. He'd gone from being another faceless customer to something different. Maybe something dangerous. And that, somehow, had attracted her. He shook his head. His sister had always told him he didn't understand women. He was beginning to think she was right.

"You okay?" Wolf said.

"Yeah. Just wiped out."

They arrived at the hotel without speaking further. As they got out, Dushane said, "I need another drink. I got a bottle in my room. Anyone care to join me?" Her voice seemed less slurred than at the restaurant, but she was still unsteady on her feet.

"L.D.," Wolf said, "the last thing you need is another drink right now."

"Fine. That's a no from Agent Wolf. Buckthorn?"

He shook his head. "I'll pass. And I agree with Tony. You should just go to sleep."

"I don't sleep, remember?" she said.

"You should try."

"Yes, dad." She slammed the car door and stalked off across the parking lot. Wolf and Buckthorn looked at each other. Wolf shrugged.

"Just as well," Buckthorn said. "I'm not really fond of angry drunks. She's going to feel like hell in the morning, though."

"She says she doesn't get hangovers," Wolf said.

"That's actually a bad sign."

"Really? How?"

"A lot of alcoholics don't."

"You speak from experience?"

"Yeah. Good night, Tony."

"G'night, Tim." They walked towards their separate rooms.

Back in his room, Buckthorn took off his shoes and lay on top of the covers, too tired to do anything more. Yet, somehow, sleep continued to elude him. He lay on his back and stared at the ceiling for a long time, thoughts racing through his head.

There was a knock at the door.

Buckthorn groaned. He considered ignoring it. Then it came again, and he heard the voice. "Tim. It's Leila. Come on, damn it, open the friggin' door."

He sighed. Getting himself up off the bed seemed to take forever, but he did it. He went to the door and opened it.

She was standing there, her hair disheveled. She held a bottle of Jack Daniel's in one hand. It was a little over a quarter full. She was crying.

"Don't get the wrong idea," she said. The slurred voice was back. "I'm not here to fuck."

"That wasn't what I was..."

She pushed past him and plunked the bottle down on the table by the door. She practically fell into one of the two chairs. "Right *now*," she said, punctuating the last word by slamming her open hand down on the table, "I just need someone to have a goddamn *drink* with me, because if I have to be by *myself* all night, I'm going to go out of my fucking *mind*, okay?" She looked at him savagely, her eyes red, the tears streaming down her cheeks. "*Okay*?" she asked again, her voice breaking.

"Okay," he said. He went and got two cups from the sink. "You want ice?" he said. She shook her head. She poured two fingers of the dark amber liquid into each one.

She drained off half of hers in one gulp and looked into the cup. "You killed anyone before this?" she said.

"Yeah," he said. "A couple right after I met your boss. Then one a few months later. On Christmas Day, in fact."

"Bet that sucked."

"Yeah," he said. "It really did."

"Lot of action for such a little place."

He took a sip. The whiskey made a pleasant burn in the back of his throat. "Yeah."

"You getting used to it? Killing people?"

"No," he said. "At least not yet. I hope I never do."

She looked up. "So how do you deal with it?"

He set his cup down. "I remind myself that I'm an officer of the law, and that they were lawless men, who'd drawn weapons either on me or on someone I'd sworn to protect, with the intent to kill."

She drained off the second half of her whiskey, poured another two fingers. "And that made it all better?" she said bitterly. "That they were 'lawless men'?" She made air quotes with her fingers on the last two words.

He ignored the sarcasm. "No. But it helps some."

She took a drink, a smaller one this time. She closed her eyes and rolled the whiskey around on her tongue a bit before swallowing. "You know what the worst part is?"

"That it felt good?"

Her eyes opened in shock.

He finished his own drink in a gulp. "Yeah. I know. When that man fell dead, killed by your hand, part of you was scared to death, part of you was cranked up like an engine running full throttle, but part of you—a big part—thought that was the most alive you'd ever felt in your life. Am I wrong?"

"No," she breathed. "You're not wrong." A tear ran down her face. She wiped it away with her hand.

"And you can't talk to anyone about it, because you're afraid it makes you sound like some kind of monster."

She nodded, her eyes closed again. He leaned over, took both of her hands in his. "Listen to me," he whispered. "You killed, but you are not a killer. Someone tried to kill you. You lived anyway. That's *supposed* to feel good, Leila."

Slowly, her eyes still closed, she leaned forward, until her forehead was resting on top of his hands, which were still holding hers. "Thank you," she whispered. She raised her head slightly and nuzzled at his hands, turning slightly to rub her cheek against his knuckles. "You have nice hands," she murmured. Then she was still.

"Leila?" he asked. There was no response. "Leila?" he said, a little louder. She was asleep.

"Damn it," he muttered. He gently pulled his hands out from under her head. She wriggled her nose and leaned forward further, raising her arms and resting her head on them like a student napping at her desk. He stared at her in frustration, then looked at the bed. She wasn't very big; he considered picking her up and carrying her back to her room. But he was just too tired, and he couldn't remember her room number. Sighing, he stood up. He tried to shake her awake, but she just squirmed and made small sounds of annoyance. Eventually, his shaking put her off balance and she started to slide to the floor. He grabbed her before she could collapse and manhandled her to the bed. He laid her down on top of the covers and pulled her boots off. He arranged her in the recovery position, on her side, one knee bent, with a pillow at her back. He moved the wastebasket beside the bed where, he hoped, she could find it easily if she had to throw up. When he was done, he stood back, looked at her, and shook his head. There wasn't an easy chair to sleep in; the only chairs in the room were the straight-backed chairs at the table. He found a thick, scratchy blanket on the shelf in the closet. Taking a pillow off the bed, he took his own shoes off and lay down on the floor in the narrow space between the bed and the wall, wrapping the blanket around him. He rose once, to snap the lights off, then lay back down. Exhaustion overcame him almost immediately and he fell into a deep, dreamless sleep.

He awoke in the dark, momentarily disoriented. He thought he was lying in a ditch. After a moment, his wits returned. He lay on his back for a moment, staring at the ceiling. It occurred to him he ought to check on Dushane. Before he could sit up, she stuck her head over the edge of the bed. "Hey," she said. "What are you doing down there?"

He sat up. "You passed out. I didn't know how to get you back to your room."

She looked around. "But why are you on the..." comprehension dawned on her face. "Oh." She shook her head, then smiled. "You really are something else, Tim Buckthorn."

"Um. Thanks."

"Come on," she said. "Get up here." She rolled over and pulled aside the covers on his side. He got to his feet. "You're going back to your room?"

She smiled again. She made no move to get out of the bed. "No," she said. "Not right now."

Chapter Twenty-nine

Donovan arrived shortly after midnight. Patience let him in.

"He's sleeping," she whispered, then she threw her arms around him. "Oh my God," she said into his ear, "I was so worried about you."

"I'm fine, love," he said. "I'm totally fine." He kissed her. "How's he been?"

"Raging. Until he thinks I'm not looking. Then he's crying."

"Huh. Who knew he actually cared about the eejit?"

"He's also been making a lot of phone calls. To Lofton's people. Making sure they know he's still in charge."

"And is he?"

She smiled. "Well, that would depend on you, wouldn't it? Maybe now would be the time to make your move?"

He thought it over for a moment. "Not this second," he said. "But soon. I expect I'll be the one overseeing all of Lofton's old businesses. And his people. Let me get them on my side first."

"Most of them already are."

He nodded. "Yeah, that's true. Some of the others may need persuading."

She snuggled closer. "And I know how persuasive you can be," she whispered. "Some might not be on board, though. Some might think they can break away."

"Well," he smiled. "I'll just have to show them different, won't I?" He looked at the closed bedroom door. "How long will he stay out?"

"A while," she said, then smiled a smile rich with erotic promise. "I gave him a little something to keep him under till morning."

"Good," he said, and his hands on her became more demanding. She closed her eyes and moaned. "I knew what you'd want the second you got home," she whispered. "And I knew I wanted to give it to you. Anything you want, Sean. Anything."

***

Dushane nestled into Buckthorn's arms and sighed happily. "*Very* nice hands," she said. She kissed his bare chest. "And everything else, too."

Her braid had come loose while they were making love. He brushed a lock of hair away from her forehead. "Thanks." He didn't know what else to say, so he kissed her again. She broke the kiss first and looked up at him. "Thank you," she said. "For everything." She nestled against him again. "So. Tell me what you're thinking."

"About what?"

She scowled. He wondered how someone could look so beautiful even with that expression on her face. "Oh no," she said. "You keep shutting down on me. Don't do that. Not now. Especially not now."

He considered for a moment. "I think I'm happy."

"You say that like you're surprised."

He ran his fingers through her thick hair, loving the feel of it. "It doesn't happen much."

"I thought you liked where you are."

"I do. I mean, it's home. It's where I belong. It's just that..." he stopped.

She struck him lightly on the chest with the flat of her hand. "Keep going."

"It's just that I'm worried. All the time. It never stops."

"About what?"

"About everything. About everybody."

"In general? Family? What?"

He raised a hand, let it fall helplessly. "Everybody."

"Ahh," she said. "You want to keep everyone safe. Like that girl."

He nodded. "Yeah."

"And you worry that you can't do it."

"I know I can't. Not everyone."

"And it makes you crazy."

"I try not to let it."

She hugged him tight. "I don't know what to tell you, Tim. It's part of the job. It's why we do what we do." She pulled away a little and propped her head on her hand. "But with you, it's just a little more intense that most people. Even most cops. I get the feeling there's a story there you're not telling."

He didn't answer. He felt himself tensing up, willed his muscles to relax as he stared at the ceiling. She put a hand back on his chest, gently. "Your heart is pounding," she said. "And I don't think it's pounding in a good way."

"I'm okay," he whispered.

She sighed, clearly irritated. "Okay. You don't want to tell me, don't tell me." She started to sit up.

"Wait," he said. She stopped, then settled back down against him. "I'm sorry," she said. "I shouldn't push."

"It's okay," he said. "It's just something I don't talk about much." She didn't answer, just kept stroking his chest with her fingers. After a moment, he spoke.

"My dad died when I was three. He was a long-distance trucker. There was an accident. He slid on some ice. He was killed. My sister was six months old."

"I'm sorry," she murmured.

"Thanks. But I don't remember him."

"Still."

"Yeah. Still. My mom got some money from worker's comp, and he had some insurance. But the accident...did something to her. Or maybe she was like that all along."

"Like what?"

"I guess you'd call it 'bipolar'. Some days, she was great. She played with us, she cooked great meals, she was laughing and happy."

"And some other days..." she prompted him.

"Some days she wouldn't get out of bed. For days at a time. If I or my sister was hungry, I had to get us fed. I'd have to get both of us up and dressed and off to school."

She sucked in her breath. "How old were you when you started doing this?"

"The earliest I can remember was when I was seven."

"Jesus," she said, "didn't anyone try to help?"

"My uncle...my Dad's brother...tried. He'd come get us sometimes and take us to his house. We'd stay there a few weeks, then Mom would show up, all bright and shiny, and tell him she was better, she was seeing a doctor, then everything would be fine."

"And he'd let you go."

"And he'd let us go." He fell silent. "Things got worse when she started drinking."

"They usually do," she said softly.

"Yeah. She'd get abusive. Not physically. She didn't hit us. I think she knew that'd leave the kind of marks that would show. The kind someone would have to do something about."

"Damn," Dushane said.

"We were running low on money at that point. The house almost got repossessed. That was our fault. She couldn't hold a job. That was our fault. The power got turned off, until my uncle paid the bill and got the lights turned back on. That was our fault, too, because I was the one that called him and told him. I was eleven."

"Oh, Tim," she said. She hugged him tighter.

"I don't mean to say it was all bad times. When she was up, she was great. We'd go places, she'd buy us stuff, even though we couldn't really afford it. She was our best buddy."

"But never your mom."

"No." He paused. "When Loretta...my sister...started growing up, things got really bad."

"How?"

"You've seen her. Loretta was really pretty. Still is. Mom was, too. Or she was before...everything. But with all the drinking and...everything, her looks were starting to go. Loretta started getting interested in boys. And they got interested in her. That made my mother really crazy. She'd scream at Loretta. Say she was a slut, a whore...all sorts of things."

"And you'd try to protect her."

He nodded. "Yeah."

"Tim," she said, "have you noticed how much those pictures of Callie Preston look like your sister?"

He was silent for a moment. Then, "I do now." Another pause. She almost didn't hear the next thing he said: "Well, I'll be damned."

She couldn't help but laugh softly. "I mean, like I told my boss, it's not a long-lost relative kind of thing, but you have to admit..."

"Yeah," he said. "I get it now." He laughed, a little ruefully. "Looks like I don't know myself as well as I thought I did."

"No one does," she said. "You said you had to come home from college to take care of your sister."

He took a deep breath. "Yeah. I suppose I might as well tell you everything."

"Yeah," she said. "Might as well. This opening up thing works both ways, cowboy."

"Okay. My freshman year in college, my sister was a sophomore in high school. This older guy asked her to prom. Loretta didn't drink, she didn't get high, she didn't sleep with the guy. She even got home in time for curfew."

"The guy must have been pissed."

"Probably. But not as pissed as my mom was when she saw how good Loretta looked in her prom dress. She started drinking. Hard. When Loretta got home, my mother jumped out from behind the door and slashed her face with a box cutter."

Dushane sat bolt upright in bed, her hand to her mouth. "Oh, my God."

"Loretta ran to a neighbor's house, covered in blood. They called the cops. Mom got locked up overnight, and she went into rehab the next day." Buckthorn's voice had gone flat and dead. "She walked out 10 days later, after she got done detoxing. They called my uncle to come get her. Before he got there, she walked into the highway, directly in front of an eighteen wheeler." Buckthorn was trembling. His voice shook, but his eyes stayed dry. "I should have stopped her," he said. "I should have been there."

Dushane threw her arms around him. "No. No. It wasn't your fault, Tim. It wasn't."

"I keep telling myself that," he said. "Someday I may actually believe it."

"Your sister," Dushane said. "She looked fine when I saw her."

"She had a bunch of plastic surgery," Buckthorn said. "When she got engaged to Bru Starnes, he paid for a bunch more. What's left of the scar, she can cover with makeup. Mostly. You have to be looking for it. But it's there."

"Is that why you became a cop?"

"Probably. I didn't know it at the time, though. I came home to look after my sister, and I needed a job. My uncle knew Sheriff Wheeler—he was in office at the time, before Stark—and he got me on."

"And after a few years at it, your sister doesn't need looking after any more. She's got a family of her own. So now you look after a whole county."

"I guess."

"Yeah. But who looks after you?"

He shook his head. "I don't need looking after."

She blew a raspberry. "Bullshit." She propped herself back up on her elbow. "What do you want, Tim?"

He thought the answer over. The silence lay between them. As he opened his mouth to answer, a knock came at the door. "Tim?" a voice said.

"Oh, fuck," Dushane said, sitting up and pulling the sheet around her. "It's Wolf."

"Tim?" the voice asked again. "I can't find Dushane. She's not in her room. Have you seen her?"

"Just a second," Buckthorn called out.

"Shit. Shit. Shit." She jumped up, the sheet still wrapped around her naked body. "Hide me."

"Why?" Buckthorn said, but she had already bolted for the bathroom, leaving the bed bare. She closed the door as Buckthorn was pulling his jeans on. He went to the door and opened it. Wolf was standing there, looking confused.

"Hi," Buckthorn said.

"I can't find Dushane," Wolf said, "Have you seen..." He stopped and took a sniff. Comprehension dawned on his face. He shook his head. "Jesus," he said. "How long have you two been going at it? It smells like a New Orleans cathouse in here."

"Um," was all Buckthorn could think of to say.

Wolf called over his shoulder. "L.D.," he said, "you can come out now." He pushed past Buckthorn into the room. "There's been a development."

Buckthorn sat on the bed, hoping the heat he could feel in his face didn't mean he was blushing, but knowing that it probably did. In a moment, Dushane came out of the bathroom, the sheet still covering her. She was looking at the floor, unable to meet anyone's eyes. "Sorry, boss," she murmured.

He shrugged. "I'm your partner, L.D., not your dad. You're a grownup. What you do on your own time is your own business. Unless you're sleeping with a suspect."

She wrinkled her nose. "Euuuw."

"Or a defense lawyer."

She made a gagging noise. "Double euuuw."

"Or..."

"Okay, okay," she laughed, "I get it." She looked at Buckthorn and laughed harder. "Tim," she said, "you look like you want to sink through the floor."

"I'm fine," he said. "This just isn't how the morning staff meeting usually goes."

"Christ, I hope not," Dushane said.

Wolf turned serious. "I got word from Watson," he said. "Art Preston was found dead in his cell last night."

"What? How?" Dushane said.

"They don't know," Wolf said. "They said suicide, but he'd been on suicide watch. No sheet, no shoelaces, the whole protocol. Somehow, he got hold of a belt and hanged himself."

"Or someone did it for him," Dushane said grimly.

Wolf nodded. "One of the deputies who was supposed to be on duty at the jail walked away from his post sometime during the night. Now they can't reach him at home."

"You were wondering about whether Monroe had people in the local police. Or the FBI," Dushane said. "Looks like you were right."

"It doesn't make me happy."

"When does being right ever make anyone happy in this job?"

"Someone's cleaning up," Buckthorn said. "Trying to get rid of anyone who had connections to the kidnapping."

"Anyone who might be able to take things further than Lofton Monroe," Wolf said.

"Only one who'd have any reason to do that," Dushane said, "would be this Donovan character. Or Granddaddy, the Lizard King."

Buckthorn felt fingers of ice closing around his heart. "What about the girl?" he said. "Callie. And her mother?"

"The girl's fine," Wolf said. "The mom insists she doesn't know any names. It was all just voices on the phone. But they've got someone guarding her, just in case."

"So everything dead ends with Lofton Monroe," Buckthorn said.

"For the moment," Wolf said. "In any case, it looks like we're done here. I say we go home." He stood up. "I'm getting us plane tickets back to Charlotte," he said. "Tim, you think you can get home from there?"

Buckthorn nodded. "I can get someone to come pick me up."

"By the way," Wolf said, "the news media's picked this one up. You're probably going to have a few phone messages when you get back."

"Including one from your girlfriend?" Dushane said.

Wolf looked annoyed. "Probably."

Dushane turned to Buckthorn. "He wants you to call her back first."

"I didn't say that."

"I will," Buckthorn said. "She'll get it right."

"Whatever," Wolf said, still clearly nettled. He got up. "Plane leaves at 2:45. Checkout time's at 11:00. Let me know if you want to go get breakfast." He let himself out.

"So that's it, then," Dushane said. "Case closed. At least for us."

"Leila," Buckthorn said, "I'd like to see you again. When we get back, I mean."

She raised an eyebrow. "Well, yeah," she said. "I don't do one night stands."

"I didn't think you did," he said.

She smiled and kissed him on the cheek. "That's settled, then. Call me when we get back." She stood up and let the sheet drop. "For now, I think breakfast can wait."

***

"The ones that killed my grandson," Lampton Monroe said. "I got names. Some hick deputy and two FBI people."

"I heard," Donovan said.

"I want them dead." He was sitting up in bed, a tray table across his lap. A bowl of oatmeal sat untouched on the tray, next to a cup of coffee.

Donovan shook his head. "Don't be daft," he said. "Taking out a cop is bad enough, even a small town deputy. But you're talking about killing federal agents. You've got to know what kind of shit-storm that'll bring down."

"Not if you don't get caught." Monroe's hands trembled as he picked up his coffee cup.

"They won't let up until they do. They'll hound us to the gates of Hell."

"You won't get caught. I know you can do it. I got papers for you. A whole different identity. You go in, you do it, you get out, we burn the ID. An' I got half a dozen people'll say that Sean Donovan was a hundred miles away when any of it happened." He picked up a packet off the table next to him. "It's all here. New driver's license, social security card, credit cards, the works. Cost me a damn fortune to get it all done so fast, but I want this done. An' I got names an' addresses of those three." He held it out to Donovan.

He didn't take the packet. "It's not a good idea."

The old man slammed the packet down on the tray. Coffee sloshed over the lip of the coffee cup. His voice was hard. "When I want your opinion, boy, I'll tell you. This is family. No one touches my family and gets away with it." He picked up the coffee up again and smiled slyly. "Besides, with Lofton gone, I'm lookin' for someone to replace him. But it's gotta be somebody with some hair on his balls. Someone who ain't afraid." He took a sip, looking at Donovan over the cup. "I was thinkin' that might be you, Irish. Was I wrong?"

Donovan stared back at him without expression. "No," he said finally. "You're not wrong."

Monroe nodded. "Thought so." He put the cup down and held the packet out again. Donovan took it. "There's one more name in there," he said.

"Of course there is," Donovan sighed. "Who?"

"Just a fella I know. He worked at the jail where that Preston asshole was bein' kept. The one that smuggled him in a belt an' tole him what would happen to his wife an' lil' girl if he didn't use it."

"Great," Donovan said. "Another cop."

Monroe shook his head. "Not any more. He's on vacation, you might say. I want you to make it a permanent one."

"The last link to you," Donovan said.

Monroe nodded. "He goes first. He's down at the beach, spendin' my damn money. I want it back."

"Right, then. I best be on my way."

"Yeah. An' send that red-haired gal in here to clean up this mess."

Donovan walked into the living room. Patience was at the bar in the kitchen, eating a bowl of cereal. "He wants you," Donovan said. "He spilled his coffee."

"Okay." She got up. "What were you talking about?"

"Business," Donovan said. "Nothing you need worry about."

She looked surprised at his sudden abruptness. "Oh. Okay." She looked past him at the open door. "Just...be careful."

"I will." He didn't embrace her as he walked past, out the front door.

She looked after him, frowning. He could have just been being cautious, with the old man so near. But he usually let her in on what he was up to. It worried her.

She plastered a professional smile on her face and grabbed a towel before going into the bedroom. "Oops," she said in a bright cheerful voice, "did you spill?"

"Take this shit away," he said roughly. "Then help me into the bathroom. I gotta go."

"Yes, sir." She did the requested tasks, never letting the smile leave her face. When she had the old man situated, she closed the bathroom door behind her. She glanced back once as she walked over to the bedside table and pulled out one of the drawers. She took out the small black digital voice recorder she'd slipped into the drawer when she'd gone in to wake the old man up. She turned the volume down to a whisper and ran the playback back to the beginning. The device was voice-activated and wouldn't start recording until there was some sound to record. She heard the conversation as she awakened Monroe. The voices were faint, muffled slightly from being in the drawer, but they were distinct. She could make out every word. The recording jumped to the time when she brought in breakfast. She heard the old man's wheezing complaints about the blandness of the meal, as if his system could handle anything else. She heard Donovan come in, then the door closing behind him.

"Those people that killed my grandson," she heard Monroe say. When he got to "I want them dead," she closed her eyes and breathed the sigh of someone listening to a dream come true. She shut off the recorder and looked at the bathroom door. "I own you, you old bastard," she whispered fiercely. "And Sean Donovan, too. I fucking own you. And you don't even know it."

"Gal?" Monroe's cracked voice came through the door. "Gal? I need help here."

"Coming, hon," she said with a smile.

Part Two

Chapter Thirty

Loretta Starnes met them at baggage claim in Charlotte. Dushane noticed her first, standing by the carousels, talking on her cell phone. She poked Buckthorn in the arm to get his attention, then pointed.

"Oh. Okay," he said. He hesitated.

"There's Gaby," Wolf said. Buckthorn saw her standing a few feet away from Loretta. She waved.

"Glad she didn't bring a camera crew," Buckthorn said.

"I asked her not to."

"Thanks."

"But she is going to ask for an interview. You being a hero and all."

Buckthorn sighed. "Okay. But tell her later, all right? I'm betting there's a shit-ton of work on my desk."

Wolf nodded. "Done." He walked off towards her.

Buckthorn turned to Dushane. "I guess this is goodbye."

"Yeah," she said, her face expressionless. On impulse, he bent down and kissed her. She stiffened with surprise at first, then relaxed into the kiss. People shuffled around them, muttering impatiently, until they broke apart.

"I'll call you," he said.

"You damn well better," she whispered. "I know where you live." He laughed and turned to find Loretta standing there, her eyes as bright with interest as a bird's.

"Well, hey," she said. She hugged Buckthorn tightly, never taking her eyes off Dushane until she broke away and held Buckthorn by the shoulders, at arm's length, looking at him appraisingly. "Welcome home, hero," she said.

"Lord, sis, don't you start too," he said.

"Well, it's true. Everybody's talkin' about it." She held out a hand to Dushane. "Good to see you again."

Dushane took it and smiled. "Thanks, ma'am. You, too."

"Oh, hush with that 'ma'am' nonsense," Loretta said. "You make me sound like an old lady. Call me Loretta." She smiled more broadly. "Only right, with you two getting to be such good friends and all."

"Loretta," Buckthorn said.

"My God, Tim, are you blushing?" She laughed with delight and turned to Dushane. "He's blushing! Look."

"Yep," Dushane said with a grin. "He sure is."

"Isn't he just the cutest thing?"

"Yeah," Dushane said, and winked at Buckthorn, "he sure is."

"Can we just go?" Buckthorn said, feeling the heat in his face.

"Sure," Loretta said. "Can we give you a lift, hon?"

"Um..." Dushane looked at Buckthorn. "I was going to get a cab."

"Well, now you're not," Loretta said.

"It's kind of across town. I don't want to be any trouble..."

"No trouble at all," Loretta said. "Come on. We've got a lot to talk about." She handed a set of keys to Buckthorn. "You drive, hon. I still feel like that big ol' SUV's about to get away from me. It's more of a man car, anyway."

As it turned out, Loretta did most of the talking, about the boys, her husband, what had been going on in Pine Lake since they'd left, the scandal erupting in the Sheriff's department and judiciary over in Blainesville. Dushane, sitting in the back seat of the huge luxury SUV, mostly nodded, made sounds of agreement, and interrupted occasionally to give directions. Buckthorn stayed silent and drove. Finally they pulled up to Dushane's house in a neatly kept residential neighborhood.

"Oh, sweetie," Loretta gushed. "Your place is just adorable."

"Thanks," Dushane said as she opened the door. She paused, one leg out of the car. "Um...you want to come in?"

"Oh, no thanks," Loretta said. "We've got to get on the road. But I tell you what, you doin' anything Friday?"

Dushane looked at Buckthorn. "I, ah, don't think so."

"Great. Come to the house for dinner. Seven thirtyish sound okay? Don't look at him, hon, I'm the one askin'.'"

Dushane smiled. "Okay. Thanks." She got out. Loretta turned to Buckthorn. "Well?" she said.

"Well what?"

"Tim Buckthorn, you get out of this car and kiss that girl goodbye. My God, have I got to do everything here? It's like you're fifteen all over again." He shook his head, unbuckled his seat belt, and got out. Dushane was halfway up the walk to her house when she turned at the sound of the door opening. She dropped her bag on the ground as they kissed. When they parted, he still held her in his arms.

"It's okay that I said yes, isn't it?" she murmured.

"It's great," he said, and meant it. "Sorry my sister put you on the spot like that, though. It's kind of what she does."

"I like her," Dushane said. "She reminds me of my Aunt Viola."

"Better not tell her that."

She laughed. "See you Friday."

"Looking forward to it."

When he got back in the car, Loretta said, "Now, you have got to tell me all about it."

"No," he said. "I don't."

She stuck out her tongue. "You're no fun at all." Her face grew serious and her voice lost the bantering tone. "Seriously, Tim," she said, "how are you doing?"

He thought it over. They'd been through too much together for him to give his sister a superficial answer. "I think I'm okay. Shook..I mean shaken up. No nightmares. Yet."

"You gonna talk to someone? Our pastor'd love to be able to help."

"I'm sure he would," Buckthorn said. He'd never trusted Pastor Cutler, the unctuous, pompous minister at the First Church of Christ in Pine Lake. He changed the subject. "So just how mad is Bru?"

"Oh," she said. "He was in fine form when he came home, believe me. We had a nice little set-to about him leavin' you behind. But when the reports started comin' in on the news about what happened, he got over his mad in a hurry."

Buckthorn's heart sank. "The news?"

"I wasn't jokin' when I said you were a hero, Tim. That pretty little Mexican girl from Channel 12? The one that was here a couple years ago?"

"Gaby Torrijos," Buckthorn said. "She was standing a few feet away from you in the airport."

Loretta gasped. "Are you *serious*? Why didn't you *say* something?"

"I didn't want to talk to her. Not right then."

"Well, she's been wantin' to talk to you. She's been callin' the house lookin' for you, askin' when you'd be back. Bru's been takin' the calls, and I got to tell, you big brother, he's actin' like he's already your campaign manager. To hear him tell it, you're Jack Reacher come to life."

"Who?"

"Dang it, Tim, haven't you read *any* of those books I lent you?"

"I've been busy."

"Hmph. Anyway, Bru's already settin' up meetings with some of the local big boys. I told him he should wait and talk to you, first, to, you know, make sure you're actually runnin'. But you know how he is when he gets a head of steam up."

"Yeah."

"So. Are you?"

"I haven't decided," he said. "But I guess it wouldn't hurt to talk to some people."

"Well, that's farther than you've ever gone before," she observed. "Why the change of heart?"

He thought about Dushane, the way she'd held his hand on the plane, the way she'd looked at him in the morning, after they'd made love again.

"I just figured I needed to start thinking about the future," he said.

***

Inside the house, Leila watched the big SUV pull away. She blew out a long breath. *What have I gotten myself into*, she thought. She ran her fingers lightly over the tiny bruise Buckthorn had left on one wrist. She'd been surprised during their lovemaking when he'd pinned her down, then surprised by how much she'd liked it.

She remembered a drunken conversation with her cousin Darlene, what seemed like ages ago. It had been the night before Darlene's wedding to a slight, shy young man named Casper Boudreaux. "Honey," Darlene had slurred after her fourth Cosmo, "get one of the quiet ones if you can. They're goddamn tigers in bed." Leila and her friends had laughed at the idea of Casper, who could barely look a woman in the eye, turning into any kind of tiger, in bed or out. But now Darlene was on her fourth pregnancy, so maybe she had something there. Leila smiled at the thought. Then she remembered what she'd seen in the car, and the smile fell from her face.

She'd been surreptitiously studying Loretta Starnes from the back seat, looking for the scar Buckthorn had told her about. It was a few minutes before she spotted it. The scar was a thin, almost invisible line, nearly completely covered by Loretta's heavy but skillfully applied makeup. But it wasn't the makeup that had fooled her. She'd been looking in the wrong place. The scar wasn't across Loretta's cheek or jaw; it ran under the curve of her jawline, starting just below the right ear and ending just short of the front of her throat.

Her mother hadn't been trying to disfigure Loretta; she'd been trying to kill her.

The memory sent a shiver of fear and uncertainty through Leila. She wondered if Buckthorn's outward calm hid the same kind of rage and madness, if maybe his sudden passion with her had been something more than that, something darker. What would happen to her if he really did snap?

She shook the feeling off. *He's just a quiet guy who's unexpectedly great in bed*, she thought. Which brought her back to her original problem. She'd been trying to work on her career. A woman had to work twice as hard as a man to get to the same places. If men liked the way she looked, as men seemed to, make that three times as hard. A relationship wasn't going to help, especially one with someone else in law enforcement.

Well, she didn't have to figure it all out now. Right now she needed a long, hot shower. Things would work out, or they wouldn't. But she'd think about it later. Tomorrow, as the lady said, would be another day. And she and her partner would be back on the hunt for the guy that had gotten away.

Chapter Thirty-one

J ack Carville, formerly known as Gene Thurman, stumbled out of the noisy strip club and into the hot, humid, garishly lit neon of the parking lot. Hours of tossing down overpriced drinks and watching nearly naked women bumping and grinding on the stage had left him befuddled and horny. He needed to get laid, and for once, he had the means to do it.

They'd given him a new identity and a suitcase full of cash, just like they'd promised. It was only fair, he thought, in light of the years of service he'd given the organization. He'd been mostly a conduit for information, a mole inside the Bartlett PD, for years. But they'd been telling him that someday, he might need to do something really big for them, something that would mean he'd need to disappear, but something for which he'd be well rewarded. He'd looked forward to that day, dreamed about it, only occasionally dreaded it. He had always hated that little jackleg town anyway. He was exactly the kind of rootless, angry, and dissatisfied loser who made a perfect soldier for Lampton Monroe's army.

When the day came, he was almost disappointed at how simple it was. Just deliver a leather belt to a prisoner who was supposed to be on suicide watch. That was all, Monroe had assured him. The prisoner would know what to do. And then, it would be time for Gene Thurman to disappear and Jack Carville to take his place. It had been so easy, he'd told Monroe, that he'd be glad to do other, more complicated things if he was needed. He'd felt the itch of ambition, the desire to be more than just a foot soldier. Monroe had told him that day might come, and sooner rather than later, but for right now, he should just take his payment and his new I.D. and have a good time. Preferably some place far away. He'd taken the advice and made a beeline for the Grand Strand on the coast of South Carolina. His family had always made the same pilgrimage, once a year, staying a week in a succession of beach-front rentals. He still had fond memories of the place. The smell of Coppertone suntan lotion, the lights of the Myrtle Beach pavilion, the screams from the rickety Hurricane roller coaster. He'd gotten his first pussy there, a quick pump and squirt in the dunes with a skinny black-haired girl from Valdosta, Georgia named Carmen something. She'd been staying with her folks in a room three doors down from his family's room in a shabby motel a block from the beach. He'd pursued her all week, finally nailed her on the night before everyone went home, and given her a bogus phone number when they parted. He'd never seen or heard from her again, but sometimes he thought of the way she'd looked, lying back on his spread out jacket, looking up at him with those big scared dark eyes, biting her lip in pain as he entered her...

The thought sent a jolt of arousal through his groin that cut through the alcohol fog. He pulled out his cell phone and fumbled up the number of the escort service he'd been using off and on since he'd gotten down here. He leaned against plaster statue of a rearing horse that gave the place its name as the phone rang. He thought about who he might ask for. The sassy little black girl with the big tits? The emaciated blonde who looked like a junkie, but who gave amazing head? Someone new? Someone new, he decided. He made the call, made the arrangements, then called for a cab to take him back to his rented condo.

After the cab dropped him off, he staggered up the stairs and fumbled for his keys. The place was beach-front, of course. Not hugely luxurious, but miles above any of the places he'd stayed as a kid. He entered, threw his keys on the table by the door, and opened the sliding glass door to the balcony. He leaned on the metal rail and took a deep breath of the salty ocean air, closing his eyes with the pleasure of the rich, sharp smell and the feel of the cool breeze on his cheeks. *This is the way a man ought to live*, he thought.

He heard a soft knock at the door. It surprised him. Most whores were never this prompt. Maybe being a repeat customer had its perks after all. He was whistling as he sauntered over to the door.

It wasn't a woman standing there. It was a man, dressed in a long coat that was too heavy for the weather. "Who..." he began, then stopped, blinking in confusion. "Hey," he said, as he saw the man raise his arm. He had only a second to register the sight of the gun in a gloved hand before there was a soft cough, a moment of incredible pain, then nothing.

***

Sean Donovan stepped over the body lying in the doorway, then bent to drag him out of the way so he could close the door. It didn't take more than a quick search of the apartment to find the suitcase full of cash that he'd been sent to recover. It looked to Donovan as if the fellow had been making quite a dent in his retirement fund. Well, now he wouldn't have to worry about running out. Donovan let himself out and walked to the SUV he'd parked around the corner of the building. As he pulled away, he hit a button on the cell phone in its holder on the dash. "It's done," was all he said when the call connected.

"Good," the raspy voice on the other end said. "You get the money?"

"Yeah."

"Use it to finance the next steps," Monroe said. "Keep what you don't use."

"Got it." He disconnected the call. He had some stops to make, and supplies to obtain.

***

"Everything all right?" Patience asked. She laid a hand on his shoulder.

"Fine, fine," the old man said. He patted her hand with one of his.

"Time for your medicine," she said. She held out the cup with the pills in it.

"Whatever." He'd gone back to focusing on a reality show on the television. He took the pills without looking and she handed him a glass of water. He downed them quickly with the ease born of long practice. He went on watching the show. She watched him. After a half-hour or so, he began to nod. She got up and went to the bedside table. She took a sheaf of papers out of a drawer and approached Monroe, kneeling down next to his wheelchair.

"Hon?" she said softly. "Remember those papers we talked about? About the insurance?"

He turned his head slowly to look at her. His eyes were cloudy and confused. "Eh?"

"I've got to get those signed, hon, or the insurance won't pay me to come here anymore. I'd have to leave."

"Leave?" he said, and his eyes widened in fear. "Can't...leave. Don't."

"I don't want to," she said. "So you need to sign these." She put the papers on his TV tray and stood up. "Let me get you a pen." She got up and left the room. When she returned a few moments later, it was with a middleiaged woman in tow. The woman's hair was drawn back in a severe bun and she was carrying a small briefcase. "Sorry to keep you waiting," Patience said.

The woman gave her a professional smile. "It's no trouble," she said. "Our firm prides itself on being available to our clients, at their convenience."

With the fees you charge, Patience thought sourly, *you'd better*. But certain kinds of legal help didn't come cheap. The kind she needed, the kind with the more flexible ethics, was the most expensive of all. And it wasn't like she was paying for it.

"Here you go, hon," Patience said. She picked up the papers off the TV tray as the woman was taking another set out of the briefcase. Patience put the second set on the tray and handed Monroe a pen.

"He's reviewed the draft copies?" the gray haired woman said.

"Yes he has," Patience replied. Monroe was trying to sign his name in the middle of the top sheet of paper. Patience guided him back to the signature line at the bottom. The gray-haired woman pretended not to notice, just as she pretended not to notice that the papers Monroe was signing bore no relation to the ones Patience had showed him. "You looked at the papers, right, Mr. Monroe?"

"Unnh-hunhh," he mumbled. Patience guided him through the rest of the signing process. When he was done, she picked them up briskly and handed them to the gray haired woman. "Thank you," the woman said. "I'll notarize them back at the office, and they'll be in your file."

"Mr. Monroe's file," Patience corrected her.

The woman smiled. "Of course. I'll let myself out. Have a pleasant evening, ma'm."

"You too."

Chapter Thirty-two

Buckthorn returned to find his department in much better shape than he'd expected. Janine, along with Duane Willis, the young ex-Marine sergeant who'd joined the department after his tours in Iraq and Afghanistan, had kept things running smoothly. Janine had even cleaned up his desk, so that the paperwork he needed to tend to immediately was organized and easy to complete. The detectives had made a couple of big drug arrests and turned things over to the local DA's office in what looked like good shape. Things had finally come to a head between Jubal Tyree, uncle to young Gerrome, and the wife he'd been knocking around for years; she'd put him into intensive care at the hospital in Chapel Hill with a fractured skull. Duane had taken her into custody himself, shepherded her through the booking process, and seen her home with a written promise to appear in lieu of bail and an unwritten promise to call him or Buckthorn if Jubal showed his badly bashed face around their trailer home again. Other than that, things had been quiet. The jail was even under capacity for the first time in five years. Buckthorn wondered wryly if there'd really been any need for him to come back. He didn't ask the question out loud, however; he was afraid of how Janine would answer.

His second day back, he got a message that Sheriff Stark wanted to see him. He was apprehensive; his trip to Tennessee hadn't had any kind of official sanction, and while none of it had been on the county's dime, he had been wearing the county's uniform.

As he came into the Sheriff's luxurious, wood-paneled office, with its subdued lighting and lingering smell of cigar smoke, Buckthorn was struck all over again by the contrast with the bustling, cramped offices downstairs.

Stark rose to his feet and extended a hand as Buckthorn approached. Buckthorn noticed that since the last time he'd seen the Sheriff, his hair had gotten thinner, the bags under his eyes had gotten more pronounced, and his nose redder. His voice, when he spoke, was raspier than the last time. "Good to see you, Tim," he said.

Buckthorn took the offered hand and shook it firmly. The skin of Stark's hand felt dry, almost papery. "Thank you, sir," he said.

Stark sat down, waving Buckthorn to one of the leather chairs opposite. "You've been on a little adventure, I hear."

Buckthorn took his seat cautiously. "I guess you could call it that," he said.

"Runnin' around with the FBI, savin' a kidnapped little girl...you're the talk of the county. A hero, even." Stark examined him from under his bushy gray brows.

"I don't know about that, sir," Buckthorn said. "There were a lot of people involved."

Stark grimaced. "Includin' that FBI agent that made all that trouble here a couple years ago."

Buckthorn started to say something in Wolf's defense, but closed his mouth. He sensed that his wasn't what the meeting was about.

"Anyway," Stark said, "I've got something for you." He reached into his middle desk drawer and pulled out a small jewelry box. He slid it across the empty desktop at Buckthorn.

"Well?" he said as Buckthorn looked at the box. "Open it."

"We getting married, Sheriff?" Buckthorn joked as he picked it up. He had a suspicion what was inside, and his heart pounded with the thought.

He was right. The double silver bars of a Captain glinted up at him from the cotton padding.

"It's long overdue, Tim," Stark said, and the apology in his voice sounded real. "You should have been at least a Major by now."

Damn right, Buckthorn thought. But Captains drew higher pay, and Majors higher still. Whatever failings Stark had as a lawman, he made up for in the eyes of the County Commissioners by keeping his budgets lean. And if a Lieutenant who actually did a Major's job would stay even without advancement, well, that was one place the budget could be cut. So there had to be another reason he was getting this now. All this raced through Buckthorn's mind as he regarded the silver bars. "Thank you, sir," was all he said.

"Fact is, Tim," Stark said, and that apologetic tone was still there, "I haven't been keeping up with the job as well as I used to." Buckthorn stayed silent. "I've been thinking. Talking with some folks."

Here it comes, Buckthorn thought.

"I've got enough time in for full retirement. And frankly, I don't need the aggravation of another campaign. So..." he paused for dramatic effect.

"Would my brother-in-law be one of those people you've been talking to, sir?"

Stark paused, his brows drawing together. He was clearly nettled by the interruption in his dramatic presentation. "Bru Starnes was one of the people I talked to, yes."

"And both of you would like me to run because you won't be filing next year."

The scowl deepened. "Yeah," he said.

"Thank you, sir," Buckthorn said. "I think I'd like that."

Stark's eyes widened in astonishment. "Well I have to say, this is a surprise," he said. "I thought I was going to have to twist your arm. You never showed any interest before."

"I know, sir," Buckthorn said. "But the past few days have made me think. Life's short."

Stark nodded. "That it is, Tim, that it is. And men like us need to grab as much of it as we can, while we can. Right?"

Buckthorn wouldn't have put it that way, but he kept it to himself. "Yes, sir," he said.

Stark reached into his left desk drawer. He pulled out a half-gallon bottle of Knob Creek bourbon, about one-quarter full. A pair of rocks glasses followed. "Well, now that's decided, let's have us a drink to celebrate." He poured two fingers of the dark amber liquid into each glass.

"I'm on duty, sir," Buckthorn said.

"Tim," Stark said, "when you get to this level, you're never really off duty. That's a burden, Tim, and a heavy one. But one of the perks of being at this level is that there are certain rules you can bend." He raised the glass. "To Sheriff Tim Buckthorn."

Buckthorn hesitated, then picked his glass up. "Thank you, sir," he said.

"You should say it," Stark said. "Get used to the idea of hearing it." His voice became more insistent. "To Sheriff Tim Buckthorn."

"To Sheriff Tim Buckthorn." The two men drank. The liquor burned smoothly going down.

***

"All I can say is, it's about time," Janine said as she pinned the bars on his lapel. She stepped back and squinted, assessing her handiwork.

"Congratulations, sir," Duane Willis said. He was standing in the door of Buckthorn's office. He was smiling broadly, a change from his usually serious demeanor.

"Thanks," Buckthorn said. "Feels pretty good, actually. By the way, you two, thanks again for keeping things running while I was gone."

"No problem, sir," Willis said.

"Duane, could you give us a minute?"

"Yes, sir." For a moment, Buckthorn thought he might actually salute, but he just turned and left.

Buckthorn took a seat behind his desk, motioning to Janine to do the same. "I wanted you to be the first to hear the news."

"Stark's not running again, and he's picked you to succeed him."

Buckthorn looked at her sourly. "You already knew."

"Pfft," she said. "Of course I knew."

"Should I ask how?"

"Probably not, because I wouldn't tell you."

"Whatever. I want you to be my assistant. Assuming I win, of course. There's still an election to go through."

"Of course you'll win. Stark's picked you, and Brubaker Starnes is backing you up. I'll bet anything you care to wager that no one else will even run."

"You sound like you think some sort of fix is in."

"Tim, this is Gibson County. The fix is always in. Just be glad it's in for you this time. Not that you don't deserve it."

"Thanks."

"Don't mention it," she said. "By the way, that girl reporter from WRHO keeps calling. She wants an interview."

"Okay. Go ahead and set it up for next week."

She looked surprised. "Really?"

"Yeah. I promised."

"Promised who?"

"Agent Wolf."

Janine made a face. "Him again."

"He's a good lawman."

"He's nothing but trouble. And that reporter, too." He started to say something, but she stopped him with an upraised hand. "Never mind. You're the boss. I'll call her back." She stood up. "Congratulations again."

"Thanks."

"Just don't go getting a big head over this."

He laughed. "Don't worry. If I do, I have someone to set me straight."

She smiled. "Depend on it."

Chapter Thirty-three

Donovan pulled his vehicle up into the narrow concrete parking area in front of an aircraft-hangar-sized metal building, a few miles out in the countryside near Fayetteville, North Carolina. The big rust-flecked metal doors in the front were rolled to one side in their shaky tracks, opening into the cavernous dimness inside. As he got out of the car, he could hear the high-pitched whine of a saw cutting metal from deep within.

Donovan didn't enter; he stood outside and waited by the front fender of the SUV. He folded his arms across his chest, his expression unreadable behind his dark sunglasses.

After a few moments, a man came out of the building. He was short, with a shock of salt-and-pepper hair that stuck out at various angles from his head. He walked with a pronounced limp, and one eye was covered with a black patch. The whine of the saw continued from inside.

"Hey," the one-eyed man said.

Donovan looked over the man's shoulder, to where the sounds of metal against metal stopped, then started again. "We were supposed to meet alone."

The one-eyed man looked apologetic. "My nephew," he said. "He showed up, unexpected like. Had some work he needed to do with the saw. Don't worry. He don't know nothin'."

Donovan grunted reluctant assent. "Okay. You got what I need?"

"Yeah," the one-eyed man said. "Wasn't easy at that kind of short notice, though." He licked his lips nervously. "I had to, ah, pay a little extra."

Donovan looked at the man. He took his shades off. "I'm willin' to make some allowances for a rush job," he said, "but I won't be taken advantage of. We clear on that?"

The man swallowed. "That's not how it is," he said. "You know I wouldn't do that. But hurryin' means some of my sources have to cut corners. They run higher risks. Risks cost money. You know how it is."

"Yeah," Donovan said. "I do. So. Where's the order?"

"In back," the one-eyed man said. He turned and started to walk into the building. Donovan stuck his shades in his pocket and followed.

Inside, the building was cluttered with haphazard stacks of boxes arranged around wooden workbenches. Various kinds of tools and machinery sat on top of the benches, from hand tools to large machines taller than a man. They passed by a bench where a young man with a thick unruly bush of red hair was bent over a saw, doing something Donovan couldn't identify with a length of metal tubing. The young man looked up as they passed. His eyes were hidden behind thick plastic goggles. He took no further notice of them and turned back to his work. Sparks flew in a bright cascade, flaring and dying as the blade sheared through the metal.

They came out of the back door, into a kind of courtyard bounded on three sides by more metal buildings. The ground in the center of the square was pounded flat and hard as pavement. The one-eyed man led Donovan across the lot, to the smallest of the outbuildings. He pulled a sliding door, like the door of a garage, up into its tracks with a noisy rattle.

In contrast to the other building, this one was empty, save for four wooden boxes, three large and one small, sitting in the center of the work space. The only light was what came through the open door. The air smelled musty and old.

The one-eyed man walked over to one of the crates and raised the lid. Donovan leaned over and picked up a long, thick package wrapped in plastic. He hefted it in his hands as if testing the weight, then grunted again in apparent satisfaction.

"All there?" the one-eyed man said.

"It'll do," Donovan said. He drew his pistol from the back of his waistband and shot the one-eyed man through the forehead. The man fell backwards without making a sound, crashing to the floor. He kicked and spasmed for a moment as his outraged brain fired its last signals randomly though his nervous system. Then he lay still, staring up at the ceiling.

Donovan walked back across the courtyard, leaving the boxes behind him. He re-entered the workshop, gun extended before him. The red-haired man was still bent over the workbench. The noise of the saw masked Donovan's approach. The man never saw him coming. Donovan shot him in the back of the head, then put another bullet in his ear after he fell to the floor.

He knew that what he was about to do with the contents of those boxes was going to bring down heat the likes of which the Monroe organization hadn't seen in years. Everyone who'd had even the most tenuous connection to them would be squeezed, and squeezed hard. Some might find the pressure unbearable and want to give him up. He'd always made it a point to eliminate any weak links, and in this situation, he presumed any link to him was a weak one. The red-haired man had seen Donovan's face. That was his bad luck.

Donovan pulled the SUV around into the courtyard and loaded the boxes into the back, covering them with a thick blanket to hide them from casual passers-by. He slid into the seat and started the vehicle. The GPS system on the dash was the latest model, equipped with voice command. He spoke slowly and clearly, as he'd learned to do.

"Navigate," he said. "Pine Lake. North Carolina."

***

Wolf was on ice again, stuck in a windowless office, paging through files of busywork while the Bureau figured out what the hell to do with him. He'd been there before, but familiarity didn't make it any easier.

The phone on his desk buzzed. He tried not to snarl as he answered. "Wolf."

"Tony," a voice said. "Pat Steadman."

Wolf relaxed slightly. "Hey. Any news?"

"A lot, actually. What do you want first?"

"What's going on in the kidnapping investigation? How's the girl?"

He heard a sigh on the other end. "That's not your case, Tony."

"Yeah, but let's just say I have an interest."

"She's out of the hospital. Home and resting. And keeping her mouth shut. Like her mother."

"They're scared. And they probably ought to be, with Donovan still out there. Any luck finding him?"

"Don't you want to know whether or not you're going to have a job? You or your partner?"

"Do we?"

"Yeah. I talked to OPR. They're not happy with either of you. But I persuaded them that cashiering a couple of heroes who saved a kidnapped girl and killed the kidnapper wouldn't make very good press."

"That's why you're a Deputy Director. Always seeing the big picture."

"Spare me the ass-kissing. You're terrible at it."

Wolf laughed. "True. So when do we get back to work? We need to find Donovan. I'd like to interview Monroe. Squeeze him a little."

"No."

Wolf frowned. "What do you mean, no?"

"I mean, you stay the hell away from him. And Donovan, too."

"What? Why?" His voice rose. "Sean Donovan tried to kill my partner, Pat. He's ours."

Steadman's voice rose. "What part of 'it's not your case' do you not get?" He got himself back under control. "Look, Tony, part of the price of you and Dushane not getting delivered up to OPR is that you're not to be involved any more. You pissed in too many people's corn flakes this time."

"Now look..."

"No, *you* look, Agent Wolf," Steadman said, and there was steel in his voice. "I've been to the well for you a bunch of times. You're one of the best agents I've ever seen, and the Bureau owes you a lot. But the well. Is. Dry. Do I make myself clear?"

"Yes sir," Wolf murmured.

"Good. I'll let you break the news to your partner."

"Just tell me one thing," Wolf began, but the line was dead. He stared at it for a moment, teeth gritted in frustration, then set the receiver into the cradle, gently, repressing his desire to slam it down. He pulled out his cell and hit Dushane's number on his speed dial. He considered the best way to give her the news. But the call went straight to voice mail. He frowned. He'd never known her to cut her phone off. "L.D.," he said when the outgoing message was done. "It's Tony. Call me."

Chapter Thirty-four

The bodies were laid out around him in a circle like the spokes of a gruesome wheel. Loretta. Janine. His nephews, Brandon and Ethan. Callie Preston. There were no marks on the bodies. They lay peacefully, eyes closed, their hands folded reverently across their chests. *Leila*, he thought. *Where's Leila?*

As if in answer to his unspoken question, she walked into view, pacing slowly around the circle. He tried to call her name, but the words stuck in his throat. She stopped and turned to look at him. Her eyes were gone, replaced by pools of deep red blood.

You're dreaming, he said to himself. *Wake up.* WAKE UP. Even though he was paralyzed, frozen helplessly in place, he could feel himself struggling. He heard a loud buzzing sound and looked up. A chainsaw had appeared as if by magic in Leila's hands. She was holding it above her head, running at full speed. Tears of blood ran down her cheeks. She walked forward, bringing the saw down towards Loretta's body....

Buckthorn sat up straight in the bed, gasping for breath. His body was drenched with sweat, heart pounding, the blood throbbing so hard in his temples he had a brief flash of greater fear that he might be having a stroke. He heard the buzzing sound from his dream again, loud and insistent. He looked over to find the source and saw his cellphone, lying on the bedside table, the screen glowing with the incoming call. With shaking hands he picked it up and looked at it.

INCOMING CALL FROM: LEILA.

He pressed the button and put the phone to his ear. "Hey."

"Hey. Did I wake you?"

He looked at the clock. 3:37. "Yeah," he said. "But it's okay. I was having a nightmare." The dream was fading so fast, he was starting to lose the details, even as the physical effects lingered. The sweat drying on his chest and brow felt cool and clammy.

"I'm getting those too," she said. "I couldn't sleep. Not that I did it that much anyway, but now I really can't." She sighed. "Sorry."

"It's okay, really," he said. "It's good to hear your voice."

"Yours, too." She said it so softly he could barely hear her.

"Look, what we're going through is totally normal, okay?"

"Doesn't feel normal. They're trying to get me set up for an appointment with one of the Bureau shrinks."

"That's good."

"Not really. You know how it is. If I tell him what's going on, I'll be behind a goddamn desk for the rest of my career. So I feed him a line of happy horseshit, tell him I'm fine, and hope he lets me get back to work."

"Well, you know you can talk to me," he said.

"That's good. I'm glad. I didn't know if you'd started feeling...you know, kind of weird about what happened."

"I do. But not about what happened between us. Well, maybe a little weird about it. But in a good way."

"So...you still want to get together this weekend?"

"Of course," she said. "Why would you even ask that?"

"I don't know. I'm just...You know, some guys..." she stopped.

"That's not me," he said. "Ever."

"Jesus," she said. "Listen to me. I sound like a damn teenager. A crazy one."

"You really don't," he said.

"Anyway, what's going on with you? Everything okay at work?"

"Yeah," he said. "In fact, I've got some news." He told her about his conversation with Stark.

"That's fantastic!" she said. "You deserve it."

"I don't know," he said. "I've never been much of a politician."

"And this is a problem why?"

He laughed. "I guess I'm just suspicious. If this is something my brother-in-law wants so badly, I can't help but think it's a bad idea for me."

"Trust that instinct," she said. "But do it anyway. You're a good man, Tim. If you don't do it, God knows what kind of empty suit he'll try to put in the job."

"You're probably right." A thought occurred to him. "Listen, if you'd like to stay through Saturday, there's a kind of reception Saturday night. To sort of introduce me around to people."

"Don't they know you already?"

"Not as a candidate."

"Blecch," she said. "Sounds awful."

"It does. But it might not be so bad if you were there."

"Seriously? You really want me to come with you to this political thing?"

"Yeah," he said.

"You're not worried I'll say the wrong thing? I tend to do that, you know."

He laughed. "I know. But you can say anything you like. You're part of my life now, Leila. At least I want you to be. And if people have a problem with you, then that's just too damn bad. I don't want the job that bad."

There was a long pause, so long that he glanced at the screen to see if the call had been dropped. "You still there?"

"Yeah," she said. Her voice sounded choked. "I'm here."

"You okay?"

"Yeah. I am. I really, really am."

"So you'll come?"

"Sure," she said. "I'll get the LBD out of the back of the closet. It'll be fun."

"LBD?"

"Little Black Dress," she clarified.

He chuckled. "I cannot wait to see you in that."

Her voice dropped to a whisper. "I can't wait for you to see me out of it."

The image made his mouth go dry. His heart started pounding again, this time in a good way. It took him a moment to work up the courage to say what he wanted to say next. "I want you so bad it hurts," he said.

"Me, too," she said. "Me, too. Get some rest, cowboy. You're gonna need it."

"Oh, like I'm going to be able to sleep now," he said.

"Listen," she said. "Like I said, I'm doing busy work till the shrinks and OPR clear me. I can take a personal day. It's a two-hour drive to where you are, give or take. I can be there by the time Lulu's opens. I've got a craving for some good coffee and a biscuit. Afterwards."

"After..." he paused. "Oh."

"You game?"

"Damn right I am," he said.

***

"I never did get that biscuit," Dushane said. She was lying on her stomach, her head on her folded arms.

Buckthorn leaned over and kissed her naked shoulder. "Or any sleep either," he said.

She rolled over and sat up, pulling the sheet up to her neck. "Neither did you," she said, smiling.

"Well, you can stay a while and sleep if you like."

Her eyes widened in surprise. "Really?"

"Sure. Why not?" He chuckled. "I figure I can trust you. There's coffee in the tin on the counter. Not much else, I'm afraid. But I've got to go."

She looked at the clock, dismayed. "Oh, hell. You're late for work."

"Yeah," he said, buttoning his uniform shirt. "First time in twenty years. They'll get over it, I think."

"Sorry."

He smiled and sat down on the bed. "I'm not." He kissed her.

"Mmmmm," she said, then broke the kiss. "But I'm not going to let you make a habit of it. I know how important the job is to you."

"You are, too." He leaned over to kiss her again.

She smiled and swatted him away playfully. "You keep talking like that, I'm going to do something to make you even later. So go."

"Okay." He stood up. "Want to do lunch? Or do you have to get back?"

"I'll come by and meet you. How late does Lulu serve those biscuits?"

"No idea. But he makes a mean burger, too."

She shook her head. "Who knew the little town of Pine Lake was such a culinary oasis?"

"North Carolina's best kept secret, that's us."

She laughed. "Get to work, Sheriff," she said. "I..." she trailed off.

He stopped in the door. "What?"

Her face had suddenly grown serious. "Nothing," she said. "Go to work."

He blinked in confusion. "Okay." But by the time he got to the door, he was whistling.

***

Donovan sat in his car, parked a few doors down from Buckthorn's driveway. He saw the police cruiser come down the driveway and pull away. He started the engine and pulled out, keeping his distance. He frowned as he passed by the small frame house with its tiny front porch. There was another vehicle parked in the driveway, a Toyota Camry. The deputy had company, it seemed. That might complicate things. Then he spotted her, standing half in and half out of the front screen door. She was dressed in a man's robe, presumably Buckthorn's, that nearly swallowed her. He stiffened with shock as he recognized her. It was the agent who'd shot at him. She didn't notice him; her eyes were fixed on Buckthorn's car as it drove away.

"Ahhh..." he said softly to himself. "You old dog, you." He considered breaking in, catching the little bitch by surprise, and teaching her a lesson, leaving her broken and dying for Buckthorn to find. Maybe a punishment and lesson from the old days: bullets in both ankles, both knees and both elbows, none fatal, all agonizing, spaced out over time to increase the anticipation and the pain, until the victim begged for the release of death. Then two in the head to finish it. He smiled at the thought, then sighed. That could take hours. Plus, this was a quiet neighborhood, with small houses spaced close together on tiny plots. Even with a gagged victim and a silenced pistol, he might attract attention. Not only that, there were always traces left behind, DNA and hair and skin.

No, best stick with the original plan. The plan, properly carried out, would barely leave enough evidence behind to identify the victims, much less who'd done them in. And with two of the three together, his job would be that much easier.

He was humming as he drove away.

Chapter Thirty-five

"Agent Wolf?"

Wolf looked up from the computer screen he'd been looking at without really seeing. He tried to place the young agent standing in the doorway holding a file folder. The man had sandy blonde hair, cut short, and the kind of earnest, all-American face that should be on a recruiting poster. He was fresh out of the Academy, and to Wolf's eyes, he looked barely old enough to shave. What the hell was his named. Benson? Branson?

Wolf's confusion must have registered on his face. "Bailey, sir," the kid said. "Clark Bailey."

Wolf nodded, trying to hide his embarrassment. "Yeah. Sure. What can I do for you, Clark?" He motioned to office's only other chair. "Have a seat."

Bailey sat down. "I was going through some of the reports from around the state. Routine stuff from other agencies. Ran across something that you might be interested in." He took a sheet of paper out of the folder and handed it across the desk.

Wolf scanned it. The Cumberland County Sheriff's Department had discovered the bodies of two men in a machine shop in the countryside near Fayetteville. The victims were an ex-soldier named Russell Pennington and his nephew, Donald Furr.

"ATF took an interest," Bailey said, handing another sheet of paper. "Pennington's ex-Special Forces. Demolitions guy. Got blown up in Iraq and sent home on a medical discharge. Since then, the ATF guys have been looking at him in connection with some missing explosives."

"Missing? From where?"

"Fort Bragg."

"Military-grade stuff."

Bailey nodded. "Yeah."

"So someone offed this guy. And the nephew. Was the nephew supposed to be involved?"

"ATF doesn't think so. They think he was just in the wrong place at the wrong time." Bailey leaned forward and pointed at the report in Wolf's hand. "But check out the list of possible and known associates."

Wolf looked back down. There were several names in that part of the report, but one jumped out. Sean Donovan.

Wolf looked up, his eyes narrowed. "Donovan?"

Bailey nodded.

"How'd you know I was interested in Donovan?"

It was Bailey's turn to look embarrassed. "My office is right next door. And these walls are kind of thin."

Wolf put the paper down. "Was I that loud?"

Bailey nodded. "You were pretty pissed off. Not that I blame you. Someone tried to kill my partner, I'd want their ass, too."

"Okay," Wolf said. "Thanks for this, Bailey. Good work."

"Could be nothing," Bailey said.

"Maybe. Probably, in fact. 99 percent of stuff like this does turn out not to mean anything. But don't ever let that stop you from paying attention and sharing it."

Bailey nodded and got up. "Thanks."

"I'll be sure and mention your name when I talk to Deputy Director Steadman," Wolf said.

Bailey looked worried. "What if it turns out to be a dead end?"

"Don't worry. Steadman's the one who taught me what I just told you."

Bailey smiled. "Okay." Wolf picked up the phone and dialed as the young agent left. He asked to be connected with Steadman.

"Yeah?" the Deputy Director said when he came on the line.

Buckthorn ignored the tone. "One of the new guys ran across something that might have something to do with Monroe and Donovan."

Steadman sounded exasperated. "I thought I told you..."

"You didn't tell me to keep it to myself if something fell into my lap, did you?"

Steadman sighed. "Okay. What is it?"

Wolf told him, making sure to mention that it was Bailey who'd given him the information. He left out how Bailey had known of his interest in Donovan.

There was a brief silence. "This means something, doesn't it?" Wolf said.

"Maybe," Steadman said. "There...might be some connections here."

"Come on, Pat," Wolf said. "If there's something we need to know, you need to tell me."

"Okay," Steadman said. "The jailer who disappeared after Art Preston committed suicide, a guy named Thurman, turned up dead in South Carolina. He'd apparently been spreading a lot of money around. More than he made in a year on a deputy's salary."

"How did he die?"

"Shot in the head at point-blank range. The hooker he'd called found him and called 911. She tried to leave, but the cops caught up with her. She said one of the other girls who'd been there before told her he'd had a suitcase full of cash."

"Let me guess. The cash was gone."

"Yeah."

"And any connection with who paid Thurman off vanished with it."

"Looks like it."

"And then a guy with connections to Donovan turns up dead in North Carolina. Why do you think that is, Pat?"

Steadman's voice was tight. "Could be a lot of things."

"He's coming after us."

"Maybe."

"Bullshit. You know it and I know it. Donovan's tying up loose ends. Anyone who's seen him dies. That includes both me and my partner. And Buckthorn. So we're back on this."

"I'll talk to..."

"You misunderstand," Wolf said. "I'm not asking." He hung up the phone. He pulled out his cell and speed-dialed Dushane. Voicemail again. He called Buckthorn.

The deputy picked up on the first ring. "Buckthorn."

"It's Wolf. I've got some information." He filled Buckthorn in. "And I can't reach Dushane," he finished.

"Um," Buckthorn said. "She's...ah..."

"What?"

"She's at my house."

Wolf sighed. "Okay, fine. Get her to turn her phone back on." The phone in Wolf's hand vibrated. He checked the screen. "Never mind. She's calling in now."

"Okay."

"Tim?"

"Yeah."

"You be careful. This guy is serious."

"You do the same."

"I will." He connected with Dushane's incoming call. "Hey."

"Um..." she sounded hesitant. "You left a message. Sorry. I was, ah..."

"I know where you were. We can talk about it later. We've got a problem." He filled her in.

"Can you think of any other reason Donovan would be in the area?" she said.

"Monroe's got business interests up and down the I-95 corridor," Wolf said.

"The truck stop hookers."

"Yeah. And maybe something going on there needs a hitter like Donovan. But the guy that was killed's suspected of dealing explosives. And Donovan was a customer."

"Maybe."

"Maybe. Then there's the guy connected with Preston's death..."

"Maybe."

Wolf was losing patience. "Yeah. Maybe. You think this is coincidence?"

"I think there may be a pattern in this, but right now the evidence is pretty thin. We got ballistics on the weapons in the two killings?"

Wolf didn't answer. He hadn't thought to ask Steadman. "I'm just playing devil's advocate, boss," she said. "Like you taught me."

"I know," he said. "Keep doing it. It's just..."

"What?"

He couldn't put it into words, and the frustration on it made him grit his teeth. Finally he blurted out, "It *feels* wrong."

"Ahhh," she said. "Now I *am* worried."

He barked out a short, humorless laugh. "About me? You think I'm going nuts?"

"No," she said. "I'm worried you're most likely right."

"What?" he said. "I thought you were the skeptical one here. And you're right. We don't really have any hard evidence. Just some stuff that may or may not be connected, and my hunch."

"I am skeptical," she said. "But I also know your hunches kept you alive a long time, through some pretty hairy stuff, right?"

"Yeah," he said. "They did."

"There you are, then. So let's assume Donovan's coming after us. He's packing some pretty serious heat. And he's in my neighborhood. What do we do?"

"Get the hell out of there," Wolf said automatically. "Get back here where we can protect you."

"Really? Is that what you did the last time someone was hunting you?"

Wolf fell silent again. "No," she answered for him. "You went hunting for them. You broke cover, but you didn't run away. You went straight at the bastards' throats."

He felt a lump of fear turning to ice in his gut. "That was different."

"Why?" she demanded.

"Because I didn't have a partner," he said.

"Well, now you do," she said. "So maybe you need to get your butt down here so we can do some hunting. Sir."

He rubbed his eyes. "L.D...," he said.

"Think about it, boss. You used to live here. Everyone knows everyone. A stranger stands out like a zit on a prom queen's nose."

"Cute."

"Thanks, I got a million of 'em. But you know I'm right. If he's tracking any of us, we stand a better chance of seeing him coming in this burg than we do in the city. And if we see him coming, his ass belongs to us. Am I right or am I wrong?"

"You're right," he admitted.

"Okay," she said. "I'll get down to the Sheriff's department and help brief Buckthorn's people. See you soon." She broke the connection. He took a deep breath. It looked like he was headed back to Pine Lake. He'd often thought about returning, but not like this.

Chapter Thirty-six

The tiny "motor court" on the edge of town had seen better days, but at least the rooms were clean. It was better than some places Donovan had stayed, especially back in the old days. He took a bite of the biscuit he'd taken off the tray on the front desk. The lady who ran the place made a fresh batch every morning, and since the place was nearly deserted, he hadn't seen any problem with taking two, since the need to lay low meant he'd be taking as many meals as he could in his room. He knew the ID's Monroe had procured for him were solid; they were the best, in fact, that money could buy. But he was a stranger here, in a place that didn't see many strangers.

He took another bite of the biscuit and turned his attention back to the work he was doing on the small table next to the door. Three slabs of plastic explosive rested on the table, small but potent. The explosive was safe to handle; it was the detonators and fuses that lay beside each of them that made the devices lethal. Each of the fuses was an old-style "tilt" fuse: a tube with a glob of mercury in one end and a pair of separated electrical contacts on the other. When the fuses were wired to the detonators and placed in a vehicle, the movement of the vehicle would soon send the liquid metal to the far end of the tube, complete the circuit, and trigger the plastic explosive. For safety's sake, he'd wired a crude timer so that the electrical contacts wouldn't go "live'" until he was well away. It was the type of device he'd learned how to fix up in his early teens, back during the Troubles. He was pleased that he hadn't lost his touch. *Like riding a bike*, he thought. He stashed the explosives in a small canvas shoulder bag he'd picked up at an army surplus store, wrapping the detonators separately in cloth to keep them apart from the explosive until the time was right. He thought of leaving the bag in the room while he scouted his targets, but decided he wanted to be prepared if opportunity presented itself. The bag went onto the passenger side floor as he slid into the driver's seat of the SUV. His pistol went into the center console. He was ready.

***

"The suspect's name is Sean Donovan," Buckthorn told the men crammed into the department briefing room. He was standing behind a small podium set on a work table, sweating lightly in the stuffy room. The group was a mix of uniforms from patrol and plainclothes officers from the detective division. He'd pulled some of them in on their days off, and some of them looked less than pleased about it. They'd brightened up a bit when he'd mentioned overtime. Stark would probably be pissed off, he thought, but he figured he had some goodwill left, and now would seem the time to use it. And if that didn't work, he didn't think the Sheriff would publicly undercut his newly appointed heir apparent.

"This man is wanted by the FBI," he went on, gesturing towards Dushane seated next to him. "He's a known terrorist, formerly with the Irish Republican Army." The word terrorist got their attention; several of them sat up straighter and leaned forward. "He's now working for a multi-state criminal enterprise headed up by a man named Lampton Monroe. We think he may be in our area."

"What for?" a skinny, beak-nosed deputy spoke up. Duane Willis, leaning against the wall with arms folded, shot him a look that could have flash-frozen a cup of boiling water. The deputy winced as he realized he'd spoken out of turn. His name, Buckthorn recalled, was McCall, and he'd been with the department less than six months. Buckthorn started to answer, but Dushane spoke up first. "He may want to kill your boss here." That provoked a murmur around the table. Now it was Buckthorn's turn to stare daggers. Dushane looked back at him and whispered "motivation". Willis raised his hand.

"Yeah, Duane," Buckthorn said.

"This have anything to do with that business in Tennessee?"

"It might," Buckthorn said.

Dushane stood. "May I, Captain?" she said politely. Buckthorn nodded. She turned to them.

"Donovan, and through him the Monroe organization, have links to a couple of people who were found shot recently. One in Myrtle Beach, and another just outside of Fayetteville. These areas are outside of his and the organization's usual stomping grounds. What we've got right now is mostly conjecture. We don't know for sure if he's coming here. But if he is, he's got no other reason to be here other than going after Captain Buckthorn, who's responsible for the death of a member of the organization. Lampton Monroe's grandson, in fact. His heir apparent." She looked at Willis, who had his hand raised again. "Yes, Deputy?"

"Didn't you have a part in that, ma'am?"

"Yeah," she said. "I did."

"So he's probably after you, too."

"Probably."

"Well..." he hesitated.

"Speak your mind, Duane," Buckthorn said.

"Shouldn't the two of you be in some kind of protective custody? At least Miss Dushane here?"

Buckthorn darted a glance at Dushane, expecting her to react to the implied sexism. But she was smiling at him. "Thank you, Deputy," she said. "But I'll be fine." Her smile broadened. "I've got to keep up the reputation of the Bureau, don't I?"

He dropped his eyes, his face reddening. "Sorry, ma'am," he mumbled. "No offense intended."

"And none taken," she said. "Truly."

"No one's going into hiding," Buckthorn said. "But keep a lookout. Ask around. See if anyone's seen anything or anyone suspicious."

Dushane picked up a sheaf of copies from the work table next to the podium. "This isn't the greatest picture," she admitted, "but it's the best one we have of Donovan." She began passing them out. Several officers looked dismayed. "This could be anyone," someone muttered.

"Right," Buckthorn said. "So if something turns up, you call me or Agent Dushane. We stand a better chance of recognizing Donovan. Any more questions?" There were none. "Dismissed," Buckthorn said. They filed out, some shaking their heads.

"They think it's a wild goose chase," Buckthorn said.

"I hope it is," Dushane answered. "But they'll do their jobs. Because you told them to."

"Thanks," he said. "Sorry about Willis. He's a good guy."

She chuckled. "For a Neanderthal. But you seem to trust him, so I figured I didn't need to bite his head off." She grinned impishly. "Besides, he's kind of cute."

He kept his face impassive. "Want me to set you up?"

She laughed. "Nah. My calendar's kind of full. I can only fit one caveman into my schedule at a time."

"Anyone I know?"

She laughed again and gave him a playful shove. "You promised me lunch," she said.

He looked at his watch. "That's right, I did. Lulu's?"

"Why not?"

As they walked out together into the lobby, Buckthorn heard a familiar voice. "Tim!"

He looked over. Loretta was standing at the security station, just outside the metal detector. An older deputy was going through her purse. She inclined her head at him, with a look that clearly said "do something about this." He heard Dushane's sigh beside him as he called out. "She's with me, Norris."

The deputy looked up, blinking myopically. Buckthorn walked over. "This is my sister, Loretta. Loretta, Norris Barlow."

"Sorry, Tim," Barlow said. "Don't think we ever met."

"Not a problem, Norris," Buckthorn said.

"Hmmph," Loretta said as she snatched up the purse. "Not for you, maybe."

"Or for you, either, Loretta," Buckthorn said firmly. "The man's doing his job." He stood there, looking at her pointedly, until she pasted a smile back on her face. "Sorry, hon," she said, turning the charm back on. "I'm guess I'm just a grumpy old woman."

"Not at all, ma'am," Barlow said.

She turned to Buckthorn. "I thought I'd swing by and take you out to lunch." She looked over at Dushane. "Well, hey, shug! You want to come along, too?"

"Loretta..." Buckthorn began, but Dushane cut him off. "That'd be great," she said, her smile as brilliant and artificial as Loretta's.

"Super!" Loretta was practically beaming. "I thought we'd go to the Pine Room."

Buckthorn suppressed a groan. The Pine Room was the grill at the local country club. The food wasn't bad, but the place was always full of old men in ugly pants coming off the golf course, waiting to get on, or just hanging around talking about the great rounds they'd played. It was the type of place where the movers and shakers of Gibson County met, but it made Buckthorn feel claustrophobic. "We were going to Lulu's," he said.

Loretta made a face. "Oh," she said. "That place."

"I asked Tim if we could go there," Dushane said, her smile never wavering. "I like the biscuits."

"Well, I guess a girl who gets as much exercise as you do," Loretta said, "can afford a few extra calories. Me, if I don't have a salad for lunch, I blow up like a *balloon*."

"Oh, stop it," Dushane said. "You're as skinny as a rail. A French fry or two won't hurt you."

Loretta sighed theatrically. "Well, I suppose." She dug into her bag and handed her keys to Buckthorn. "Here," she said. "You drive. I need to use the facilities." She looked over at Barlow, who'd been watching the whole exchange with a baffled expression. He pointed across the small lobby. "Through those doors, ma'am," he said.

"Thanks, hon," she said as she walked off.

Buckthorn looked at Dushane. "Mind telling me what that was about?"

"It's a girl thing," she said. "Specifically, a Southern girl thing. You wouldn't understand."

"Okay. It just seemed...I don't know, like you were fighting."

"Not at all," she said. "She pushed a little. I pushed back. Now we understand each other a little better, so maybe we can get along."

"I hope so," Buckthorn said.

"Don't worry," she said. "Now let's go eat."

***

Donovan sat across the street and watched the people who'd shot at him and killed Lofton Monroe walk out of the front door of the Sheriff's

Department, arm in arm. They walked to a beige SUV in the parking lot and got in. A moment later, a dark haired, expensively dressed woman followed, hurrying to catch up. There was a brief, awkward discussion, then they got in the car, Buckthorn in the driver's seat, the FBI agent in front with him. The dark-haired woman got in the back, looking a tad disgruntled. They pulled out of the parking lot and headed down the main street. Donovan started the car and followed. Now he knew what Buckthorn drove. All he needed was an opportunity.

Chapter Thirty-seven

Lulu's was packed and noisy. A trio of waitresses moved easily and purposefully about the room, shuttling orders to and food from the steel-silled kitchen window, pouring tea and water from pitchers clutched tight in either hand, keeping up a steady stream of conversation as they wove between the tables. The youngest of the three waved at Buckthorn. "Grab a table anywhere, Tim," she called out. He made his way to a recently vacated four-top at the far side of the room. Dushane trailed in his wake, Loretta bringing up the rear. Every few tables, Buckthorn would stop and greet someone, ask about their family or how their last fishing trip had gone, then move on. Whenever he'd stop, Dushane would bump up behind him. After the second time, she turned back to see how Loretta was taking it. She was smiling, looking at her brother fondly. When Dushane caught her eye, she shrugged with a comically exaggerated look of resignation. Dushane couldn't help but laugh, and she couldn't help but like Buckthorn's sister. For all her brittle pretension, she clearly adored her brother.

By the time they'd reached the table, the three waitresses had descended on it and cleared away the dirty dishes and debris. As they took their seats, glasses of iced tea with lemon appeared as if by magic in front of Buckthorn and Loretta. "Whatcha drinkin', shug?" the young blonde waitress asked Dushane. She had a plump, friendly face and a tiny flower tattoo peeking coyly out from the neckline of a Taylor Swift T-Shirt that hugged her curves just a little too tightly.

"Iced tea. Sweet," Dushane said with a smile.

"Comin' up." She headed back into the noise and bustle.

The tea, when it arrived, was as strong as the coffee had been and
so sweet Dushane was surprised it didn't flow like maple syrup. She cut
the sweetness with a slice of lemon and listened to Buckthorn and his
sister talk—or, more accurately, Loretta gave her brother an exhaus-
tive run-down of local events and gossip, with Buckthorn making the
occasional interested noise or asking a quick question that more often
than not sent Loretta off on another tangent. The one-sided conversation went on and on, pausing only when the waitress took their orders.
It was the sort of thing that would have normally driven Dushane to
distraction, but Buckthorn seemed to soak up every word. Once again,
he seemed relaxed and happy just to be in the presence of his family.
He belongs here, she thought. *And I don't*. The thought startled and
disturbed her. They'd been getting so close, getting along so well. Was
she trying to sabotage things before they got started? Her mind raced
ahead. Much as she enjoyed where she worked and who she worked
with, she knew the FBI career she wanted would eventually take her
out of North Carolina, where Buckthorn's career path was digging him
in deeper and deeper here. Should she put a stop to it before it got too
serious? *That horse may have left the barn, Leila*, she thought ruefully. She shook her head and put the thought aside. She realized that
Buckthorn was looking at her. "You okay?" he said.

"Yeah," she said, and smiled. "Just thinking."

"Oh," Loretta said, "where are my manners? I didn't mean to leave
you out, Leila. It's just that I don't see enough of this one here. When
we do get together, I just talk my silly head off."

"It's okay, really," Dushane said. At that point, the food arrived (chef
salad for Loretta, burgers and fries for Dushane and Buckthorn)and
they busied themselves for a moment with dressings and condiments.

"So," Loretta said. "Tell us about your family."

The question stumped Dushane for a moment. She didn't know
where to begin. But Loretta was looking at her with such guileless interest, she felt like she had to say something. "Ummm...my dad owns
a hardware store in Lafayette. Mom taught music part time. I've
got three brothers..." as she talked, she loosened up, encouraged by
Loretta's questions and comments. *Damn*, she thought in the back of
her mind. *If this woman put her mind to it, she could be a hell of an*

interrogator. All of that wide-eyed attention may be total bullshit, but she makes you want to spill your guts.

She glanced again at Buckthorn. He was smiling at her, listening. She felt a surge of warmth towards him and his sister. *I think this might just work*, she thought.

***

Donovan cruised through the crowded parking lot, eyes moving from side to side as if he was patrolling a hostile neighborhood. Here and there, people walked purposefully to their vehicles, lunch over, headed back to whatever work they did. No one gave Donovan a second glance.

He spotted the SUV parked in a line of other cars, around one side of the building. A large shiny pickup truck was pulling out of the parking spot next to it.

Opportunity knocks, Donovan thought to himself. He pulled in next to the SUV. This put him in the cool shade of the building, with the target blocking the view on one side and another of the ubiquitous oversized pickups blocking the other. He paused for a moment to look in the rearview. No one seemed to be paying him any attention. He pulled the bag onto his lap and stuck his hands inside. He found the components of the bomb by feel and started to put them together without taking his hands from the bag. Back in the day, he could put one of the deadly little packages together in pitch darkness, going by feel alone. He hoped he still could.

When he was done, he pulled the device from the bag and looked it over. After a moment, he nodded, opened the door and eased himself out to stand by the SUV.

***

The waitress was just asking if they wanted dessert when Buckthorn's phone buzzed. He checked the caller ID.

"It's Duane," he said.

"Say hey for me," Loretta said, "and remind him I still want to introduce him to that nice Higson girl from our church."

"Not now, Loretta," Buckthorn said, but without heat. "Yeah, Duane," he said into the phone.

"Captain, you remember you told the fellas to keep an eye peeled for anything out of the way?"

"Yeah."

"Well, McCall phoned from out at the Motor Lodge. He talked to the owners and they said there was some foreign-sounding guy staying there."

Buckthorn sat up straighter. "Foreign how?"

"Couldn't say. Maybe English. Or something like that."

"Like Irish?"

"Could be."

"Okay. Is the guy there?"

Buckthorn could hear a brief snatch of conversation, interspersed with the crackle of radio chatter.

"Something?" Dushane said.

"Could be. One of the officers got word of an unusual guest at the motel outside of town."

"Could be a tourist," she said, "come for the fishing."

"Bass Festival was two months ago," Loretta said. Buckthorn shushed them both as Duane came back on the line. "Naw," he said. "He's out. They don't know where."

"Okay," Buckthorn said. "Tell McCall to sit tight. Come by and get me."

"And me," Dushane said.

"I'm pullin' into Lulu's right now," Duane said.

Buckthorn looked out the window. A Gibson County Sheriff's cruiser was pulling up to the door. Buckthorn fumbled a twenty out of his wallet and put it on the table. "Hate to eat and run, sis," he said.

"Tim?" Loretta said, clearly alarmed. "What's going on?"

"May be nothing, ma'am," Dushane said.

"If it was nothing," Loretta said, "you wouldn't be calling me 'ma'am' in that cop voice."

"Okay. You're right. But we need to go."

"And you best go home, sis," Buckthorn said.

"Oh, go do your job, then," Loretta said with fond exasperation. She handed the twenty back to Buckthorn. "I'll get lunch."

Buckthorn just nodded as he and Dushane headed for the door. A chorus of "Bye, Tim" followed in their wake, replaced by a low buzz of puzzled conversation as they bolted out without responding.

"What are they in such a hurry about?" the waitress asked. "They took off out of here like their shoes was on fire and their asses was catchin'."

"Your guess is as good as mine, shug," Loretta said. "But I guess I got the check."

***

Donovan was backing up as he saw the police car pull into the lot. He paused, half in and half out of the parking space, until he saw it go past. Then he pulled the rest of the way out and drove slowly around the corner. He saw the police car pulling away at high speed. It looked like there were several people inside, but he couldn't make out who. They were heading in the same direction he needed to take to get back to the motel. He followed, barely under the speed limit so as not to attract attention and soon he lost sight of the police car in front of him. He looked back at the restaurant disappearing in his rear-view. "Hope you enjoyed the meal."

***

"What have we got on this mystery guest?" Buckthorn said as they headed towards the town limits and the Pine Lake Motor Court.

"The subject registered with a Florida license. Name of Ian McClain. NCIC's got nothing on him."

"Checked Florida DMV?" Dushane said.

"Running it right now."

"Probably just a tourist," Buckthorn said. "Like you figured."

"Yeah. Probably."

***

Loretta walked to her vehicle, a white Styrofoam box containing the leftovers from her salad in one hand. She'd have it with dinner. No matter how well-off she was now, inside was still the girl who grew up poor, who saved every scrap because there was no guarantee of food in the house tomorrow or the next day. She put the box on top of the car as she got out her keys. A wave of pent-up heated air rolled out from the interior of the car and she stepped back. She glanced at her watch. It was an hour and a half before the boys would be home from school, so she had time to drop by the library. She'd had the new Lee Child book on reserve for ages, and maybe it had come in. She adored her life and her family, but she did love getting carried away to somewhere else by a good thriller. It was all the excitement she needed.

***

Donovan's eyes narrowed as he caught sight of the police car still ahead of him. Could they be going to the same place he was? A tiny but insistent alarm began sounding in the back of his head. He didn't have any reason to feel threatened, but that feeling was still there, and he hadn't survived as long as he had, with as many people after him as he'd had, by ignoring it. He took the next right turn, not knowing where it went. He'd wander aimlessly for a few minutes. Give the cops time to get on with whatever they were about, then head for the motel. He'd left the room locked and tidied up, with nothing incriminating in plain view. But a nosy maid or manager who interfered with his luggage was going to get a hell of a surprise.

Chapter Thirty-eight

"705, County," the radio crackled to life.

"705," Willis acknowledged with his car's number.

"Be advised, Florida DMV reports no, repeat no such license number and no Ian McClain associated with it."

"Son of a bitch," Dushane said.

"A fake," Buckthorn said.

Willis keyed his mike. "709, 705," he said.

The reply came back immediately. "709, go ahead."

"Chris, you still at the motel?"

"10-4."

"You got eyes on the subject yet?"

"Negative. Lights are off. No one's home."

"Okay, listen up. Anyone comes back to that room before we get there, do not approach. Repeat, do not approach. Wait for us, you hear?"

"10-4." McCall sounded nervous but excited. "Think this might be our guy?"

"I don't know," Willis said. "But he ain't right. Sit tight. We'll be there in one."

"10-4."

***

Loretta turned the car on, sighing with pleasure as the hot air from the A/C vents turned quickly to a frigid blast. She put on her seatbelt, loosening it a bit so as not to wrinkle her dress. She fiddled with the radio, frowning with annoyance when all she could find were commercials.

Finally, she found a country station actually playing music, a Toby
Keith song she liked. Whistling along with the tune, she put the car in
gear and began backing up.

***

It sounded like the first crack of a peal of thunder, but without the long
rolling rumble that would normally follow.

"What was that?" Dushane said.

Buckthorn looked over at Willis. The younger man's face had gone
chalk white, his eyes wide, his jaw clenched. "Duane," he said. "What's
wrong?"

"I hope that wasn't what it sounded like," was the only answer.

"What?" Dushane asked. "What did it sound like?"

Willis was looking in the mirror. "Fuck," he breathed.

Dushane and Buckthorn looked back through the car's rear window.
A column of black smoke was rising in the distance.

"Last time I heard that sound," Willis said. "Was in Baghdad."

"Oh my god," Dushane said.

"Duane." Buckthorn said, his voice sounding strangled. Willis was
already turning onto the shoulder of the road. He whipped the car
around in a tight arc and headed back the way they came, towards the
smoke.

"All units, County," the dispatcher's voice came over the radio, tight
with tension and fear. "All units. Explosion and fire at 2311 Bristow
Road, Pine Lake. Repeat, all units. Respond, explosion and fire at 2311
Bristow Road, Pine Lake..."

"That's Lulu's," Willis said as he stomped the accelerator. He hit the
button for the siren and it began to wail.

***

Donovan heard the sharp sound of the explosion as he made the turn
into the motel parking lot. He froze as he saw the Gibson County
Sheriff's car in the lot. There was a young deputy standing next to it,
looking confused as he stared into the distance where the sound of
sirens was beginning to rise. At first, he didn't seem to notice Donovan

as he pulled up outside the door of his room. When Donovan opened the door and swung his legs out, he had his pistol concealed behind his back. He saw the kid's head turn towards him, saw eyes narrow and the jaw set in determination. *Bad day to be you, Sunny Jim,* he thought as the kid started towards him.

"Sir," the kid called out just as Donovan drew the gun from behind his back and fired. The bullet hit the young cop in the throat. He staggered and clawed at his neck, a gout of red blood spilling from the wound. He fell to his knees, one hand clutching at this throat as if to try and hold the blood in, the other groping for his holster. Donovan fired again and hit the kid square between the eyes just as his knees hit the ground. His body bent backwards at the waist at an impossible angle, then fell over sideways, twitching and shaking in his death throes. Donovan looked over at the door to the motel office. No one came out, but he saw the Venetian blind lift slightly in the window next to the door. He began walking towards the office with a long, determined stride that turned into a run as he saw the blind drop into place. He heard the lock click as he reached the door and dropped his shoulder to slam against it. The door shivered, but held. He stepped back and delivered a shattering side kick to the door. The frame splintered, revealing the terrified face of the old man who'd checked him in, cowering behind the high topped counter. He had the desk phone in one hand and he was fumbling at the keypad with the other. He dropped the phone and raised his hands high when he saw Donovan. Donovan shot him in the face. The old man dropped to the floor as if his bones had suddenly dissolved. Donovan went behind the counter and stepped over the body to where the phone lay on the floor. He picked it up and put it to his ear. Dial tone. Maybe the old man hadn't had the chance to call 911. He raised the phone over his head and let it drop to the Formica floor, which was worn and stained from years of use. The flimsy plastic shattered as it hit. Donovan made sure by stomping the remaining bits several times beneath his boot.

"So much for a quiet getaway," he said to the silence of the empty office. *Ah well, you couldn't have everything.* He thought of the still unused devices he had left in his room and decided to leave a few surprises behind him to further disrupt things, cover his escape, and last but certainly not least, destroy any evidence he may have left behind. *Just like the old days*, he thought as he headed back to the room.

Chapter Thirty-nine

They spotted the first signs of the chaos that awaited them as they got closer to the diner. At first, it was a small pickup coming from the direction of the place. As it flew past them, Buckthorn spotted the face behind the wheel. It was Gus Hawthorne, one of the town's two dentists. He was white-faced and wild-eyed, as if some hell-hound was chasing him. Then another vehicle, a compact sedan with a driver he didn't recognize. Then they saw the people walking, a middle aged couple with their arms around each other. The woman was weeping, the man speaking soothingly to her. Willis slowed the car and began rolling down the window. Buckthorn looked at the column of smoke rising above the trees. They were very close now. "Just drive," he said.

Willis' face was set in grim lines. "This is gonna suck," he muttered. Over the radio, they could hear the crackling, barely controlled chaos of the county's volunteer fire and rescue units converging on the scene. Finally, they rounded a long curve and caught sight of the diner.

"Mother of God," Dushane breathed.

The parking lot was wreathed in smoke, people moving to and fro in the dark gray cloud like denizens of the Inferno. As they pulled in, they could see the diner itself. The end closest to them appeared untouched, but the big windows to their right were shattered. As the siren wound down, they could hear the sounds of people crying out in pain, orders being shouted, and the keening of more sirens approaching. Several vehicles were burning, others had windows shattered or webbed with cracks. The destruction seemed to center around a single vehicle, off to the side of the lot opposite them. That was blackened and burned out, but something about it looked familiar. A bolt of cold fire went through his body like an electrical shock as he recognized it.

"No," he said, the word coming out as a moan of despair. "Oh no. Please. No."

"Sir..." Willis began.

"Tim," Dushane said, her own voice catching on a sob, but he was out of the car, stumbling like a drunk, towards the burned out SUV. He saw the blackened and twisted figure still sitting behind the wheel and he stopped, uncomprehending. He started walking again and was immediately stopped by a man in the long turnout coat and helmet of a volunteer firefighter.

"Tim," the man said. Then, more urgently, "Tim!"

He looked, uncomprehending, at the firefighter. He knew the face, but the name refused to register.

"My sister," he croaked. "My sister. In the car."

The man's face crumpled. "Oh, Jesus," he said. "I'm sorry, Tim."

The import of the words fell on Buckthorn's shoulders like a mountain and drove all rational thought from his brain. He felt his knees buckling, and the fireman grunted with the effort of keeping him upright. The cacophony of the scene receded away from him. It sounded as if he was at the bottom of a pool, the shouts and cries and sirens all far above him. He could pick Duane's voice out of the din, shouting orders, trying to get the chaos organized.

My job, he thought. *I need to be doing my job...* Then the smell hit him, the awful reek of cooked and bubbling flesh, for all the world like overcooked barbecue, but a thousand times stronger. He knew what... who...he was smelling. His guts wrenched and he vomited, his stomach emptying itself of its recent meal in one mighty convulsion. He managed to turn his head so as not to spatter the man holding him up (*Carl*, he thought as the name absurdly came back to him, *Carl Farris*), but the man sprang back in surprise, loosening his grip. Buckthorn fell to his knees, retching again, unable to bring up anything but a thin and bitter bile. The spasms and the humiliation brought tears to his eyes. He felt an arm across his shoulders and turned.

Leila Dushane knelt beside him, tears streaming down her own face. "Tim," she said softly. "Tim, I am so, so sorry."

***

She moved without thinking the moment she saw him go down, putting her arm around his shoulder to keep him from falling over. He looked at her as if he didn't recognize her. Then he shook his head, like a man recovering from a blow.

"What's wrong with him?" Dushane heard a female voice say. "Wait, is that Tim Buckthorn? Why isn't he..."

She turned. "That's his sister in that car, you stupid cow," she snarled. "Now back the fuck off."

"Well, you don't have to be nasty," he heard the woman say as she moved away. Dushane tightened her grip on Buckthorn's shoulder. He wouldn't look at her.

"My fault," he muttered. "My fault."

"No," Dushane said fiercely. "No fucking way. Do not do this, Tim. Do. Not. Do. This."

At that point he did look up. "I brought this here," he said. His voice was suddenly clear and infused with a dreadful certainty. "This time, I'm the one that brought it."

"Tim," Dushane said, "listen to me. Are you listening? Can you hear me? Good. Now, we are going to get you up, we are going to get you into one of those ambulances over there, and we are going to get you the hell out of here."

He began getting slowly to his feet. "It's a crime scene," he muttered. "I need to get it secured."

"Not you," she said, "and not now. You're in shock. We need to get you..."

"No," he said. He got to his feet. "You think you could get me some water?" he asked Dushane. He wiped his face with his hand. "And a towel," he added.

"What are you going to do?" she asked.

"My job," he said. "Now how about that water?"

He didn't wait for an answer, just strode over to where Duane Willis was talking urgently into the portable radio mike on his shoulder.

***

"Give me a sitrep, Duane," he said..

Duane looked up. "Sir, I think you need a doctor," he said.

Buckthorn tried to smile reassuringly. From the look on Duane's face, it wasn't working. "Not a scratch on me, Duane," he said.

"You're, ah..." the deputy trailed off uncertainly.

"Here," a voice said behind Buckthorn. He turned. Dushane was standing there, a grim look on her face and a bottle of water in one hand. In the other she held a small kitchen towel.

"Thanks, Agent Dushane," he said.

"Don't mention it," she said tonelessly. "Really."

He washed his mouth out, spitting the water onto the gravel, then took a drink. He wiped his face to a reasonable facsimile of cleanliness. He thought back to the way he'd felt at the collapsed house in Tennessee, that calmness he felt in a crisis. He reached down inside to try and find that control. He felt only an icy coldness at his core, in contrast to the hot summer sun beating down on the back of his neck. *Just do the next thing*, he told himself. *The next thing.*

"Come on," he told Duane. "Let's get to work."

***

Dushane stood back, her phone to her ear, waiting for Wolf to pick up on the other end. She watched as Buckthorn took over the management of the scene of his sister's murder—directing fire and emergency vehicles, assigning patrol officers as they arrived to cordon the place off and corral witnesses, giving the team that showed up from the detective division a quick briefing as they stood there looking stunned and sweating in their suit jackets and ties. She shivered despite the oppressive heat, made even worse by the grimy smoke that still hung over the scene. She knew that bomb had been meant for them, and she knew who'd set it.

There was no way she was going to let Buckthorn blame himself. That way was a sure path to madness. But she wondered, after looking into his eyes just now, if he was already headed down that path. The eyes that had once looked at her with love were dead, the smile that had warmed her heart turned to a ghastly rictus. She'd thought when she'd met him that maybe he was wound too tight. She'd worried that he might snap. Now he truly seemed like a clockwork man, going through his job like an automaton. She wondered if she'd just seen Tim Buckthorn die.

There was a click as someone picked up the phone. "Tony Wolf."

"Boss, it's Leila. I'm in Pine Lake. Someone—Donovan—just tried to kill us with a car bomb."

Wolf's voice was calm. "Okay. I assume you're all right."

"Yeah. We weren't anywhere near when the bomb went off. But it was rigged to Buckthorn's sister's car. She's dead."

"Jesus," Wolf said. "Is he okay?"

She looked across the lot. "No," she said. "He's walking, he's talking, he's doing cop things. But... her voice broke, "he's a long way from okay."

"Got it," Wolf said. His voice softened. "L.D., listen to me. You need to get out of there, and bring him with you. Donovan may be back. Or he may have rigged another device to take out the first responders. That's an old IRA trick."

"Oh, shit," she said. "I hadn't thought of that."

"Well, start. Get someplace safe and hole up. Tell the locals to secure the scene for the Bureau and sit tight. I'm getting Steadman on the line."

"And then what?"

"And then we're going full out, balls to the wall on this one. They just tried to kill an FBI agent. My partner, no less. These people are history."

"Best idea I've heard all day, boss," Dushane said. "I'll call you later."

"Do that. We'll have a team there ASAP. Just make sure the scene's secure."

"I think it will be." She killed the connection and walked over to where Buckthorn was talking to Duane Willis and a pair of detectives.

"Captain Buckthorn," she said formally. He didn't seem to hear her. She raised her voice. "CAPTAIN BUCKTHORN!"

He turned, looking annoyed. "What is it?"

"I've just been on the phone to Agent Wolf. He's asked me to inform you that the FBI is taking over this investigation. As of now."

He scowled. "I thought you people didn't do that."

"The rules are different when someone tries to kill one of us." She knew she was bullshitting, but she hoped she could pull it off. His eyes narrowed in anger. "One of you?" he said. "In case you haven't noticed yet, Agent Dushane, whoever did this did kill..." his voice faltered, "did kill one of us. One of my family."

"Which is exactly why you should not be running this investigation," she snapped, "and you damn well know it. Captain."

The two detectives looked dumbstruck, their eyes tracking back and forth between Dushane and Buckthorn like spectators at a tennis match. Buckthorn was glaring at her, his teeth clenched, lips drawn back in what was almost a snarl. That iron control was beginning to slip. Duane Willis broke the silence. "She's right, sir."

Buckthorn's gaze snapped to him. "What did you say, *Deputy*?"

Willis met the stare, his own gaze as flat and uncompromising as a stone. "You know she's right, sir. You can't be involved in an investigation where the victim's a member of your family. That's a rule. And it's a good one."

"TO HELL WITH THE RULE!" Buckthorn screamed. Other people were beginning to stop talking and stare. He got himself under control with a visible effort of will, but he was still shaking.

"Captain," Dushane said. "Tim. We need to go. Come on."

Buckthorn wouldn't look at her or Willis.

"I can take over, sir," Willis said. "Go ahead and take my vehicle." Buckthorn still didn't answer. "Please, sir," Willis said. Buckthorn still didn't answer, just turned and walked towards the cruiser.

Dushane let out a deep breath. "Thank you, Deputy Willis."

"No problem, ma'am," he said. "Take care of him, okay?"

"I wish I knew how, Duane," she said. "Oh. Agent Wolf reminded me of something. The primary suspect in this used to be a member of the Irish Republican Army. One of their techniques was to place a second device to catch first responders."

He rubbed a hand down his face. "Yeah. The hajjis used to do that, too. I've got people poking around."

"Carefully, I hope."

"You know it, ma'am. And Fort Bragg's sending over some EOD guys." He shook his head. "I came home to get away from shit like this."

She nodded. "Tim...Captain Buckthorn's...got a lot of faith in you, Duane. I can see why now."

"Thanks, ma'am," he said. Something seemed to occur to him. He spoke into the portable mike on his shoulder. "709, this is 705. Report."

There was no answer. Willis tried again. "709. Come on back, Chris."

Nothing.

"Damn it," Willis breathed. He spoke again. "County, 705."

"705, County."

"I can't raise Chris in 709. He was out at the Pine Lake Motor Lodge. See if you can get a unit out there."

"10-4."

"I don't like this," Willis said. "Not one bit."

"I don't blame you,." Dushane began, then she noticed Buckthorn. He was behind the wheel of the cruiser. They heard the engine start.

"What the hell..." Willis began, then he began waving his arms. "HEY!" he yelled. "CAPTAIN BUCKTHORN!" Buckthorn began backing up, turning the car around. "HEY!" Willis yelled again.

"Maybe he heard you trying to contact your guy," she said.

"Oh, that is just fucking *great*," Willis said. He spoke into the microphone. "Captain, where you going with my car, you don't mind my asking?" There was no response. He shook his head angrily and spoke into the mike again. "County, 705. Captain Buckthorn's got my vehicle."

There was a pause before the dispatcher responded. "Say again, 705?"

"Captain Buckthorn took off with my vehicle."

"Well, where's he goin' with it, Duane?"

He looked at Dushane. "Possibly the Motor Lodge. What's the ETA on that other unit?"

"Ten minutes," the dispatcher said. "I'm havin' to call people in on their days off. Perry Twisdale told me to tell you he ain't happy. He was takin' his wife to the doctor."

"I hate it for him. But days off are canceled right now. We got a situation developin' here."

"Ahhh...does Tim know about that?"

"He put me in charge. Just get everybody you can get ahold of out on patrol. We got a suspect in this bombing runnin' around loose. We need to get some roadblocks set up. We need..."

Dushane stopped listening by this point. Buckthorn was clearly right on the edge of losing it, and if, as she suspected, he was headed for the where he thought he'd find Donovan, he stood an excellent chance of getting himself killed. She spotted a uniformed deputy taking a roll of crime scene tape out of the trunk of his car.

"Hey," she snapped, pulling her badge out and flashing it at the deputy. "FBI. I need your car."

The deputy blinked. "What?"

She held out her other hand, snapping her fingers before opening her palm. "Your keys. Give them to me," she looked at his name tag, "Deputy Arrington."

He looked around, as if searching for someone to save him from this deranged apparition that had suddenly appeared before him.

"Lady, I can't..."

"It's not 'lady', Deputy Arrington. It's 'Agent'. 'Special Agent' if you want to be formal. As in 'Federal Agent' on a Federal investigation, which you are coming perilously close to obstructing. Do you know what happens to people who obstruct federal investigations?"

"Ma'am..."

"They go to federal *prison.* Now what's it going to be?"

He was getting angry now. "Ma'am, I'm not giving you my car!"

At that moment, the radio crackled in the patrol car. Tim Buckthorn's voice came through clearly, his words causing every officer in the area to turn their heads and listen.

"Attention, all units. Officer down. 10-33. Repeat. Officer down."

"God DAMN it," she heard Duane Willis snarl behind her. Then, "Arrington! Take Agent Dushane and get out to the Motor Court. Haul ass."

"Yes, SIR!" Arrington said. He looked at Dushane. "But I'm drivin'."

"Whatever," she said. "Let's go."

She'd barely gotten her door closed when Arrington stomped the gas pedal hard, kicking up a spray of gravel as he tore out of the lot, siren wailing. She grabbed the door as he rocketed down the road. An ambulance fell in behind them, its own siren adding to the cacophony.

"Hey," she said, "sorry I was kind of rough back there."

"Not a problem," he said. "You're that Agent Wolf's partner, right?"

"Yeah." She held on to the door, her knuckles whitening as he took a curve at tire-squealing speed. "You've met him?"

"Sorta." He grinned. "Chased him one time. He got away. Ran me right in the damn ditch. That fella can sure drive."

"I'll tell him you asked after him," she said through gritted teeth.

"You do that...oh, no." They had come within sight of the Pine Lake Motor Court. There were two sheriff's cruisers in the otherwise empty parking lot. One had its lights flashing. But what had gotten Arrington's attention was the sight of Buckthorn, sitting on the pavement beside a stretched-out body in the brown uniform of the Sheriff's Department. Arrington pulled the car to a screeching halt a few feet away and he and Dushane piled out.

Buckthorn looked up as they approached. He had his pistol out, held loosely in one hand on his knee. His face was blank, drained of all emotion.

"It's Chris McCall," he said in a dead voice. "Shot twice. Ev Carter's in the office back there. Dead." Arrington started toward the office just as the ambulance pulled in, its siren grinding down to a low growl. Buckthorn raised his voice to speak over it. "Don't touch anything," he said. "There's something wired to the bottom of Chris's car. There's probably other devices around." Arrington pulled up short, looking confused. "Wh...what do you want me to do, Captain?"

Buckthorn didn't answer at first. He looked around, then slowly got to his feet. Two paramedics, a man and a woman, ran to where McCall lay and bent over him. The man put his fingers to McCall's throat, pulled back his eyelid, then looked up and shook his head. Buckthorn didn't seem to notice. "Secure the scene," he said as he slid his pistol back into the holster on his hip. "Tell Duane to get the EOD guys from Bragg over here. Wait for the FBI. They'll be taking over. Right, Agent Dushane?"

His eerie calm was giving her chills. "That's not important right now. We need to get you...where are you going?"

He was climbing into Willis' vehicle. He acted as if he hadn't heard the question. "Tim!" she said as he started the engine. He didn't look at her as he drove off.

"Where's he going?" Arrington asked.

"No place good," she whispered.

Chapter Forty

Buckthorn sat in the patrol car, looking at the outside of Bru and Loretta's house. He knew what he needed to do. It was his news to deliver. His duty. But for once in his life, he couldn't face that duty. He reached for the keys in the ignition, intending to start the car and just drive away. He didn't know where he'd go after that. His whole life had been dedicated to protecting his town, his officers, his family. And he'd failed. Utterly. Loretta was dead, burned to an unrecognizable husk by an evil he'd gone out and found and brought back to Pine Lake with him. A young officer lay dead, slain by the same evil. He felt the weight of his failure settle on his shoulders. He remembered the story he'd had to read in high school where a man suspected of witchcraft was pressed to death by having progressively heavier stones laid on his chest. 'More weight," the man had said. But the weight was coming down on him without being asked. A strange lethargy seemed to steal over him, as if someone had slipped him a powerful anesthetic. He let his hand drop and sat there until Bru came out of the house. He walked towards the car, looking puzzled and slightly annoyed at the interruption. Finally Buckthorn got his legs to work. He opened the door and stood just as Bru reached him.

"Tim?" Bru said. "What's going on? Loretta said she was going to meet you for lunch. Did she…"

"Bru," Buckthorn interrupted. "Loretta…" he choked on the words.

Bru's face went slack with shock as he saw the expression on his brother in law's face. "What? What is it?" He grabbed Buckthorn by the shoulders. "What happened to my wife, Tim?"

"She's dead, Bru," Buckthorn said. "She was...someone came after me. They put a bomb. In the car."

Bru released him and stepped back, a look of disbelief on his face. "A bomb? What? That's crazy." His face darkened. "If this is a joke, old son, it's not funny. Not a..."

"It's not a joke, Bru. She's gone."

"You're sure?" A note of desperation crept into his voice. "Maybe you're wrong. Maybe she's just hurt. She's at the hospital."

Buckthorn shook his head. "I'm sorry, Bru. I'm...I'm so sorry."

"Sorry," Bru said hollowly. He swayed like a drunk for a moment, his eyes glazing as if he was about to collapse. He steadied himself with a hand on the hood of the car. His eyes cleared and he looked at Buckthorn. "How the hell can you stand there so calmly?" he demanded in a harsh voice. "Don't you feel anything?"

"Yeah," Buckthorn said. "I do. I...I do." He looked around, as if he was seeing where he was for the first time. "Where are the boys?" he asked. "I need to tell..."

"I'll tell my sons, Tim," Bru said, and his voice was raw with rage and pain. "You've done enough."

"Bru, I..." he trailed off "I'm sorry," he said again. They were the only words he seemed capable of forming. Bru didn't answer; he just turned and walked back towards the house, his shoulders bowed as if he was bearing the same weight Buckthorn did. As Buckthorn started to get back in the car, Bru suddenly turned. His face was a mask of fury and hate. "Useless," he hissed. Buckthorn froze. "You were supposed to protect us. And you've done a piss poor job of it."

He couldn't answer. It was an echo of the same voice he'd been hearing in his head. He felt a sharp pain in his jaw, a quick bolt of agony that made him gasp with surprise He realized that he'd clenched his jaw so hard that he'd broken a tooth clean through. The pain was like lightning pulsing through his head.

Bru went on. "You said they were trying to kill you. I wish to God they had, if that meant my Loretta would still be alive."

"I wish that too," Buckthorn whispered. Bru didn't hear him. "But they missed," he said. "What happens if they try again? Are you going to do the same great *fucking* job you did protecting us this time?"

"I'll find them," Buckthorn said. "I promise you that. I know who did this. And I'll make sure they pay."

"How?" Bru said. "You're going to *investigate*? You're going to *arrest* them? How's that worked so far?"

Buckthorn straightened up. "No," he said. "You're right."

"I can't believe...what?"

"You're right," Buckthorn said. "It's not working." He slid behind the wheel.

"What are you going to do?" Bru shouted. Buckthorn drove off without answering.

***

"Janine?" Sheriff Stark's voice coming from the intercom on her desk startled her. She was so unused to him calling down to the office that she didn't answer at first. "Janine!" he said again, a little louder.

"Yes sir?" she answered.

"Where the heck is Tim Buckthorn?"

He's doing the job you ought to be doing, you useless tub of lard, she thought to herself. "I assume he's out at one of the crime scenes, sir."

"Well, you assume wrong. Someone just saw him walk into my office and walk back out again. And he left his badge on my desk."

"He left..." she stopped. "I'm not sure where he is, then, sir. I'll see if I can find him." She pulled out her cell phone and hit Buckthorn's number on speed dial. The phone rang five times before his voicemail came on. "This is Tim Buckthorn. Leave a message."

"Tim," she said. "It's Janine. Sheriff Stark says you just walked in and left your badge on his desk. What on earth are you thinking of? Call me." She called his house, got the answering machine, left a similar message. She sat in silence for a moment, her brow furrowed, her stomach twisting with worry. She got up and went into Dispatch.

"Monica," she said, "you know where Tim is?"

"Ain't you heard?" Monica said. "He took Duane Willis' car and run off from where McCall got shot. I guess between that and his sister, he's freakin' out."

"What about Loretta?" She put her hand to her mouth. "Oh, no. Was she...oh, no."

Monica nodded grimly. "Yep. It was her car that got blown up." She shook her head. "What is this world comin' to when somethin' like this can happen in Pine Lake? Crazy bikers a couple years ago, now some terrorist is goin' around blowin' people up."

"Get Tim on the radio," Janine said. "Now. Tell him to call me. Now. Move it, girl!"

"Okay, okay," the girl muttered, turning back to her console. "You don't have to yell." She keyed her mike. "705," she broadcast. "705, County. Please acknowledge." The only reply was the hissing of the radio. She keyed the mike again. "Tim," she said, "where you at, Tim? Acknowledge." There was no answer. Monica frowned. "Now, that ain't like him."

"No," Janine said, "it isn't." She pulled out her phone again and punched another set of numbers in. The answer came after the first ring. "Dushane."

"Agent Dushane, this is Janine Porter."

She didn't get a chance to go on. "Mrs. Porter, have you seen Tim?"

Janine felt a cold chill down her spine. "I was hoping you knew where he was."

"I don't. His sister was killed. I'm on my way to his house as soon as I can get someone to give me a ride back to my car."

"He's not picking up his land line," Janine said. "Or answering the radio."

"Fuck!" Dushane said. Then, "Sorry."

"Never mind that," Janine said. "You just call me when you get there."

"Yes ma'am. I will." She broke the connection. Janine stood in the doorway of the dispatch room. For once, she had no idea what to do.

***

Dushane saw the sheriff's car parked at the curb as she pulled up. She parked behind it and sat for a moment. She wondered what she'd find inside. Buckthorn was beginning to frighten her, and she hated that feeling. Finally, she got out and walked slowly up the concrete walk to the front of the house. She tried the front door without knocking. It swung open easily at her touch. She took a deep breath and entered.

Buckthorn was coming out of the bedroom. He'd changed out of his uniform into a pair of worn, ragged jeans and a solid black t-shirt. He was carrying a small overnight bag in his left hand. A shotgun was cradled in the crook of his right elbow. He stopped when he saw her standing in the living room.

"Hey," she said as calmly as she could. "Going hunting?"

"Something like that," he said. The blank, stunned look she'd seen earlier was gone. In its place was a look that frightened her even more. His face was still calm, but she could see the muscles working in his clenched jaw. It was the eyes that scared her most. They were narrow, smoldering slits of rage.

"Tim, what's going on?"

He wouldn't look her in the eye. "I've got to go. I'll be away for a while."

"Go where?"

"Better that you not know."

The fear gave way to anger. "Oh, really? You can't tell *me*? The person you were, you know, making love to this morning?" She shook her head. "It's not like I can't figure it out. I'm not stupid, Tim."

He set the bag and shotgun on the couch and went to the closet. "I don't think you're stupid. But you shouldn't try and stop me."

"Tim," she said, "this is not you. Remember what you told me? When I was shook up? After I shot Lofton Monroe?"

He took an NC State baseball cap out of the closet and put it on. "What?"

"You said you got over killing people when you had to do it because you reminded yourself you were a sworn officer of the law, and they were lawless men."

He looked at her, and her heart broke in half as she saw the pain mixed with the rage in his eyes. "Yeah," he said. "And look how well that worked out."

"We're going to get these people, Tim. I promise you. But we're going to do it the right way."

He picked up the gun and the bag. "I wish you a lot of luck. But I'm betting I get to them first." He started for the door.

She moved to block his way. "Or they kill you."

He stopped. "Maybe. But where did twenty years of following the law get me? My sister's dead, Leila. I can still smell her burning. I can still taste the ashes on my tongue. One of my officers, a young man whose name I barely knew, is dead, too. I spent all this time, all this worry, all this work, to try and protect this town and its people. But in the end, I can't even protect my family. Or my men."

"So this is your answer? Some sort of kamikaze mission against Donovan and Monroe? I've heard of crooks committing suicide by cop, but this is the first time I've seen a cop try to commit suicide by crook."

He almost smiled at that. "Funny."

"Thanks," she said. Her voice broke as she added, "I got a million of them."

"I'm not a lawman any more, Leila," he said. "I failed at it."

A tear ran down her cheek. "You didn't. You really didn't." She put a hand on his shoulder. "Please, Tim," she said. "Don't do this."

He shifted the gun to the crook of the arm holding the bag. He reached up and gently took her hand. He brought it to his lips and kissed it softly, looking into her eyes. Then he put a hand on her shoulder and moved her aside. "Goodbye, Leila," he said as he walked past her and out the door. She went to the door and watched him walk to his pickup. The tears streamed freely down her face as he got in, started the truck, and drove away. He didn't look back.

Chapter Forty-one

"**S**o how's he taking it?" Donovan asked.

"Better than you might think," Patience said. "He started off raging and swearing that you'd missed the ones you were after. But when he found out that the deputy's sister is the one who died, he started thinking. Now he's almost happy about it."

"He thinks it's more fitting? More of an eye for an eye?"

"You'll have to ask him. He said to send you in as soon as you got here."

"Okay." He paused before entering. "See you later?"

She nodded. "I've missed you."

"I missed you too." He took a deep breath and opened the door.

Lamp Monroe was sitting in his wheelchair, watching a daytime talk show on the flat screen TV. As Donovan entered, he picked up the remote and killed the sound. He stared at the silent screen for a full thirty seconds Donovan stood silently. He knew the old bastard was trying to make him nervous, but he knew that game well. Finally, Monroe looked at him.

"Well?" he croaked. "What've you got to say for yourself?"

Donovan shrugged. "They got into another car. There was no way I could've known they'd do that. I'll get him next time."

Monroe grunted. "Maybe it's better this way. Let the sumbitch suffer."

"I agree."

Monroe bristled. "Did I fuckin' ask if you agreed?"

Donovan decided to change the subject. "Is my alibi secure?"

Monroe nodded. "Couple of feds came nosin' around. But I had three people swear you was workin' security on a riverboat casino in

Biloxi for the last three weeks." He chuckled. "We even got time cards showin' you clocked in."

"Don't those things have video surveillance? What if they ask for the recordings?"

"We tell 'em to get a warrant or go fuck themselves. An' they ain't got no reason for a warrant. Even if they do, we got a guy walkin' around the casino, about your size, with a hat pulled down so you can't see his face. That's you, as near as anyone can tell."

Donovan shook his head. "They're going to want to question me in person."

"Oh, they tried. But you walked off the job the day after the bombin' and no one's seen you since. So don't worry. We got this locked down."

Donovan wasn't convinced, but he let it go. "So what now?"

"I like the idea of an eye for an eye. That girl agent's got family down in Louisiana. Maybe you pay them a visit. And that other FBI fella, that Wolf. He's got him a pretty little Latin gal for a girlfriend." He cackled. "Maybe we can set y'all up a blind date." He waved a hand at Donovan. He seemed almost cheerful now. "But not right now. Let 'em think they're safe. Right now you take some time off. Go get laid."

"Thanks," Donovan said, thinking of Patience in the outer room. "I just might do that."

***

He'd been on the road for hours, working his way slowly down the Interstate, hitting every truck stop he could find, checking out the security. When he saw what he was looking for, he made a note of the exit in his notebook and moved on, waiting for dark. When the sun finally began to slide below the horizon, he headed back up in the direction he'd come, towards the first stop he'd marked. The girls were just starting their "shift"; they stood together in a knot, smoking and talking, looking around at the trucks beginning to fill up the lot, until the car with "Dixie Security" stenciled on the side pulled up. He couldn't hear what the man in the passenger seat said to them, but it was enough to scatter the group in all directions like frightened deer. Buckthorn got out of his truck and got ready. It was time to bring some pain to the land of the Lizard King.

Part Three

Chapter Forty-two

"So," Deputy Director Pat Steadman said, "You're telling me we've got nothing."

They were in Wolf's office. Steadman had flown down from Washington to take command of the investigation, and he sat behind the desk he'd commandeered from Wolf.

"We're still working on it, sir," Dushane said. She was sitting in the office's sole chair. Wolf leaned against the wall, arms folded over his chest.

Steadman picked up a file folder and leafed through it. "This Donovan has an airtight alibi," he said, his voice flat and emotionless.

"The Jackson, Mississippi office is trying to get a warrant for the surveillance tapes from the casino," Dushane said.

"Which they most likely won't get," Steadman answered with that same infuriating calm, "since all we have to go on is an assumption that this is connected with Lampton Monroe and his people."

"Who else would go after Buckthorn and Dushane?" Wolf said.

"How do you know they were even the target?" Steadman shot back. "Maybe the woman was the intended victim. I hear her husband's made some enemies. Have you even looked at him?"

Wolf and Dushane looked at each other. "No," Wolf finally said.

Steadman took off his glasses and rubbed his eyes. "Explain to me again why you two aren't too close to this and why I shouldn't put someone else on it." He put the glasses back on. "Especially you, Agent Dushane, considering that you're romantically involved with the brother of the victim." She opened her mouth as if to answer, then closed it. "Don't look so shocked, Agent," Steadman said. "You don't get to be a Deputy Director by being clueless. Did you think I was clueless, Agent Dushane?" the lack of emotion in the harsh words somehow made them even more intimidating.

"No, sir," she said in a small voice.

"Good," Steadman said. "And speaking of Deputy Buckthorn, have either of you heard from him? Either of you have any idea where he is?"

"No, sir," Wolf said. Dushane just shook her head.

He picked another file up. "Well, I do. We've got reports of lot security officers at three different Interstate truck stops being assaulted by and robbed by a man who identifies himself clearly to the victims as Tim Buckthorn."

"Let me guess," Wolf said. "All of the rent-a-cops were from the same company."

Steadman nodded. "Dixie Security. Owned by one Lampton Monroe."

"So he's trying to get back at Monroe...how?" Wolf said. "By stealing his money?"

Dushane spoke up. "He's trying to get Monroe and Donovan to come after him," she said. "Somewhere other than Pine Lake."

They both turned to look at her. "And did he tell you this himself?" Steadman said. Just the barest hint of anger had crept into his voice.

She shook her head. "No, sir. Not in so many words. But..." she took a deep breath. "As you say, sir, I've been...involved with him. I know him pretty well. At least I thought I did. The one thing he wants to do more than anything else is to protect his town and the people in it."

Wolf nodded. "That sounds like the Buckthorn I know."

Dushane went on. "He took his sister's death hard. Not just because it was his sister, but because he saw it as the failure of his life's work. That much he did tell me."

"So now he wants revenge," Wolf said, "but he doesn't want Pine Lake to be the battleground again."

"Agent Dushane," Steadman said, "Do you have reason to believe that Buckthorn is suicidal? Because that's what this looks like. A lot more than it looks like revenge."

She tried to keep her voice steady as she said, "I've considered the possibility, sir."

"And yet, you didn't consider sharing it with your fellow agents."

"I'm sorry, sir."

"I should make you sorrier. I should suspend you without pay for your shocking lack of professionalism."

"Sir..." Wolf tried to interject.

"Shut up, Agent Wolf," Steadman said. "You're as culpable as she is. Dushane, if you could make contact with Mr. Buckthorn, do you think you could talk him down?"

"I don't know, sir," she said. *I am not going to cry in front of this bastard,* she thought fiercely. *I am* not *going to fucking cry.* "I tried it once, and I didn't have much luck."

"Are you willing to try again?"

"Are you asking, sir, if I want to try and talk Deputy Buckthorn out of killing the person who tried to kill both of us?"

"Good point," Steadman said, "and it raises the question: do we want to?"

"Sir?" Wolf said.

"No one's denying that Lampton Monroe's a scumbag, Agent Wolf. And Donovan's a murderer several times over. We just haven't been able to prove either of those things. If Buckthorn does manage to take them out, I don't think I'm going to be losing any sleep over it."

Dushane couldn't believe what she was hearing. "And if he doesn't?" she said. "If he fails and gets himself killed in the process? I thought you liked Buckthorn. And you're sworn to uphold the law. Just like I am."

"I do," Steadman said. "And I am. So now do you have an answer to my question?"

"An answer to your..." she trailed off.

"Do we...do *you*...want to try and talk him out of this?"

"Yes sir," she said. "I'll do it."

"Actually," Steadman said, "I can't order you to do it. Officially, you're still off this investigation."

Dushane couldn't believe what she was hearing. "But sir, you just said..." the import of what he was saying sunk in. "Yes, sir."

"Good." He got up, picked his coat up from where it had been hanging on the back of the chair and started to put it on. He looked at them. "Something else?" he said.

"No, sir," Dushane said as she and Wolf got up.

"Good. Now if you two will excuse me, I have to get over to a little town nearby called Blainesville. You know it?"

"Vaguely," Wolf said. "It's the next county over from Gibson. What's going on there?"

"Some kind of mess. A friend of mine who's from there asked me to have a look at it."

After he left, she turned to Wolf. "Did he just tell us to do something we're not supposed to do?"

"Not officially, no," Wolf said.

"But he'll back us up."

"If we succeed. If we fail, we're on our own."

"Jesus," she said. "Machiavellian fucker, isn't he? Guess that's why he's a Deputy Director."

"Probably going to be the head honcho one day," Wolf said. "Which is something we ought to be praying for, I guess. In the meantime, how are we going to find Buckthorn?"

"Go where he's headed."

"And when we get there," he said, "what the hell do we do? Go to Biloxi, camp out on Monroe's doorstep and wait for Buckthorn to show up?"

"You have a better idea?"

He sighed. "I guess not."

She pulled out her phone. "You make the travel arrangements. I'll try to call him again. Or text him. Assuming he knows how to use text."

Wolf laughed. "He's that old school?"

"Yeah," she murmured. "He is." She stopped, closed her eyes, took a deep breath.

"Hold it together, L.D.," he said soothingly. "We'll get him."

"I don't think we will, boss," she said. She opened her eyes. "I think they're going to get to him before we do. And they're going to kill him."

"We're not going to let that happen," he said. "Remember, I'm the legendary bad-ass Tony Wolf who you idolize and who you begged to get teamed up with."

She laughed and brushed a tear away. "Okay," she said. "Let's get to work."

Chapter Forty-three

They were on their way to the airport. Wolf was driving. Dushane was slumped in the passenger seat, punching away at her smart phone with her index finger. Suddenly she sat up straight. "Fuck," she said in a low, savage voice.

He looked over. "What?"

She held up the phone, facing towards him. "On the CNN website."

He glanced over. "I can't read it and drive at the same time. Just tell me."

She read from the screen. "Rogue cop on interstate rampage," she read.

"Wait, what?" he said. "Is it about..."

"Yep," she said.

"Damn it," he muttered.

"It gets worse," she said. "The one reporting the story's your girlfriend."

"No."

She swiped at the screen, then turned up the volume. Gabriella Torrijos' voice came from the tiny speaker. "A North Carolina sheriff's deputy has been identified as the person responsible for attacks on security guards at three interstate truck stops..."

"Look like she's hit the big time," Dushane said.

"Turn it off," he said through gritted teeth. Dushane killed the sound. Wolf fumbled his own phone out of the center console. "Call Gaby," he snarled at it. He glanced down at the screen. VOICE COMMAND NOT RECOGNIZED. He resisted the temptation to throw the device out the window. "Call Gaby," he said again, trying to keep the strain out of his voice. He put the phone to his ear as the voice command system dialed the number. She picked up on the second ring. "What the hell are you doing?" he snapped.

"Having a cup of tea and a bagel," she said.

"Stop it, Gaby. You know what I mean."

"I'm doing my job," she said with that same infuriating calmness. "This could be big. At least that's what CNN told me when they picked it up off my station's feed and asked me to run with it."

"You realize you might get Buckthorn killed."

"No, Tony, I don't realize that. Why don't you tell me why that might be? And why one security company seems to be the target?"

"I can't," he said.

"Of course you can't."

"It's a current investigation, Gaby. It's at a delicate stage. I'll tell you about it when we're done."

"That's what you said the last time, Tony. And you never did."

"Gaby, *please*."

"Does this have something to do with the death of Buckthorn's sister? Does he blame these people for the bombing? I know the man he killed in Tennessee was the grandson of the man who owns the security company. Is this some kind of feud going on?" When he didn't answer, she continued. "I tried to call this Lampton Monroe, but didn't get an answer. Maybe I should..."

"Gaby, don't be an idiot," Wolf said. "Stay the hell away from Lampton Monroe. Or anyone having to do with him."

"Why is that, Tony?" she insisted. "Are you saying he's dangerous? That he did have something to so with Loretta Starnes' death?"

"I'm not saying anything," Wolf bit down on the words. "But if he did...Gaby, I was involved in his grandson's death, too. If he's willing to kill Buckthorn's sister for revenge..."

"So he did have something to do with it!"

"I didn't say that!" he yelled.

"If he didn't, then I'm safe, right?"

"God damn it, Gaby," he said.

"Tell me what I need to know," she said.

"Only if you promise not to run with it until the investigation's over."

"You know I can't do that."

"Just please. Stay away from this, Gaby. For just a while. Please."

"In a day or two, this could be the biggest story in the country, Tony. It could make my career."

"Is that all that matters to you?"

There was a brief silence, then her voice came back, low and furious. "You, of all people, do not get to say that." The line went dead. He stared at the phone in frustration until Dushane spoke up. "Boss," she said in a tight voice. He looked up and realized he was drifting out of his lane. He yanked the car back on course.

"She's figuring it out," Dushane said.

"Yeah," he replied, his voice tight. "She's connected the dots."

"Hell," Dushane said, "We should hire her."

"She's trying to get to Monroe."

"Oh, boy," she said. "I can't think of *any* way *that* could go wrong."

"L.D.," he said.

"Sorry. But we need to keep her away, too."

"What do you want me to do? Have her arrested? Arrest her myself?"

"It's a thought."

"You're kidding, right? Arrest Gaby. My..." he trailed off.

"Might save her life."

"It might end our relationship."

"Boss," she said gently, "I think that ship has sailed." He drove in silence for a while, then she sighed. "I guess we can't arrest a reporter unless she actually has done something stupid to obstruct our investigation."

"I guess not," he said.

"Wait, now you're mad at *me*? Do we really have time for this shit?"

They'd reached the airport entrance. As Wolf turned the car into the long, gently curving parkway that ended at the terminals, he said "No. We don't. So what's the plan?"

She shrugged. "Sit on Monroe's house and wait for Buckthorn to make a move."

"And then?"

"We stop him."

"Do we?"

She looked at him evenly. "You saying what I think you are, Tony?"

"Maybe. I don't know."

"Well, I do. If he tries to take those people head-on, he's going to get himself killed."

They'd reached long-term parking. Wolf took a ticket from the automated dispenser. He didn't answer her. "I thought he was your friend," Dushane said softly.

Wolf sighed. "I know. Stupid idea." He wheeled the car into the parking lot. "Sorry."

"Yeah. Well, you damn sure better be."

"You know we'll have to arrest him," Wolf said. "I don't know that he'll go for that." He spotted a parking space and made for it.

"I know," Dushane said. "I'm working on that."

"Working on a way to talk him out of it?"

"That," she said. "Also dealing with the thought of maybe having to shoot him."

They'd pulled into the space. Wolf put the car in park. "If it comes to that," he said. "I'll take the shot."

She shook her head. "If it comes to that," she said, "the person with the best shot takes it."

"L.D...."

"I can do the job, boss," she said, staring ahead through the windshield. "Whatever it takes."

"I know," he said. "But I don't want it to hollow you out."

"Thanks," she said. "But I think that ship may have sailed, too."

Chapter Forty-four

Donovan awoke to Patience shaking him gently by one shoulder. He smiled and reached for her, but the smile died as he saw the expression on her face. "What's going on?"

"I don't know," she said. "But he wants you. Now."

"What's his mood?"

"It's...odd."

He ran a hand through his hair. "Care to enlighten me further?"

She bit her lip uncertainly. "I can't describe it. He's furious. But he's also...it's like he's happy to be."

"Has the old fucker finally gone off his head?"

She shook her head. "Actually, it's the most lucid I've seen him in months."

"Huh. Tell him I'll be right there."

The two of them had taken over a deserted room in the unused wing, far enough away that Monroe wouldn't know he was still there, or hear him and Patience. He hadn't bothered to take the covers off any of the other furniture, only the bed. He pulled on a pair of trousers that lay puddled on the floor and pulled a shirt from his overnight bag. He realized as he walked down the long silent hallway that he was whistling. He stifled himself, then pasted a serious expression on his face. If the old man was well and truly teed off, it wouldn't do to walk in grinning like some kind of muppet.

He heard movement behind him and whirled around, his gun hand reflexively moving towards a weapon that wasn't there. A man was coming out of one of the other bedrooms. He was another one of the 'roided up types that filled the ranks of Monroe's so-called "security service." This one had a round, rather small head crowned by a ridiculous looking Mohawk. He was dressed in jeans and leather vest over a ragged red T-shirt. What drew Donovan's immediate attention was the AR-15 rifle slung over his shoulder.

"Who the fuck are you?" Donovan said.

The man puffed up at the tone. "I could ask you the same question, asshole."

"But you won't, unless you want to be learning how to fire that gun from out your arse. Now answer the question."

The man looked about to make an issue of it, but the look in Donovan's eye made him think better of it. "Mr. Monroe called us in. Said he wanted some extra security."

"Did he now?" Donovan said. "And why is that?" From down the hallway, he could hear a raised voice. It sounded like the old man, cursing. He frowned.

"Ask him yourself," the rifleman said. "I got outside duty." He turned and walked away.

The sound of shouting grew louder as Donovan approached the door to the old man's bedroom. "What the fuck you mean, he walked off with it?!" the old man was screaming as he entered without knocking. Donovan was shocked to see he was actually out of the wheelchair and standing up. He'd braced himself with one hand wrapped claw-like around one corner of a tall armoire, but it was the first time in months that Donovan had seen him fully upright. "Ain't you got a gun!?" Monroe listened for only a brief second, hardly long enough for a reply, then began yelling again. "Listen here, boy, you better find some way to track down that sumbitch and get me my money back, or I'll be takin' it off yore fat ass in strips!" He snapped the phone shut and threw it across the room. It hit the wall, rebounded and landed on the bed. He looked at Donovan. "I'm surrounded by fuckin' idiots," he snapped.

"Even me?"

"Especially you, you stupid Mick bastard! That redneck sheriff you missed? The fella whose sister you blew up?"

"Yeah?"

"He's goin' from truck stop to truck stop, robbin' my men. Pullin' *guns* on 'em. Tellin' 'em to let me know he's *comin'* for me." Patience had been right. The sheer rage that had raised Monroe from his wheelchair

like an avenging revenant was startling. But what was even more dis-
turbing was the mad grin plastered across his face that contradicted
the anger in the words. *Christ*, Donovan thought, *he really is enjoying
himself. Maybe what he really needed was a war to fight.*

"Guess he decided not to suffer in silence," Donovan said.

Monroe squinted at him. "You think this is funny, boy?"

Donovan shook his head. "No. We'll take care of him."

"And just how do you figger to do that?"

"He's coming here," Donovan said. "I wouldn't be surprised if the
FBI gave him your address. They're letting him do their dirty work. But
I say, let him come."

"And let him rob me ever'where he goes along the way? That's your
damn solution?"

"What are you suggesting? I hit the road looking for him? We don't
know where he's going to hit next. But we know where he's going to end
up. Right here. And then I'll handle him."

"You couldn't before."

"He's off his head," Donovan said. "He's not thinking clearly. He's
outnumbered. When he gets here..."

"I want him alive," Monroe broke in. "I want an example made that
people are going to remember. I want his dyin' to last for *days*."

Donovan shook his head. "Bad idea. We just kill him, we can claim
we repelled an intruder. He turns up dead somewhere, with signs that
he's been tortured..." he shrugged. "Your call. But the way you want to
do it is going to get you arrested."

Monroe looked like a sulky child. "I want what I want."

"All right. I'll do what I can," Donovan lied. "But I'm not risking my
own life, or yours, to try and get him alive."

Monroe nodded. Then he grinned and began to laugh in a nasty
wheezing gurgle. "Once we do," he said, "We have us some fun."

Chapter Forty-five

The house at 601 Grampian looked the same as when Buckthorn had been there with Wolf and Dushane, except there were no motorcycles parked outside. He parked his truck in the driveway, in the space behind the Explorer where they'd been. He sat and watched the house for a moment, then got out. As he walked to the front door, he noticed all of the curtains were still drawn. He knocked. After a minute, the door opened slightly. He could see part of a young girl's face, one dark eye peering out at him. "Can I help you?" she said.

"Callie?" he said.

The eye narrowed slightly. "Yes?"

"Callie, my name's Tim Buckthorn. I was one of the people that found you."

The door closed. She heard the girl shout "MOM!" from behind it, followed by more shouted words he couldn't make out. He stood there for a few moments, unsure of what to do. He heard the sound of a chain being unfastened, then the door opened. Myra Preston stood there. She didn't look happy to see him. "Mr. Buckthorn," she said.

"Hi, Mrs. Preston," he said. "I was just checking back to see if you folks were all right. How's Callie?"

She looked around him and over his shoulder, as if checking to see if he was being followed. "You shouldn't be here."

He tensed. "What's going on?"

She seemed to make up her mind. "Come in before someone sees you." She stepped aside and he entered.

The living room was dim, only a small table lamp providing scant illumination. Callie stood beside the couch. She looked nervous. He saw that she still had a gauze bandage on one cheek, but the other cuts and bruises seemed to be fading.

"Hi, Callie," he said.

"Hello," she said. After an awkward moment, she said "Thanks for helping get me out. I heard that you found my picture."

He nodded.

"That's pretty weird," she said.

"The lady who found it said it was a sign. She said that God meant for me to find you."

"Oh." She didn't seem to know what else to say.

He turned to Myra. "How are you holding up?" The look on her face troubled him. "What's wrong?"

"I'm not supposed to talk to you. Or any police."

"Wait," he said, "the FBI was supposed to be guarding you."

"They were," Callie said. "They went away."

"They weren't going to stay forever," Myra said. "Not like..." she stopped.

"Not like the Monroes? Or Donovan?" Buckthorn felt the anger rising in him again. "Have they been back?"

"I don't know who Donovan is," she said. "I swear it. But as soon as the FBI stopped watching us, I started getting phone calls. The same voice, every time. Telling us they were just checking. To make sure we weren't talking to the wrong people."

"Did the person calling have an accent?" he said. "Irish, maybe?"

She shook her head. "Not that I could tell."

"Did you call the FBI back? Or the local cops?" He shook his head. "What am I saying?"

"Right," she said. "I don't know who to trust."

"You can trust me," Buckthorn said.

She laughed bitterly. "You? Are you going to stay here forever? You think you can protect us from them?"

"You'll go away," Callie said, "and they'll come back." He looked at her, saw the defeat and hopelessness in her face. "They always come back," she said.

He felt a shock of agony go through his head and realized that he'd clenched his jaw on the broken tooth. The pain was so intense, he groaned involuntarily.

Myra looked alarmed. "Are you okay?"

"I'm fine," he rasped.

"You don't sound like it," she said.

"Actually, I could use an aspirin."

She nodded, still looking dubious, and left the room. He turned to Callie. "I am going away," he said. "And I'm not coming back. But neither are they."

"How are you going to stop them?"

The pain had settled to a dull throb. His voice sounded like it was coming from someone else. "I'm going to take care of them."

Myra had returned with a bottle of ibuprofen and a small plastic cup of water. "How do you plan to do that? Arrest them?"

He shook two of the tablets out into his hand and popped them into his mouth. He handed the bottle back to her, took the water and washed them down. "No," he said. "You're right. They'd just come back. Or have someone else do it. Arresting them won't protect you."

"Wait, aren't you a cop?" Callie said.

"Not anymore," he said. He walked to the door. "Thanks for the painkillers."

"You haven't told us what you plan to do," Myra said.

He paused and turned back. "I'm going to end them," he said simply. He walked out, leaving a stunned silence behind him.

***

"This isn't going to end well," Patience said.

"Not to worry, love," Donovan answered. "We've got it sorted."

She shook her head. "No," she said, "you really don't. Oh, I know you think you do. But say you really do get this man. Say you kill him. What then?"

He shrugged. "Bury him, I suppose."

She rubbed her temples in frustration. "And after? Every cop and FBI agent in the world is going to be all over this place." She looked up. "We need to get out of here. We need to run."

"No."

"Don't be an idiot. We have..."

The blow came so fast, she never saw it. All she knew was that she was sagging against the wall. It was all that had kept her from falling on her ass. Her cheek hurt so bad, she thought the bone might be broken.

"Listen to me, *darlin'*," he said, biting down hard on the last word. "You don't talk to me that way. Ever. Ya follow?"

She straightened up, her hand going to her face. "I can't believe you just..."

She didn't see him move this time, either. Suddenly she was pinned against the wall with his hand tight around her throat where he had grabbed her and shoved her backwards so fast the back of her head had rebounded off it. *He's so fast*, she thought. He began tightening his grip, cutting off her air.

"I said, do ya *follow*?" His voice was a low, vicious snarl.

She couldn't answer. He wasn't letting her breathe. She raised her hands to her throat to dislodge his grip. He pulled a fist back, ready to smash into her face again. "Don't," he said. She dropped her hands to her side, hating herself for doing so.

Her vision narrowed, black spots appearing before her eyes. *I'm dying*, she thought. *He's killing me...* "Just nod your head if you understand," he said. His voice was a deadly purr now. With her last strength, she nodded her head as rapidly as she could. Then she was gasping, taking in huge gulps of sweet, cool air. She sank to her knees and began to cough. He grabbed her by her hair and pulled her head up to look at him.

"I think I like you like that," he said. "I think, when I'm king, you'll be spending a lot of time on your knees."

She looked up at him, rubbing her bruised throat, unable to speak. She could see the bulge in the front of his pants. The son of a bitch was getting turned on.

"Things are going to change around here," he said. He turned and walked off, leaving her there.

"Honey," she croaked softly, "you have no *fucking* idea."

Chapter Forty-six

Buckthorn cruised slowly by the Monroe house. It was far out in the country, north of the city. Overgrown fields ran for a half mile either side of the house and across the road, testifying to a productivity that had long since gone by the wayside. Where cotton had once grown, the thick black Mississippi soil had nurtured thick, gnarled webs and tangles of kudzu. The plant, native to Japan, had been brought to Mississippi in the 1930's to curb soil erosion. Freed of its natural competitors, however, the tough, durable weed had overwhelmed all other native vegetation. Even the few trees that had made a try in the neglected fields had lost to the invader and now stood, wrapped in cocoons of green.

There was a stone wall at least ten feet high encircling the house proper. Access to the driveway was through a huge double sided wrought iron gate. The gate was closed and, he assumed, locked. The entranceway was paved with cobblestones that ended a few feet on the other side of the gate and gave way to a more modern concrete driveway that sloped gently upwards to the house itself. The place was huge, two stories high, with shallow porches above and below supported by pillars that had once been white, but now showed long streaks of gray where the paint had peeled away. Glass windows on both sides flanked the double front door. The heavy curtains behind the windows were closed. As he watched, a man crossed his field of vision, walking with the bored slouch of someone who'd been on guard duty too long. Bored or not, Buckthorn knew the guard could bring the rifle he had slung on his back into play before he could get halfway up that driveway. He was also willing to bet there were other armed men inside. And he had no idea how to even get through the gate. The shotgun he carried behind the seat wouldn't do much against that massive iron latch. You'd need a battering ram. Or...an idea occurred to him. He looked at the bags of money he'd collected in the floorboard of the truck. His idea would probably take all of it. *But*, he thought, it's *like they say. You can't take it with you.*

He stepped on the gas and pulled away from the driveway. He didn't see the rental car pulling in across the road from the house as he left.

***

"This one's got some miles on it," the salesman said, "but you can't hardly beat the price."

Buckthorn nodded. He got up on the step next to the driver's side door and looked into the truck's cab. The vinyl driver's seat was cracked and patched with duct tape. More duct tape held a piece of cardboard in place where the right side window used to be. A thin layer of dust covered the dash. Buckthorn stepped down. "Does it even run?" he asked.

The salesman looked indignant. "Course it runs," he said. His confidence was made somewhat less convincing by the sweat that sheened his forehead beneath the long, sparse strands of his comb-over. "The engine's been overhauled. The hydraulics all work, I tested 'em myself. And all the brakes are 50% or better, guaranteed." He pulled a set of keys out of the pocket of his short-sleeved polyester dress shirt. "Take it for a test drive." He jingled the keys as if trying to amuse a baby.

Buckthorn ignored them. "How much?"

The salesman looked surprised and dropped his hand to his side. "Thirty-five," he said.

Buckthorn squinted up at the truck appraisingly. "Shit," he said.

"It's a bargain," the salesman insisted. "The brakes are guaranteed."

"And if they fail," Buckthorn said, "you expect me to come back from beyond the grave to collect?" The man started to answer, but Buckthorn cut him off. "I'll give you twenty-five."

"Now wait..."

"Cash."

The man fell silent. His watery blue eyes narrowed in suspicion. "I'd need to see, like a cashier's or bank check."

"Maybe I didn't make myself clear. I mean actual cash. Greenbacks. *Dinero*."

The man rubbed his chin, his eyes narrowing. "You got that much cash on you?"

Buckthorn nodded towards his truck parked next to a row of Freightliner tractors. "Right over there."

"Don't believe in banks, do ya?"

"Let's just say I'm a little bit old school. Don't like to be in anyone's debt. And I'm not real fond of the tax man, either, If you catch my drift."

The salesman nodded. "I heard that."

"So if you want to sort of slow walk the paperwork, it won't bother me much."

The salesman began smiling. "I think we might be able to work something out."

"Good," Buckthorn said. He looked the big Mack dump truck over again, from the high set cab with its flaking green paint to the 20 foot long, high-sided bed. "And don't worry about the brakes. I'm only using it for one job."

Chapter Forty-seven

"The voice mailbox for this user is full. Please try again..."

Dushane killed the message with a savage punch of her finger. She felt like throwing the damn phone out the window of the car. Buckthorn's mailbox was full, all right, and she was willing to bet most of the messages were from her. Angry, warning, pleading...she'd tried every tone she could think of to get him to respond. He hadn't. She didn't know if he wasn't answering because he'd turned his phone off, because he was just being stubborn, or because he'd pushed his luck and gotten himself killed by Donovan or one of Monroe's other goons. The uncertainty was doing what uncertainty always did: it was driving her crazy.

"Nothing?" Wolf said from the driver's seat of the cheap rental they'd gotten at the airport. They were parked on the shoulder, across the country road from the front gate of Lampton Monroe's estate. There was an overgrown field to their right, with a badly tended dirt access road leading deep into the tangled growth in front of them. They'd considered pulling into the field to set up, but when they'd tried it, they saw that the jungle of vegetation all around obscured their peripheral vision. Besides, Dushane said, if Buckthorn came, they wanted him to know they were there. Maybe that would stop him from his mad quest.

They could see a bit of the front of the house from between the iron posts of the huge swinging gate. It was silent, all shades drawn. From time to time, men would enter or come out of the house. They could see other men walking the grounds. All were armed. If Buckthorn showed up, he was going to be walking into a hornet's nest.

"No," she said, shaking her head. "The bastard."

Wolf grunted and looked at his own phone sitting in its hands-free rack on the dash. "Gaby's not returning calls either."

"Sorry."

"Why?" he said. He looked straight ahead. "You never liked her."

She was surprised. "When did I say that?"

"You didn't have to."

"Boss," she protested, "I like her fine."

"Skip it," he said curtly.

She wasn't going to let it go. "Look, Tony, you know as well as I do what surveillance can be like if one of the partners has a bug up his ass about something. It's a special kind of hell. If you're mad at me, let's have it. If you're just mad…"

He sighed. "You're right. I'm sorry. I'm worried about her. No reason for me to take it out on you."

"You got that right."

He looked at her, one corner of his mouth quirking. "You know, you can be a hard person to apologize to."

"Oh, I know. But I truly am sorry that you're hurting."

"Thanks." He raised the binoculars again, peered at the house. "You actually think he's coming here?"

"I don't know," she admitted. "But it makes sense."

Wolf nodded. "If he really is after the people who killed his sister, this is where he'll be."

"Oh, he's after them, all right. I saw the look in his eye."

"We've got another visitor," Wolf said.

She felt the approach of the big truck as much as heard it, the rumble of the big, badly tuned diesel engine sending a deep bass vibration ahead of it. She turned around in her seat to look, the relaxed slightly. "Dump truck," she said as it rolled into view.

"I didn't see any construction around."

She raised her binoculars to her eyes and peered through the back windshield. The man in the driver's seat was wearing dark glasses and a ball cap. As the view came into better focus, she could read the lettering. "Oh, shit."

"What?"

"It's Buckthorn."

"In a dump truck? What the hell is he..." Wolf looked at the iron gate. "Oh, no."

Dushane lowered the binoculars. "Oh, yes."

"He wouldn't."

"He is."

"We need to stop him," Wolf said.

"Any ideas?"

He started the car. "Get in his way?"

She shook her head. "I wouldn't."

"You seriously believe he'll run over us?"

"I don't know," she said. "I'm not sure I want to find out."

"Shit. It's too late anyway." Buckthorn had pulled even with them. He looked down and saw Wolf in the driver's seat. He didn't change expression. After a moment, he waved.

"BUCKTHORN!" Wolf shouted. "TIM!" he started to roll the window down. Buckthorn had turned around and was backing the truck up, into the dirt road in front of them. When he was done, the front of the truck was pointed directly at the iron gate across the street. The rumble went up and up in pitch as Buckthorn revved the engine higher and higher until it had turned into an all-consuming roar like some raging prehistoric beast.

Wolf and Dushane piled out of the car and started to run towards the dump truck, shouting and waving. Buckthorn didn't look at them as he popped the clutch. The tires kicked up a choking cloud of thick, gritty black dust as the wheels spun, then bit deep into the soil. The truck leaped forward, headed straight towards the gate.

***

Buckthorn felt the impact through the soles of his boots as well as his hands on the wheel and gearshift as the truck smashed into the iron gate. It held for a split second, then the barrier gave way at the latch and burst open with a scream of rending metal. The left half of the gate was torn from the hinges and flew off to one side, while the right swung hard to the limit of its traverse, then bounced back, slamming against the right side door. The mirror shattered, spraying tiny slivers of glass through the hole where he'd taken the cardboard off the window. The metal frame of the mirror caught for a moment on the gate, then ripped off.

Pushing through the resistance of the gate had slowed the truck's forward motion, so Buckthorn shifted down, the engine coughing and belching smoke, the transmission whining as he began a ponderous climb up the slope towards the house. He saw the front door open and a pair of men ran out, assault weapons at the ready. He reached over with his left hand and picked the shotgun up off the seat beside him. He hung it out the window, pointed at the running men, and fired one-handed. The recoil felt like it nearly broke his wrist, and he almost lost his grip on the shotgun. The shot went wild, as he knew it probably would, but it had the desired effect. The two men scattered in opposite directions. He saw another figure disappear from the open door. He pulled the shotgun back in, laid it on the seat, and shifted again. He'd reached the front of the mansion, but instead of turning towards it, he spun the wheel and turned away, towards the trees. He took the truck out of gear and stopped, the air brakes hissing. He could hear the sound of shouting, then a gunshot. A loud bang came from the side of the truck, just behind the cab. Buckthorn reached down, with his right hand this time, and picked up his pistol from where it lay alongside the shotgun. An angry, yelling face appeared in the window. One of Monroe's braver goons had leaped up on the running board, pointing an ugly black semi-automatic pistol at him. Buckthorn didn't fire; he transferred his own gun from his right hand to his left, then back-handed the man across the face with the long barrel. A bright red gash spurted blood across his sleeve as the man screamed and fell away from the truck. Buckthorn laid the pistol in his lap and grabbed the wheel. He completed the three-point turn, looked in the remaining mirror to confirm he was lined up with the dump bed centered on the front door, then jockeyed the gearshift into reverse. A loud piercing beep began to sound. The engine roared, the transmission whined, and the tires spun for a moment on the driveway before they again found traction. The truck gave a convulsive leap backwards, then picked up speed, headed for the double front doors, the backup alarm blaring.

***

"What the fuck?" Lamp Monroe said as he sat bolt upright. He'd been lying on the bed with Patience. They were both fully clothed, but he'd been dozing with his head pillowed between her breasts. Recent events had made him more frisky; she'd had to gently move a roaming hand away as he'd pawed at her before drifting off. She didn't know what he was going to do if he got more demanding.

There was the sound of shouting and of running feet outside the bedroom door. She heard a single hard, firm knock, then Donovan burst in. He had a pistol in one hand. His brow furrowed as he took in their position on the bed, then turned to Monroe.

"It's the front gate," he said. "Some crazy bastard just drove a dump truck through the front gate."

"A dump truck?" Patience said.

They heard more yelling, then a faraway series of gunshots.

"It's got to be Buckthorn," Donovan said.

"No shit," Monroe sneered. "What are you going to do about it?"

Donovan racked the slide on the weapon. "Don't worry," he said. "I'll take care of it."

The floor under their feet trembled as the whole house shook, as if in the grip of an earthquake. Another shock ran through the place, harder than the first.

"Oh, my God," Patience said.

There was an immense crack, then a long low rumble that shivered through the floor again. A fissure appeared above the lintel of the doorway, then ran upwards to the ceiling. They could hear an insistent, rhythmic beep through the closed door.

"Mebbe we ought to start worryin'," Monroe said.

Chapter Forty-eight

"Well, there's something you don't see every day," Wolf said. They were outside the ruined gate, watching as the big truck smashed backwards through the front door and the surrounding doorway. The front of the building crumbled before the onslaught, bricks and mortar tumbling down like an avalanche. The sound of the collapse was like thunder, overriding the engine. The truck stopped, then the engine coughed and grumbled like a giant clearing his throat. There was a clash and a horrible metallic rasp of gears. The truck began to move forward, the backup alarm falling silent. The air brakes hissed, the brake drums squealed, and the truck came to a stop with the dump bed half in and half out of the building.

"Looks like probable cause to me, Agent Wolf," Dushane said, her mouth set in a grim line. She drew her weapon and racked the slide.

He did the same. "I agree, Agent Dushane. With exigent circumstances, even."

They started up the driveway at a jog, weapons at the ready. They heard another alarm, then the high pitched grind and whine of hydraulics. As they drew closer, they saw that the entire middle section of the front wall had collapsed, rubble spilling out of the huge hole. There was a loud metallic clatter from inside. They saw the dump bed begin to rise.

"Oh, fuck," Dushane whispered.

A loud hissing sound filled the air, followed by a deep rumble. Clouds of gray dust billowed from the hole on either side of the truck. A long-haired, bearded man in a leather jacket stumbled out of the cloud, next to the driver's side door. He stood up, weaving slightly, as if drunk or stunned. He was holding an assault rifle down by his side.

"FEDERAL AGENT! DROP THE WEAPON!" Dushane yelled. The man looked at them as if he couldn't believe what he was seeing. He shook his head as if to clear it, then looked up at the cab of the truck. He scowled, then stepped closer to the truck, raising the assault rifle. Dushane and Wolf stopped simultaneously and took aim, each one dropping into a perfectly synchronized combat crouch. Before they could fire, however, the truck door flew open, slamming into the end of the rifle barrel. The man stumbled back, fumbling with the weapon. Buckthorn leaped from the truck, holding a shotgun pointed straight at the man's face. The man tried to bring his weapon to bear again, but Buckthorn spoke a single word that they could hear from where they stood: "Don't." There was the promise of a world of hurt contained in that one word. The man froze.

"DROP THE WEAPON!" Dushane yelled again. It wasn't clear which of the two men she was shouting at, but only the bearded man dropped his rifle. Buckthorn stepped on it with one booted foot and gestured with the barrel of the shotgun. "Over there," they heard him say. The man started to rise, but Buckthorn placed the barrel of the shotgun against his leather-clad back. "No," he said. "Crawl." The man rose to all fours and began scuttling towards Wolf and Dushane like a bug.

"YOU TOO, TIM!" Dushane shouted.

"Come on, man," Wolf urged in a more normal voice. "Don't do anything stupid."

"Little late for that, Tony," Buckthorn said. He bent down to pick up the assault rifle. Wolf heard Dushane suck in her breath, then mutter something under her breath. He couldn't make out what she said clearly, but it sounded like "please, no." He realized he was holding his own breath, waiting for the shot. It didn't come. The bearded rifleman had reached them. He looked up at them, for all the world like a whipped dog. They took their eyes off Buckthorn for a moment to look at him, and in that moment, Buckthorn had slung the shotgun on his back and headed into the house through the ruined front, crouched over, holding the assault rifle in front of him.

"I'm going after him," Wolf said. "Secure the prisoner..."

"No," Dushane said flatly. "You take this lowlife. I'm going after Tim."

"Agent Dushane, I'm giving you a direct order."

"And I'm disobeying it, Agent Wolf," she said. "You can bring me up in front of OPR if you can stand the wait in line. But I'm still the person he's most likely to listen to." They could hear the faraway wail of approaching sirens. She gestured with her pistol in the direction of the sound. "And unlike those guys, I probably won't shoot him by mistake."

"By *mistake*," he repeated, emphasizing the last word.

"Yeah." She started towards the house. "Follow me when you get this lamebrain squared away, okay?"

"Wait," Wolf said. He looked down at the man cowering in the grass. "Maybe he can give us some intel."

She didn't stop. "If he does, let me know. But there's no time." A flurry of shots sounded from inside. She broke into a run.

"All right, asshole," Wolf said to his prisoner. "On your feet. And start talking."

Chapter Forty-nine

The half-ton of pea-sized gravel that he'd dumped in the front hall of the big mansion had overflowed out the hole he'd punched in the front wall, forming a short slope. Buckthorn climbed it easily, holding the rifle at his shoulder, looking at the world through the front sights. He'd trained with a similar weapon when he'd taken selected members of his department through a grueling week of tactical training at the Justice Academy in Salemburg. It all seemed like a long time ago, almost another lifetime, but he was relieved to feel it all coming back to him. *Even if I'll never be a law enforcement officer again*, he thought. That sent a pang through his chest, but he shoved the regret aside. There was work to be done. He reached the top of the tiny hillock he'd created and entered.

The gravel had smashed into the front hall like a wave, crushing everything before it. The hall ran a good distance on either side of the front door, ending in large glassed-in French doors on either side. The doors led to what looked like a parlor of some kind to his left one side and a dining room on the right. Both rooms appeared to be unused, most of the furniture covered with white sheets. The place looked deserted. The ceiling of the hall ran up to the second floor, with a long railed gallery overlooking the entranceway. Stairways on either side led up to the gallery.

Buckthorn heard a low moan. He swiveled the rifle towards the sound.

A man lay against the wall, half buried in the gravel that had piled up against it. He was only semiconscious, his head lolled back against the wall. He had grimy olive skin and stringy black hair combed

inexpertly over his considerable bald spot. Buckthorn could see the
splintered remains of what looked like an antique chair sticking up
around him. He stepped over. "Hey," he said. He nudged the man in the
chest with his boot. "Hey. Wake up."

The man's eyes opened blearily. "Who..." he rasped.

"Where's Sean Donovan?" Buckthorn demanded. "And Lampton
Monroe?"

The man seemed to be recovering some of his faculties. "Fuck you,"
he said, his voice still hoarse and fuzzy. He flailed around on top of the
gravel with his hands, obviously searching for something.

Buckthorn raised the rifle. "You looking for a weapon under there?"

The man looked up, his eyes widening. "No," he said in a small
voice.

"Son," Buckthorn said, "you are the worst damn liar I have ever
seen. And that is saying something." He raised the rifle. "I don't think
I should leave you behind me."

The man threw up his hands in front of this face. "Please," he
whined. "Please don't kill me."

Buckthorn hesitated, then sighed. He lowered the rifle. He caught a
sudden movement out of the corner of his eye and looked up. Another
man, in jeans and a leather vest and sporting a Mohawk, was aiming
down at him from the gallery above. Buckthorn brought his own
weapon up and fired, just as the man let off a three-round burst. The
sound of the shots was deafening in the enclosed space. The screaming
of the half-buried man added to the din. Mohawk's shots thudded into
the gravel at Buckthorn's feet, just as one of Buckthorn's shots struck
the gunman under the chin. The bullet passed upwards through his
skull, exiting out the back of his head in a spray of blood, skull fragments, and gray matter. He fell over backwards and lay still. Buckthorn
swept the gallery from one end to the other with his rifle sight, looking
for more guards. He saw none. He swiveled the rifle back down to bear
on the half-buried man, who squealed and thrashed frantically, trying
to get up. The action apparently caused him great pain. His panicked
cry turned into a howl of agony that trailed off to sobbing. "I think I got
a broke leg," he whimpered.

"I'll get you some help," Buckthorn said, "If you tell me what I want to know." From outside, he heard the approaching sirens. Help was on the way anyway, but not for him. "Where's Lampton Monroe?"

"Upstairs," the man said. "To the left."

"Then?"

"Take the left-hand hallway. All the way. The bedroom at the end. That's Monroe's room."

"What about Donovan?"

The man shook his head. "I don't know," he said. "I swear. I think he and the redhead have a room, but I don't know which one. Please, man, get me a doctor. I feel...I think I might be bleeding."

"I'll see what I can do," Buckthorn said, "but I got something to do first."

"What might that be, Captain Buckthorn?" a voice said behind him. He whirled, his finger tightening on the trigger.

Leila Dushane stood there, by the back bumper of the dump truck that projected so surreally into the genteel living space of the front hall. She had her gun hand down by her side.

"Leila," he said.

"Hey," she said. "You didn't return my calls."

"Sorry," he said. "Been a little busy."

"So I can see." She gestured at the truck next to her. "I've got to give you points for style, at least."

"Shock and awe, you know?"

"I know," she said. "I'd actually congratulate you for creative thinking if I didn't have to arrest you for it."

"You can do that later," he said.

"Sorry," she said. "Can't wait." She reached into the pocket of her suit pants and pulled out the zip cuffs. "You're going to need to put the gun..." she stopped in mid-sentence and raised her own weapon. "GUN!" she shouted. Buckthorn's finger tightened instinctively on the trigger, and he came within a hairs-breadth of shooting Leila down. But when she fired it was up and over him. He turned to see another man with an assault rifle duck back into a doorway along the gallery, Leila's shots turning the wood of the jamb to splinters.

"Thanks," he said, scanning with his sights along the gallery for more targets.

"Maybe we need to continue this conversation outside," she said. Her voice trembled a bit, even as she tried to keep it calm.

"You know I have to do this," he said.

"I don't know any such goddamn thing..." she fired off two more shots as the door of the room where the man had taken refuge began to open. "STAY IN THE ROOM, KNUCKLEHEAD!" she yelled, "AND SLIDE THE WEAPON OUT ON THE FLOOR!"

"No!" the man in the room shouted back. "You'll kill me!"

"No I won't," Buckthorn called up. "I won't shoot an unarmed man."

"Yes he will!" the half-buried man yelled. "He almost shot me! He's crazy!"

"Shut up," Buckthorn and Dushane told him at the same time. He fell silent, staring at the two of them wide-eyed.

"Come on, Tim," she said, lowering the gun. "This isn't you. You're a sworn officer of the law, remember?"

"We've had this conversation," he said. "I couldn't keep Loretta safe. I couldn't keep my town safe. I can't keep you safe."

"I'm sorry about Loretta. I really am. I liked her. I could see us being friends. I could...I could even see us being sisters. But she wouldn't want this. She loved you. And as for me, I can take care of myself."

"No," he said, "You can't." He gestured up the stairs. "They're going to keep coming. The law can't stop them. They've got walls of people they've paid off, a whole maze of lies and corruption they hide behind. They come out and strike like snakes. Then they slither back here. Well, I'm cleaning out the nest."

"That's real poetic, Tim. Dramatic, even. But all this is going to accomplish is to get you locked up. Or killed."

"It's a price I'm willing to pay."

"Well that's great," she said. "That's just fucking fantastic. And I guess I was just a passing thing to you?"

"No," he said. "That's not..."

"Oh, shove it," she said. "You'd rather martyr yourself like this than live with what you stupidly think is your own failure, not to mention being with me. It's bullshit, Tim. It's cowardly bullshit, and I'm calling you out on it." She raised her pistol and pointed it at him. "Now drop the fucking weapon and put your hands on top of your head."

"If I don't, are you going to shoot me?"

"I might shoot you anyway," she said. "I'm that pissed off."

He shook his head and chuckled. "You are really something, Agent Dushane."

"Too bad it took you so long to realize it. Now...GUN!" she turned and began firing up at the gallery again. Buckthorn pivoted and fired blindly. Another gunman, this one wielding what looked like a stubby MAC-10, had come out of the side hallway. His covering fire gave the man in the room a chance to scuttle out and join him. He heard Leila cry out in pain. He looked to see her stumbling backwards, behind the cover of the truck bed. A snarl twisted his face as the turned and began shooting back up, moving sideways towards her position as he fired. The men took cover again, and he darted around the truck.

Leila was sitting on the floor, just inside the ruined doorway, leaning back against one of the truck tires. She had pulled her jacket off. The right sleeve of her white blouse was soaked in blood. She rolled up the sleeve, grimacing. More blood pulsed from a hole in her bicep. Her face was white with shock.

"Happy now?" she snarled.

Chapter Fifty

Donovan moved down the hallway, listening to the sounds of combat from below. He saw one of Monroe's security guards at the end of the hall, where it connected with the gallery over the front entrance hall. He was breathing hard and his face was chalk-white. His weapon, a MAC-10, was cradled uselessly in his arms.

"What the fuck are you doing?"

"The crazy bastard backed a goddamn truck through the front door," the man said, "and dumped a fucking load of gravel in the front hall. Now he and some bitch are down there, shooting at anything that moves. I think they killed Boyle."

"So you're hiding up here like a little girl?" Donovan snarled. "Get the fuck back in the game, boyo, before they come up those stairs after you." From below, he could hear shouting from downstairs. It sounded like an argument.

"Keep their attention up here," he ordered the guard. "I'll go down the back stairs and flank them through that front parlor, off to the side of the entrance."

The man shook his head. "They'll shoot me."

"What's your name, son?" Donovan asked.

"Moody," the man said. "Bill Moody."

Donovan raised his own weapon. "Well, Bill Moody," he said, "I'll shoot you myself if you don't get your arse in gear."

Moody swallowed. "Okay." Donovan turned and broke into a jog back down the hallway. He heard the rattle of gunfire behind him and a shout of pain. He wondered who'd been hit.

He stopped first at the old man's bedroom. "Buckthorn smashed a truck through the front..." he stopped. Monroe was lying on his back on the bed, his breath coming in a ghastly rattle. Patience sat in a chair beside the bed. She was holding one of the old man's hands in hers, gently stroking it. "Hush now," she whispered. "Hush now."

"What's happening?" Donovan said.

"Heart attack, I think," she said. She looked at him and smiled. The sight made him uneasy. He saw the bruises rising on her cheek and her throat and felt a quick flash of guilt. He shouldn't have lost his head like that. He wondered if what he'd done had unhinged her. "It won't be long now."

The old man looked over at him. Spittle flecked the sides of his mouth. "Med..." he croaked. "G'me...med..."

"He wants his medicine," Patience said with that same uncanny smile.

"But you're not going to give it to him."

She shook her head. "No. It's his time. Go do what you have to do."

He looked over her shoulder at the man on the bed. He was flailing weakly, his eyes filled with impotent rage.

"Let me worry about him," she said. "Go. Do this. And then you'll be king."

It was an easy decision to make. Donovan wanted nothing more at that point than to be out of that room with the dying man and the woman who was his angel of death. He'd had dreams of being king, with Patience as his queen. But he didn't know if he'd ever be able to lie next to her and close his eyes again. Not after seeing that smile. As he exited the room, he looked back to see her seated again in the chair.

"Uck...ucking...itch..." Monroe was trying to speak, but the words couldn't make it past the dying parts of his brain. The light in his eyes was dimming.

"Hush now," Patience murmured. "Hush now."

Donovan fled.

Chapter Fifty-one

"Sorry," Buckthorn said. He stepped over her and knelt down, keeping one eye on the gallery.

"Sorry isn't going to plug this hole," Dushane said. "So I guess you have to call off this nonsense and get me out of here."

He raised the rifle and fired off a couple of quick shots. The man who'd been inching down the gallery, trying to get a shot at them, scuttled back. He looked at her pistol lying next to her. "Can you shoot?"

She shook her head. "Everything below the elbow is numb. Everything above it hurts like hell. Come *on*, Tim!"

Instead of answering, Buckthorn opened the door of the truck and stood up on the running board for a moment, reaching inside. He came back out with the rifle in the crook of his arm and a brown paper bag in the other hand.

"What the hell are you doing?" she said.

"I need to get rid of those people up there," he said. "This'll help."

"What about me?" she demanded.

"Once these people are taken care of," he said, "you can get out on your own." He pulled two 2-liter soda bottles out of the bag. Each was half filled with a cloudy liquid.

"What are those?" she said.

"Distractions." He set the bottles down in the gravel, rotating them back and forth to seat them more firmly. He looked up to make sure the gunmen above were still hanging back, then quickly unscrewed the caps.

"Having a drink?" she said.

"Not of this," he replied. He pulled two rolled up cylinders of aluminum foil out of the bag. He looked up quickly, then shoved the cylinders into the necks of the bottles.

"Oh, no," she said. "You are not..."

"Learned this one from a kid I know," he said as he quickly screwed the caps back on. "A little Drano, a little water, pop in some aluminum foil..." He plucked the bottles up out of the gravel by the necks and shook them vigorously. Dushane looked on in horror as the liquid inside the bottle began to fizz and give off a white smoke. The plastic began to visibly stretch and expand. Buckthorn stepped to the end of the truck bed, then leaped out from cover and slung first one, then the other bottle up into the gallery. There was a stutter of gunfire and bullets clanged off the metal of the truck bed as Buckthorn leaped back. "Instant grenade," he said.

***

Moody was getting frustrated. He was glad when Boyle had bolted from the room along the gallery and joined him, not dead as he'd first thought. But he could still see the body of Mofield lying near the far door. The people below needed to pay for that; he'd known Mofield since they were in Kuwait in '91. But they'd retreated back behind the truck that filled the hall below, and every time he and Boyle tried to move down to get a better angle, they were driven back by a fusillade of bullets. It was a damned stalemate, and it was pissing Moody off. The Irishman had said he was going to try and flank their adversary, but Moody figured he'd just used that as an excuse to haul ass.

Suddenly, the man below, the one they were pretty sure was Buckthorn, stepped out from cover. Moody was so startled, he didn't raise his weapon until two objects he couldn't identify were arcing through the air towards him. Boyle, crouched beside him, got off a couple of shots, but surprise had spoiled his aim as well, and the bullets ricocheted harmlessly off the truck. Moody looked down as one of the objects landed between him and Boyle. He barely had time to re-sister that it was a soda bottle before it exploded. The report deafened him, and his face and hands were immediately covered with an awful, caustic liquid that burned and fizzed. He could feel his flesh blistering, and he couldn't see. He could hear Boyle screaming, and another voice crying in pain that he realized was his own. He heard the thunder of steps. *He's coming up the staircase,* Moody thought. He fired blindly, unable to see who or what he was shooting at through the haze of agony that held his face in its awful grip. Then the shots slammed into him and took the pain away.

***

Dushane slowly got to her feet as Buckthorn pounded up the staircase. From where she stood, she couldn't see the gunmen on the second floor, but she could hear them screaming. There was a short burst of fire that blew bits of plaster out of the ceiling above Buckthorn's head. She saw him crouch and fire, and the screaming stopped. Cursing under her breath, she bent down to pick up her gun with her left hand.

"L.D.," a voice said.

She turned and stood up without picking up the weapon. Tony Wolf was standing in the rubble of the doorway, a shocked expression on his face. "You're hurt," he said.

"Yeah," she answered, her voice tight with pain.

"Where's Buckthorn?"

She gestured with her good hand. "Took out two goons with a homemade grenade and ran upstairs. What's going on out there?"

He holstered his weapon, stepped forward and gently took her arm to examine the wound. "Local PD's cordoned off the area. Waiting for the SWAT team."

"Sounds familiar," she said. "But it'll be too late by the time they get here. He's not taking hostages."

"I know," he said. "We need to get you out of here."

She looked back at the staircase, fighting back the urge to scream and pound the side of the truck in frustration. "I couldn't talk him out of it, boss," she said. "I thought I could."

"You tried," Wolf said.

"And don't think I don't appreciate it," a voice said. They turned. Wolf reached for his holstered weapon, then froze. They saw a man with dark curly hair standing in the open doorway. He had a rifle raised to his shoulder and pointed at them. Dushane recognized him as the man from the construction site.

"Mr. Donovan, I presume."

He smiled. "The same," he said. "Now step away from that pistol on the ground, sweetness, before you get any silly ideas. And you," he gestured at Wolf. "Take yours out of the holster, two fingers, very careful."

"Why?" Wolf said. "You're going to kill us anyway."

"Maybe," he said. "Maybe not. But if you don't do as I say, you'll definitely die. Then her. And I'll make sure she does it slowly."

Wolf stared at him. She could see the hatred burning in his eyes. He reached down to his holster and pulled the gun out between two fingers.

"Boss, no," she said. But he dropped the gun into the rubble at his feet.

"Now," Donovan said, "let's take a trip upstairs." He gestured with the rifle. "You first."

They preceded him out from behind the shelter of the truck. The man who'd been half buried in the gravel had worked his way free. He was hobbling on one leg towards the opposite side of the house, bracing himself on the wall. The bottom of his right leg was canted at a sickening angle from the rest of it. He stopped and turned as he heard them.

"Donovan," he said. "I need a doctor."

"No you don't," Donovan said. He fired quickly, three rounds smashing the man into the wall. He slumped to the floor, a look of shock and agony on his face.

"You fucking animal," Dushane whispered.

"Loose ends, dear," he said. "Now walk."

Chapter Fifty-two

H e'd emptied the last of the assault rifle's magazine when he'd charged the last two guards. He considered stripping the ammunition from the three dead men in the gallery, but he found himself unslinging the shotgun as he stepped over them and advanced down the hall. It somehow felt righter. It was his own weapon, one he'd grown up with, and its familiar heft felt reassuring in his hands. He felt his heart racing, and his head was light with a reckless, unshackled feeling, as if he was racing down a dark road at maximum speed. He entered the bedroom, the gun held high in front of him.

A red-haired woman sat by a hospital bed across the room. Her hands were folded in her lap, and she was smiling sweetly. There was a red, angry bruise on her cheek, and a ring of red marks around her throat. The man in the bed was still, unseeing eyes staring up at the ceiling. One side of his face was pulled down in a grotesque leer.

"If you've come to see Mr. Monroe," she said, "I'm afraid you're too late."

"Stand up," Buckthorn said. "Go over there by that wall."

Still smiling, she got up and complied. He moved across the room until he stood beside the bed.

"He's quite dead," the red-haired woman said.

"You don't seem that upset about it," Buckthorn said.

She shrugged. "As jobs go, I've had worse. But it's time we all moved on, don't you think?"

"Where's Donovan?"

"He went to fetch your friend," she said. "He'll be along directly."

"What do you mean?" he said.

"You'll see. But first, I want you to hear something."

He narrowed his eyes suspiciously. "What?"

"In the bedside table," she said, "there's a small voice recorder. I want you to get it out. It's already cued up."

"What's on it?"

"Something I think you'll be interested in," she said.

He sidled over to the table, never taking his eyes off of her.

"Top drawer," she said.

He opened the drawer, felt around inside with one hand until he felt something made of hard plastic. He pulled it out.

"Play it," the woman said.

He looked down until he found the "play" button. He pushed it. A wheezy old man's voice came out of the tiny speaker. "The ones that killed my grandson," the voice said. "I got names. Some hick deputy and two FBI people."

"I heard," another voice said.

"I want them dead..."

***

He marched them down the hallway, two abreast, keeping his distance with the rifle. "That door there," he said.

The door was open. Wolf entered first, Dushane behind him. Before she could pass through the doorway, however, she felt Donovan's hand snake around her neck and pull her against him. She felt something metal pressing against her temple. Donovan had either slung his rifle or put it down in favor of his pistol, the better to use her as a human shield.

"Now, darlin'," Donovan whispered in her ear. "Remember, no foolishness. Someone might get hurt."

She considered the odds of a quick snap of her head back into his nose, and decided she didn't like them. The moment she moved, he was likely to pull the trigger. She was also beginning to feel weak and dizzy. She'd lost more blood than she thought.

Donovan pushed her ahead of him, still holding her close from behind. As she entered the room, she saw Buckthorn. He was standing beside a red-haired woman sitting in a chair. She took in the woman's bizarrely serene smile and the bruises on her face and neck. Buckthorn had a strange expression on his face. He was holding the shotgun in one hand and a small black object she couldn't identify in the other. She looked behind them and drew a quick, shocked breath. An old man lay in the bed behind them. He was clearly dead.

"Well now," Donovan said. "Looks like we're all here for the party. Mr. Buckthorn, put the shotgun on the floor."

Buckthorn didn't move. "I'm not going to ask you again," Donovan said.

"He has something you might want to listen to," the red-haired woman said.

"I said..." Donovan began, but Buckthorn clicked a switch and a voice came out of the object in his hand. "The ones that killed my grandson," and old man's voice said. "I got names. Some hick deputy and two FBI people."

Dushane could feel the shock run through Donovan's body. Then he tensed, and she felt the gun at her temple move, ever so slightly. "Patience?" he said in a tight voice. "What are you playing at, love?"

Buckthorn snapped off the recorder and raised the shotgun in both hands. "Sean Donovan," he said, "I'm arresting you for the murder of Loretta Starnes, conspiracy to commit murder, and...he gestured towards Dushane, "assault on a Federal Agent."

Donovan's laugh was a quick bark of disbelief. "You can't be serious."

"I am," Buckthorn said. "Let Agent Dushane go."

"I don't think so," Donovan said. "And I'll be wanting that tape. Patience, I don't know what you think you're doing..."

"It's not the only copy," she said. "There's another one I've put away for safekeeping. And I just called the local FBI office to let them know where."

"What? Why?"

"Because you hit me, you son of a bitch."

"I didn't mean..." he began.

She cut him off. "Maybe not," she said, "but I'd already been thinking. Why be a consort? Why not be the real queen?" She stood up. "I originally made the tape as a shield. In case you ever wanted to cast me off. But then I also thought, why not a sword? And then you hit me, and you treated me like..." Her voice broke. "Like one of those whores in the truck stops, and I decided the time to pull that sword had come." She walked over to the old man's bed, laid a hand fondly on the dead chest. "You're done, Sean," she said. "The king is dead. Long live the queen."

"Look at it this way, Donovan," Buckthorn said. "She saved your life. I don't have to kill you now. There's the evidence I need to put you away legally. You don't have to die. Unless you don't put that gun down. "

"You fucking BITCH!" Donovan roared. The pressure of the gun barrel was suddenly gone from Dushane's temple. From the corner of her eyes, she could see the weapon pointed at the redhead. He was distracted, and Dushane seized the moment. She snapped her head back, as hard as she could, trying to break Donovan's nose. He'd moved too quickly, however; the back of her head smashed him in the cheek. But it was enough to spoil his aim. The bullet thudded sickeningly into the corpse in the bed. Dushane stomped hard on Donovan's instep. He howled with pain and rage and let go. She dove forward onto her face, screaming as she landed on the wounded arm. The pain was so intense it took the wind out of her. The world went red around the edges. She heard the roar of the shotgun, once, twice, and the sound of a body hitting the floor. Then she spiraled down into darkness.

Chapter Fifty-three

She'd interviewed a fair number of prisoners, in a lot of sad and shabby rooms, their faces pale and pinched with desperation behind the scratched and pitted Plexiglas. She had to admit, Buckthorn looked better than most. Calmer, more at peace. She took a deep breath and tried not to grasp the black phone receiver she held in her good hand hard enough for him to see the white-knuckle tension she felt.

"I've got to say," she said, "orange is not really your color."

Buckthorn looked down at the prisoner jumpsuit and chuckled. "I know," he said. "But you know what? It's actually kind of comfortable." His face turned serious. "How's the arm?"

She shrugged, then winced as the movement sent daggers of pain through the abused muscles. "They got the bullet fragments out. It's going to take a butt-load of physical therapy, but they say I'll get most of the function back."

"That's good." He paused. "How's the fallout? Back at work, I mean."

"I've got a hearing scheduled with OPR. But Tony tells me that the fix is in. I'll be back on regular duty inside a month."

"Friends in high places," Buckthorn said.

"Yeah." There was a brief awkward silence. "How about you?" she said.

This time it was his turn to shrug. "Stark dumped me like a bad habit," he said, without rancor. "But I guess I can't blame him. I may be here in Mississippi for a while. That sort of thing can really conflict with a political campaign."

She felt her throat tighten. "How long is a while?"

"Well that's kind of an amazing thing," Buckthorn said. "Apparently, the locals weren't all that fond of Monroe and his operation, either. They won't say it, but I think they're happy I cleaned the place out. At the same time, they don't want a whole lot of questions being asked about how he went so long operating under their noses."

She tried to keep from sounding too hopeful. "So they're cutting you loose?"

He shook his head. "No. There's the matter of four men, dead from my gun. They don't feel like they can just ignore that."

"Self-defense."

He smiled, a little sadly. "Doesn't really apply if you go looking for the fight."

"Then...I don't know..." she stopped, unwanted tears of frustration pooling in her eyes. "Doesn't the fact that they killed your sister carry any weight?"

The smile vanished. "Yeah. Some." He looked down at the floor, as if lost in thought.

"So?" she said. "Are you going to keep me guessing all day?"

He looked up, startled out of his reverie. "Sorry," he said. "My lawyer says he can get a deal for manslaughter. Two years."

Dismay and relief began warring in her heart. "That's not too bad," she said.

He rubbed his hands over his face. "It doesn't seem like enough."

"Oh for God's SAKE, Tim!" she exploded. She wanted to slam the phone down.

He looked surprised. "What?"

The words caught in her throat. He went on before she could untangle them. "I betrayed my oath, Leila. I was a sworn officer of the law. I..."

"Oh will you PLEASE shut up!" she snapped. He did. They glared at one another through the Plexiglas for a few moments. This time, she broke the silence. "Tim," she said in a subdued voice, "I fell in love with you because you were a Good Guy. I don't just mean a good man, I mean a Good Guy with a capital G-G. You were the guy in the white hat. All you needed was a big white horse to sweep me up onto and ride off into the sunset."

"Leila, I..."

"Shut up and let me finish," she said. "Then something awful happened, and you weren't the guy in the white hat any more. You went off the straight and narrow. Yeah, you failed. You betrayed your oath as a," she made air quotes with one hand, "'sworn officer of the law.' And yeah, I was pissed at you for that. But you know what? I can get over it. And so should you. You're human. Big fucking deal. But you took some seriously evil people off the face of the earth. That's a good thing, Tim. You may have gone about it in a way you think is wrong, but I swear, if you intend to nail yourself to the cross over this, I will walk out that big steel door behind me, and I won't come back. And that would be a damn shame."

He looked stunned. He didn't answer for a long moment. Then he said, "Can you repeat the part about how you're in love with me again?"

That made her laugh. "Yeah. I love you, Tim. God help me, I know it's the worst possible thing I could do on so many levels, but yeah. I love you."

He took a deep breath, let it out. He closed his eyes. She watched him in silence. Finally, he opened them. "I love you, too," he said, and her heart started beating again. "But I can't ask you to wait for me."

"Frankly, Buckthorn, I haven't decided if I will. Just because I love you doesn't mean I might not still decide you're too much of a pain in the ass to deal with."

This time it was his turn to laugh. "Okay. Fair enough."

"Write me," she said.

"Every day," he replied.

She felt the tears welling up in her eyes and put her hand against the glass. He did the same. "And come home as soon as you can."

"I will," he said. "Because home is anywhere you are."

Epilogue

"I 'm afraid the documents are genuine," the lawyer said. "Not only were they notarized, but we've had the signatures independently verified. By a top document examiner, I might add."

"I don't believe it," Mary Monroe Sheffield told him. She was a bony, fierce-looking little woman with snow-white hair cut severely short. "My uncle would never have willingly signed over his house and his stock in his businesses to some..." she looked down the long conference table to make sure there was no mistake as to who she was about to mention. "Whore."

Patience, seated at the end of the table, didn't react to the insult. She was dressed entirely in black. Even the handkerchief she held in one hand was black silk. She dabbed at one corner of her eye with it.

"Miss Matthews..."

"If that's even her real name," Harlan Monroe, Lampton's nephew and the only other potential beneficiary of the estate spoke up. Mary shot him a look and he subsided back into his seat.

The lawyer looked pained at the interruption. "Miss Matthews was Mr. Monroe's caregiver for his declining years. He apparently spoke very fondly of her. It's only natural that he should reward her for her years of faithful service."

"She tricked him," Mary said. "Or coerced him."

"From what I hear of Mr. Monroe's...forceful personality," the lawyer said, "I highly doubt either was the case."

Mary stood up. Harlan followed. "We'll fight this," she said. "We'll fight this, and we'll win." She looked at Patience. "And when we do, you'll be back peddling your ass on street corners. Or better yet, in prison." She stormed out, Harlan in her wake.

The lawyer took off his glasses and rubbed his eyes. "It's not just an idle threat. We've already received a communication from a law firm...a quite well-connected one in fact...who they've retained."

Patience stood up. "Thank you for your time, Mr. Suddreth," she said. "Please keep me informed."

"I will," he said. "And please call me Malcolm."

"Malcolm, then."

He licked his thin lips nervously. "I was wondering," he said, "if you might be free for dinner tonight?"

She looked down at him, still seated. She gave him the barest ghost of a smile. "Isn't that a conflict of interest?"

"Oh no," he said. "Not really. The estate is my actual client."

"And I'm executrix, correct?"

"Well, yes..."

"It doesn't matter," she said. "I'm still in mourning." She wiped at her eyes again. "For the best friend I ever had."

"Yes, yes, of course," Suddreth said. "My apologies. Perhaps some other time."

"Perhaps." He caught the barest whiff of her perfume as she left the room.

That night, Mary Monroe Sheffield received a phone call at the hotel where she was staying in Biloxi. Her home in the Atlanta suburb of Marrietta had been firebombed by a person or persons unknown. It had burned to the ground.

Harlan Monroe received a call that evening that his five-year old granddaughter had missed her ride from her preschool in Baton Rouge. Her frantic parents had called the police, but by the time they arrived the girl was home. A nice man "with drawings all over his arms" had given her a ride. He'd been funny, she said, telling her lots of jokes and promising her a ride on his motorcycle. When he'd dropped her off down the street from her house, he'd made her promise to send a message to her Grandpa Harlan about what a lucky little girl she was.

The next day, the receptionist at the law firm Harlan Monroe and Mary Monroe Sheffield had retained called. They were returning the retainer in full, and would not be able to pursue the case further. Later, the two saw on the news that when the firm's staff showed up for work that morning, they'd found every door standing open. In the conference room, they'd found what looked like several sticks of dynamite strapped together with a timer device attached. The bomb squad had determined that the "dynamite" was actually several empty cardboard tubes and the "timer" was a cheap digital watch. The reporter also said that the fake device had been sitting on top of a client file taken from one of the attorneys' locked file cabinets. Nothing else had been touched. Subsequent phone calls revealed that no other law firm in Biloxi was inclined to take their case. The promised lawsuit was never filed.

Business went on as usual.

THE END

Other Books By J.D. Rhoades

The Jack Keller series:
The Devil's Right Hand
Good Day In Hell
Safe and Sound

The Tony Wolf/Tim Buckthorn novels:
Breaking Cover

Others:
Storm Surge
Lawyers, Guns and Money
Gallows Pole

As J.D. Nixx:
Monster: Nightrider's Vengeance
The King's Justice: Two Taras Flinn Stories

About The Author

J.D. Rhoades lives, writes, and practices law in Carthage, NC. His first book, *The Devil's Right Hand*, was published in 2005 and was nominated for the Shamus Award for Best First Private Eye Novel by the Private Eye Writers of America. His weekly newspaper column in the Southern Pines, NC *Pilot* has won two North Carolina Press Association awards for Best Column. Follow him on Twitter at @jd_rhoades.

CPSIA information can be obtained
at www.ICGtesting.com
Printed in the USA
LVOW10s0340080118
562131LV00009BC/597/P